A COLD AND
SILENT DYING

ELEANOR
TAYLOR
BLAND

ST. MARTIN'S MINOTAUR........NEW YORK

www.minotaurbooks.com

Library of Congress Cataloging-in-Publication Data

Bland, Eleanor Taylor
    A cold and silent dying / Eleanor Taylor Bland.—1st St. Martin's Minotaur
ed.
        p.   cm.
    ISBN 0-312-32665-3
    EAN 978-0312-32665-4
    1. MacAlister, Marti (Fictitious character)—Fiction.   2. Homeless
women—Crimes against—Fiction.   3. Police—Illinois—Chicago—Fiction.
4. African American police—Fiction.   5. Chicago (Ill.)—Fiction.
6. Policewomen—Fiction.   I. Title.

PS3552.L36534C64 2004
813'.6—dc22
                                                                2004050947

First Edition: December 2004

10 9 8 7 6 5 4 3 2 1

Congratulations to Chuck and Jan Suidikas on their fiftieth wedding anniversary.

Special thanks to my agent, Ted Chichak, not just for his unwavering support and encouragement, but for an insight that had a major impact on this story. Also, to my editor, Kelley Ragland. Their rigorous but gentle honesty are indispensable.

My gratitude to Nanette Boryc, researcher extraordinaire, for her curiosity, expertise, and friendship.

Special thanks to John Lyman for conscientious attention to detail and a thorough, professional copyedit.

Thanks and love to Geronimo Bland, American Staffordshire terrier and gentle companion, and Maxine Louise Boryc, dancer, interior decorator, and German shepherd.

As always, a special thank-you to my family for their patience and support.

Many thanks to Super Fans Karin Gordon, Barbara Eaves, and Sisters Reading Books; Sandra Atwater; the Red Herrings who never hear 'the rest of the story'; and Tamara Yancy, Ruth Miller, and Jo Ella and John Doggett. And to old and dear friends Barbara Kelly, Beverly Parsons, Jack and Dolores Doyle, Joanne and Carlo, JoAnn and Dennis Piper, Louise Powell, and Beverly in Toronto.

For technical assistance: Joan at Top in Dog Training Kennel; Raymond Breen, U.S. Army; Mark Dobrzycki; John Rorabeck, Assistant Coroner, Lake County, Illinois; Frank Wynans, Lake County Sherriff's Dept., Retired; Nancy Jo Rich, partner, environmental department, and John Villa, national director of paralegals for Katten Muchin Zavis Rosenman.

A COLD AND
SILENT DYING

1

FRIDAY, NOVEMBER 7

There is no time here. I don't know what day it is or how many days I have been here. I have not had a shower in at least a week, maybe longer. I cannot remember the last time I ate a hot meal. Everything is sand—between my teeth, in my throat. It invades my socks, my boots, gets under the elastic in my underwear and grates against my skin. The heat is like standing in a furnace that is turned on full blast. But long after I have forgotten how hot it is here, I will remember the sand.

Strange, isn't it? You and I and Grandpa can sit down now and tell the same stories. The people we talk about will be different, the places might not be the same, the price of a beer or a whore will change, but our stories will still be the same. And with each telling we will be able to kill more people with less effort. One day my children will tell these stories, and then their children. Only the details will change. The world did not begin with war, and might not end with war. But there will be no peace in the time between. The sand shimmers in the heat and there are no mirages.

Fred read the letter one more time, then folded it along creases so worn the paper was beginning to tear. Was this why he survived the Gulf in '91? To get this last letter from his only son over a decade later? To read this

1

for the first time a week after they came to tell him that Andy was dead?

He took out Andy's picture. Wallet size, unframed, frayed. Andy. Marine-blue uniform. Corporal's stripes on his sleeve. The American flag behind him. The fifth generation in their family to serve this country. The first one to die. Fred looked at Andy's picture, but remembered him the way he was when they brought him home. So still, as if a voice had said, "Attention," and forgot to say, "At ease." Fred looked at his son until his eyes hurt, and then he looked away.

When the dog came and sat beside him, Fred reached down and stroked his fur. It was quiet here in the woods. Far from the sand, far from the heat, a long way from the desert, but not too far away to remember. He had once thought that if he just kept moving, didn't stay in one place long enough for it to become familiar, that if everything around him was different, strange, that and a little wine, or perhaps a few shots of bourbon, and he could escape the memories. Instead, the only distance he had created was between him and Andy.

Fred reached into his pocket, got a few treats, fed them to the dog. They had found each other when Geronimo was a pup and someone left him by the side of the road. In the months they had traveled together, having Geronimo with him had become much more than not being alone.

Now they were here, Lincoln Prairie, not that the name of the place mattered. Trees, woods, no sand. That was all that was important. It was a narrow strip of land, maybe two blocks wide, and six long. He had been here for a week, hadn't planned to stay that long, but had just been too damned depressed to move on.

The burr oaks grew so close together that even with just a few brown leaves on thick, bare branches, they blocked out most of the daylight and insulated him from everything but nature's noise. The path was maybe a foot wide, but the underbrush was so thick that the hard-packed dirt trail had all but disappeared.

There were ravines with narrow, rocky beds nearby, with cold, swiftly flowing water for him and Geronimo.

Fred reached out to Geronimo, felt the warmth of his tongue as the dog licked his hand. Then he looked at Andy's picture, touched the letter, returned both to an envelope, and put that in his pocket. *There is no time here.* Today was Andy's birthday. He would have been twenty-one.

It was dark when DeVonte Lutrell left the building on Boswell Street where he rented an apartment. He was only a few blocks from the lake and the wind had picked up. Chicago was cold for early November. He put a knit cap on his head and jammed his hands into his pockets. He hated Chicago, except for the Cubs. But baseball season was over. And thanks to Sharon, his wife, and her cop friend, Marti MacAlister, he could never go back to the West Indies, the island of his birth, the place that was always warm, the place that he loved. Even here, in Juneway Terrace, where he could hear the voices and dialects and music of the Islands, and eat the foods he had savored since childhood, even here, perhaps especially here, he was not home. Worse, it reminded him so much of home that sometimes his anger became an orange haze. Then, more than at any other time, he wanted to kill, he knew he would kill. But everyone he killed was just a substitute for the woman he wanted to kill. He spoke her name aloud: "Marti MacAlister." Just saying it made him tremble with rage.

He knew it was dangerous to let the rage control him. He made mistakes when it did and had to move on. And this time he couldn't just up and leave. There were things he had to do. He took several deep breaths, tried to concentrate on the cold air that entered his nose. He had planned everything this time. He had spent weeks finding out what he needed to know. He had even bought a little house in Louisiana. For the first time, he would have someplace to hide. Always, until now, he just ran. Always before, it didn't matter much who he killed. But this time he would finally get the woman who had ruined his life.

He had traveled back and forth from Grand Bahama Island to Fort Lauderdale for three years before Sharon came along. He married her because it was the only way he could get to her money. He preferred to meet a woman in the States, get as much of her money as he could, then invite her to his island condo for a few days of sun, surf, and gambling at the casinos. Somewhere between Florida and the island, the woman would go quietly to the depths of the Atlantic. And because older women who had wealthy husbands had to be careful about who they were seen with, nobody on the ship knew that any of these women were with him.

Sharon was the fourth woman he had to marry. The deaths of the first three had made divorce unnecessary. He had intended to kill Sharon, but almost died himself when a hurricane struck the island. Looking back, he knew it had been a mistake to get involved with her, but at the time, she was irresistible—so needy, so eager, so helpless. Sharon was the kind of woman his mother—for whom he hoped hell was a real and never-ending place of torment—had warned him about. Like his other wives, Sharon was totally useless to herself and the rest of mankind. It almost made him smile to think of her.

DeVonte crossed the street before he reached the corner of Jonquil, and paused to look at the large, multiunit building he had just left. He could see the bedroom windows in his apartment. The light was still off in Lynn Ella's room. Lynn Ella was the bait in the trap that would catch Sharon, and Marti MacAlister. She was Iris MacAlister O'Neill's daughter; Iris was Marti's long-lost sister-in-law. She was such a strange child, though, too tiny to be eight years old, afraid of everything. She insisted on sleeping in the closet even though she had her own bed. Yes, Lynn Ella was a strange child indeed. Was she imagining things that were not there, or was she a conjurer? He would have to find out, although he wasn't sure he wanted to know.

His car was parked near the cemetery a few blocks away. It was an older model Chevy Cavalier, four cylinder, with a few dents, a little rust that blended with the brown chassis, and a trunk big enough to hold a body. It was not the kind of car that would get beat cops' attention or attract thieves. By the time he reached it, he was shivering. He should have worn a warmer jacket, even though it seemed too soon to dress for winter. He took the gun out of the glove compartment and tucked it under his seat. He didn't like guns. They made everything too easy. The challenge was in persuading someone to do what he wanted, not ordering them to with a fake gun. The car started at once, but the heater wasn't likely to kick in until he was halfway to Lincoln Prairie. He couldn't kill that cop yet, the bitch. Until he could, someone else would have to do.

Traffic was light and it was only an hour's drive to the first shelter DeVonte planned to check out. It was almost ten o'clock and the shelters had closed their doors for the night, but he might be able to pick up a straggler. He would have preferred to arrive earlier, but he had wasted almost an hour trying to convince Lynn Ella that she should eat the cheeseburger and fries he had picked up at Po' Boys, the take-out joint down the street.

"No. It be in there," she said.

He wondered if someone had spit on the burger and the child had the eye and could see that but was unable to explain what she saw.

She pointed to the sandwich, said, "It be in there," again and backed away from it.

He wished the hell he knew what "it" was, what she could see that he couldn't. If she wasn't a conjurer and didn't have special sight, maybe someone had worked root on her.

"What's in here?" he asked. "This is just food. You need to eat. Aren't you hungry?"

She shook her head. As skinny as she was, she looked as if she must be close to starving. Not that it wouldn't be easier for him to get rid of her if she starved to death, but he needed her, at least for a while. If she was a conjurer or a seer, it would be best just to let her be. If she wasn't, there were places here where she could rest forever undisturbed.

DeVonte drove past several shelters before he saw the woman standing in the doorway of a storefront not far from the church. He slowed and rolled down the window. The wind had picked up and the air was cold.

"It's late," he called. "They won't let you in now."

The woman was hugging herself and he could see that she was shivering. Long dark hair hung below her shoulders and a knit hat almost reached her ears. Her skirt stopped just above her knees, but she was wearing slacks underneath. Her jacket looked thin, but the turtleneck of a sweater covered her throat. Layers, he thought, a good way to keep warm. He pulled over to the curb.

"The church over on Bellingham will take you in if you get there before eleven and they're not filled up. Get in and I'll drop you off."

The woman took several steps back and turned away. She was young, with honey-colored skin like his mother's. Unlike his mother, her face was marred by pimples and several small black moles. She wasn't pretty like his mother either. There was something almost masculine about the line of her jaw and the thickness of her eyebrows.

"All right," he said. "But if the police see you here they will arrest you for vagrancy."

She stared at him for a moment, then looked away.

"I've got to take this to my mother." He held up a prescription bottle filled with aspirin. "Bellingham isn't too far out of my way."

She looked again, hesitated.

"Come on," he said. "I've also got to walk the dog before I can call it a night."

When she took a step toward him he leaned across the seat and opened the car door.

"Cigarette?" he asked. He himself didn't smoke and hated the odor.

The woman shook her head.

"Maybe you could do something for me?"

6

She sort of laughed.

"What's funny?"

"Life. Nothing's ever free."

"This ride is," he said. "I just thought maybe you could let my girlfriend know I'm on my way. I don't like to drive and talk at the same time." He nodded toward the glove compartment. He hadn't spoken to Sharon since that day on the island two years ago, when the storm surge had swept him away before he could kill her.

"Her name is Sharon. You'd better tell her you're Johnny's sister, Iris. I wouldn't want her to think . . ." He smiled. "Anyway, just tell her you're with me. I'm DeVonte by the way. Tell her I'll be there as soon as I can."

He gave her the number, then listened, smiling as she repeated what he had told her to say. When she said, "But it is me, Sharon. Iris, Johnny's sister."

"Iris MacAlister O'Neill," he whispered. The woman repeated it, then said, "I wouldn't—"

He took the phone. "Hi, hon, it's me. Just giving Iris a ride home."

"DeVonte! You're lying." Her voice was high pitched, sounded shaky. "That can't be Iris. She's dead."

"Is she?"

"Please, whoever she is, don't hurt her."

"You know me well."

"What do you want?"

"Look, I've got to get Iris home. I'll give you a call back when I'm on my way."

"Don't hurt her," Sharon said. "Please."

He laughed and turned off the phone.

"Thanks. I'll just drop this off at my mother's on the way." The woman didn't answer.

"What's your name?" Again, she said nothing.

"That's okay. I'll just call you Marti."

He drove to a street that was familiar, and pulled into the driveway of a house he had been to before. This time a man wearing army fatigues was standing beneath a tree in the woods nearby and urinating into the undergrowth. Just another bum, DeVonte thought. Just like in the city. The man looked in their direction, then disappeared among the trees.

DeVonte pulled out the fake gun and pointed it at the woman. He put one finger to his lips and toward the side door of the darkened house. The woman nodded. She slid across the seat after he got out. He looked into her eyes, expecting to see fear, but her expression was closer to indifference, as if she didn't care. He enjoyed killing them more when they were afraid.

As soon as she hung up, Sharon rushed to her daughter's room. She eased the door open and saw Lisa, all of sixteen, still sleeping with that shaggy old teddy bear. She sagged against the door frame. That couldn't have been Iris. Johnny's sister had taken off years before he and Marti got married. Johnny had tried to find her until he died, and then, periodically at least, Marti had continued the search. But Marti had as much as admitted that she thought searching for Iris was hopeless, that she believed Iris was dead.

That woman couldn't be Iris. She and Johnny and Marti were sixteen that summer when Iris went out one morning and never came back. She was doing drugs, got caught up in the life, that was what everyone assumed. What had she told DeVonte about Iris? Everything. He was always so interested in her past, her friends.

No, that wasn't Iris. It couldn't be. Marti would have found her by now if she was still alive. Whatever *was* going on now was all her fault. She had brought DeVonte into their lives. No, she had welcomed him. DeVonte Lutrell, the ultimate Mr. Wonderful: kind, thoughtful, handsome, charming. A real killer, as Marti had said, "to die for," and she almost had. She had put them all in danger when she married him. She was endangering them again. Her daughter didn't deserve this. Neither did Marti. They had been children together, friends since kindergarten. Even then Marti shielded her from the other children's teasing, and by the time they were in third grade, the older boys she flirted with.

No, that couldn't have been Iris, but that was DeVonte. How she hated him, hated herself for wanting to be with him. She had thought he was out of her life, prayed he was dead, tried to convince herself that after two years without a word, he was dead. Safe. Had she really thought she was safe, that she could ever be safe from him? Dear God, whoever that woman was, she wasn't safe either. Why did he call her? What did he want? What was she going to tell Marti? Once again, Marti would have to save her. There was no way she could save herself. She didn't even know how to try.

DeVonte sang "The Sound of Music" to a reggae beat as he drove back to Chicago. Traffic was light. He tapped his fingers on the steering wheel as he drove. He did not think of Lynn Ella until he turned onto the street where he lived. Did she sense what he was going to do to her and her mother and her sister as well? If he could find her sister. Kim's whereabouts still eluded him. It had taken almost four months to locate Iris. She wasn't a MacAlister anymore. She had gotten married in Indiana. Her name was now Iris Mary O'Neill. She had kept her middle name but dropped MacAlister, although it was on her marriage application, a more detailed document than a marriage license.

It hadn't taken him long to think of marriage records, but there was nothing in Chicago. He had tried Milwaukee next, then St. Louis, then Nashville. Then he decided on points closer to home rather than the nearest big cities: Gary, South Bend, Mishawaka. He had found the record of Iris's marriage in Valparaiso, Indiana, a college town of all places. That was also where she applied for a Social Security card.

Finding her was easy, once he had the right name. Marti MacAlister's sister-in-law was locked up in a nuthouse downstate. She would be released on Sunday and he would be there to meet her. Iris and her daughters were the means by which he would gain what he wanted, Sharon's money and MacAlister's death.

Sharon would go to her oldest and dearest friend, Marti. She would need Marti to rescue her again. When he was ready for Marti to come after him, Sharon would be the bait in the trap. For a moment he thought of the man in the woods. He had seen him with the woman. Just a bum, he reminded himself, but he had killed men before who had noticed too much.

Lynn Ella opened the door to the closet and looked out. This wasn't anything like Mama Dee's. There were no rats, no roaches. Two dolls sat in a chair. She didn't like dolls. When she saw them on television, they moved and talked and hurt people.

She listened, but did not hear DeVonte snoring or walking around. He said he would bring her mama to see her soon, her real mama. She wasn't sure what a real mama was and she didn't want no more mamas no way. Maybe DeVonte was a daddy. Maybe she could just have a daddy for a while.

It was quiet here. There was just her and DeVonte, not all those other people like at Mama Dee's. There was no television here. No music with the banging noises. Nobody coming in and out all the time talking loud and laughing. No hollering and fighting. Sometimes the children who lived upstairs ran and played, and sometimes she could hear talking and laughing next door, but there was no fighting. She wasn't scared here.

And DeVonte didn't give her whumpings like Big Mama or tie her to the bed like Mama Dee. He let her sleep in the closet and close the door. He brought her paper bags with food inside, but she didn't get hungry much anymore. Even if she was hungry, she had never seen food on television that came in paper bags without pictures. She wasn't going to eat anything that didn't come from McDonald's. Big Mama told her folks were trying to poison them and then she ate ribs that had come in a bag with no picture. Then Big Mama went to sleep and didn't wake up no more. No way she was gonna do that. She sat cross-legged on the blanket and wondered when DeVonte would come home, and if maybe he was her daddy.

* * *

DeVonte let himself into the apartment and stood just inside the door, waiting. If the child was not in the closet, she would need time to get there. Lynn Ella was a good, obedient child in most things. It was important that she was not afraid of him, that she would stay here when he went out and not try to get away.

He went to the kitchen first, checked to see if she had eaten, annoyed to see that she had not. He didn't need a sick child. If she became ill he would have to get rid of her. Replacing Lynn Ella with another child would be risky in many ways, not the least that Iris would know that the child wasn't hers. He tossed the bag with the burger from Po' Boys into the trash. He should have picked up a milk shake on his way home. He patted his pocket, a candy bar. Maybe he did have something she would like. When he went into her room, the closet door was ajar.

"Come, child," he whispered. "I've brought something for you."

There was no movement from inside the closet, but he did not believe the child was sleeping. Often, when he came home late, after he went to bed, she would stand in the hall outside the door to his room. Sometimes she watched him for a long time.

"I brought you some candy."

She came out with a little more coaxing. He held out the candy bar. She looked at it but didn't touch it.

"I have something else, too." He took the cell phone out of his pocket.

"It is in there," she said.

"It can talk," he explained. "Just like I can, just like you can." She nodded.

"Do you know what this is?"

"Phone."

"Have you ever talked on one?"

She shook her head.

"Do you want to talk on the phone?"

She hesitated, then gave him a short, quick nod.

"Good. I'm going to call my friend Sharon and let you talk to her, okay?"

11

DeVonte punched in Sharon's number. When she answered he said, "Hi, hon, it's me again. I've got someone here who wants to say hello."

Lynn Ella looked at the phone, then took it and listened. "Lynn Ella," she whispered. Then, "DeVonte." Then, "Yup."

He took the phone and said, "Good talking to you again. I'll call back soon," and clicked off.

Sharon sat on the edge of her bed. She felt light-headed, as if she would faint if she tried to stand up. The phone fell from her hand. She stared at it, reached out to pick it up, but didn't. She pushed the caller I.D. button instead. Blocked call. Her stomach churned. Acid rushed to her throat. A child. Dear God. He had a child. And she didn't know where he was. She picked up the phone to call Marti, but put it down. That was what she always did. This time she wasn't going to ask for help. Not yet.

2

It was almost four in the morning when Marti turned onto Hemlock, a street that was one block long and dead-ended at Deer Woods. She could see half a dozen squad cars lined up near the clearing at the entrance to the woods. It was a quiet neighborhood. Long driveways led to sprawling brick ranches. There were no fences, no swing sets, no basketball hoops or bicycles left in the driveways. Just lots of lawn and bird feeders. Not like her neighborhood. Lights were on in a few homes, but Marti didn't see anyone looking out the windows. Nobody was standing outside either. When it came to crime, nosy neighbors were the best kind.

Deer Woods was a long, narrow strip of land dense with trees and underbrush. Hemlock Street and five other streets dead-ended on the south side. There was a major east-west thoroughfare to the north. Marti spotted Vik's car and parked behind it. According to dispatch the bodies had been found in one of the houses, but the suspect was at a campsite somewhere in the woods.

Marti grabbed her camera case and wide-beamed flashlight. She zipped up her jacket and pulled up the hood. In northern Illinois, fall weather always came with a question mark. It was cold tonight, more like mid-December than early November.

There weren't any streetlights near the entrance to the woods. Marti switched on her flashlight. A rutted trail went east so she headed in that direction. Just off the trail, she could see one of the ravines that had been carved out ten thousand years ago by a

13

retreating glacier. The water was low now, but with winter snow and spring showers there would soon be a deep, fast-moving stream.

As she walked she watched for other flashlights and listened for the sound of voices. Dead leaves reached her ankles and crunched beneath her thick-soled shoes. The underbrush that extended into the footpath tugged at her slacks. It was quiet until a fox began to bark and, from somewhere in the distance, a dog answered with a howl.

She saw flashlights, then five or six uniforms standing just below the branches of a conifer, where a tent big enough for two had been set up. Another few minutes and she heard voices. The tent flap was open and a Coleman lantern lit the interior. There were two sleeping bags and a rucksack. A camping stove had been set up beneath another tree, along with a metal cooler. A four- by six-foot American flag hung from the horizontal branch of an oak tree.

Vik was talking with a man wearing green camouflage fatigues. From where she was standing, Marti could make out a patch on the knee. As she came closer she could see that it was a stain. The man was sitting on a tree stump with his hands cuffed behind his back.

Vik, four inches taller than Marti's five feet ten inches, was leaning over the man in what Marti called his vulture pose. His face was craggy, his beak nose skewed by a break. He tended to intimidate most people, but not children or animals. This man didn't seem impressed either.

"So," Vik said. "Tell me again about this body."

"Ain't no body," the man said. "Ain't nobody here but me."

His speech was slurred. His eyes were bloodshot and several empty beer cans and a half-filled bottle of whiskey lay on the ground nearby. Straight brown hair hung below his ears but not quite to his shoulders. He needed a shave. As thin as his face was, his body was bulky. Marti took a closer look and saw a turtleneck and the collars of two sweaters beneath the fatigues. The man was wearing military boots as well.

"What's your name?" she asked.

"Fred."

"Fred what?"

"Just Fred."

He wasn't belligerent and she didn't want him to become belligerent. She didn't persist.

"Fred here got a little rambunctious," Vik said.

"Just had a few drinks," Fred said.

"Woke up the neighbors," Vik added. "The lady who called it in said it sounded like someone was screaming, getting hurt maybe."

"Who was screaming, Fred?" Marti asked.

"Me."

"Why?"

Fred didn't answer.

"Why?" Marti asked again.

He looked up at the treetops. "Dreams." He spoke just above a whisper. "Just dreams."

"What did you dream about?"

"I don't remember."

Vik waved over a uniform. "Keep an eye on him."

He nodded toward the flag-decorated tree and Marti fell in step beside him. When they were out of earshot, he said, "Uniforms checked out a vacant house on Hemlock that's for sale. Place had been broken into. They went in and found a recently deceased female in an upstairs bedroom and another not so recently deceased female in the basement. We're waiting for the medical examiner and the evidence techs now. Fred is going to be our guest at the county jail."

"Any evidence to connect him with the victims?"

"That could be a blood stain on his pants. Otherwise, nothing yet."

Marti thought for a moment. There had been a lot of changes in Lincoln Prairie since the mayor died in a boating accident Labor Day weekend. An interim mayor was chosen from among the twelve aldermen, otherwise known as the City Council. The chief of police retired and the new chief promoted Marti's boss,

Lieutenant Dirkowitz, to deputy chief. Dirkowitz's replacement, Lieutenant Gail Nicholson, had arrived two weeks ago. She had been on a two-year leave of absence to work as a consultant with a software company that was developing new systems for police departments. One of the new chief's goals was to have the latest in computer technology, so Nicholson seemed like a good fit. So far, Marti had not found her easy to work with.

"I bet she'll want to know why we didn't put out an all points bulletin," Marti said.

"For whom?" Vik asked. "Jack Frost?"

"How about 'suspect or suspects unknown'?"

"Why not? Have you got a witness? A description?"

Marti ignored the sarcasm. "Did we do a canvas yet?" she asked. "Is anyone searching the woods?"

"There are two search teams out there, Marti. And a couple of squads driving around looking for anyone suspicious."

He looked at her for a moment, then said, "Nicholson is getting to you, isn't she?"

"Maybe," Marti admitted. She wanted to ignore Nicholson's criticisms, dismiss them as pettiness or envy. She also knew that as much as she disliked the woman, there would be times when Nicholson would be right. She couldn't reject everything Nicholson ragged on her about without listening first.

"Look, MacAlister, I know she rides your ass, but who knows what she'll find fault with next? She's about as predictable as a junkie on shit. Point is, we don't know what happened to the victims yet. It could be a murder-suicide. Nicholson's just a career paper pusher with a new job. She wants everyone to think she's on top of things. You know how it goes."

She did know. And she had known other cops like Nicholson. Climbers. They didn't care who they stepped on as long as they got where they were going. "Dirty Dirk" Dirkowitz was her kind of cop. He had worked the streets, come up through the ranks; he wanted results, and wouldn't tolerate any breaches of anyone's constitutional rights.

* * *

"Fred's worried about his dog," the uniform said when Marti and Vik returned.

Fred looked at Vik, then Marti. "You've got to take care of my dog. Put him in one of those boarding places. I can pay. I get a pension from the military. Desert Storm. And my gear." He almost fell off the tree stump as he leaned forward. "Leave it here and somebody finds it and it's his."

The man still wasn't sober. Marti didn't bother to explain that everything was now potential evidence and would be impounded.

Vik looked about the meager campsite and shrugged, as if to say he didn't know why anyone would want any of it. Then he looked at Fred. "We'll take care of it," he said, voice gruff.

"Thanks. It's not easy, finding a place like this with nobody around to bother you. You're sure I've got to go to jail? The V.A.'s got a detox program."

"Jail," Vik confirmed.

"I haven't done anything but have a few drinks."

"A few too many," Vik reminded him. "Where is your dog?"

"Trying to find a fox or a rabbit to chase, most likely. Wildlife is really scarce here. He'll be back about daybreak. He's a good dog."

"What kind of dog?" Marti asked.

"Pit bull."

"What's his name?"

"Geronimo."

As they walked to the house where the bodies had been found, Vik said, "Pit bull. About as bad as a rottweiler. Better to get him to the pound than to leave him on the street to maim or kill somebody. We'll have to call animal control. And, MacAlister, don't even think about taking this mutt home. At your house, Trouble is the alpha dog. If a pit bull shows up, it'll be war."

"Doesn't sound like he's been trained to fight."

"Doesn't matter."

In spite of her decision not to anticipate Nicholson's complaints, Marti said, "Maybe we should go over to the jail when they take Fred in, and question him while they check out the victims and go through the house."

"MacAlister, the man's still half-drunk."

"Drunks talk."

"And defense attorneys get what they say under the influence thrown out. Look, no matter how we handle this, Nicholson will find fault, so let's do our job, same as always, and pretend she doesn't exist."

Marti kicked at a tree branch that was blocking the ribbon of path that led back to Fred's tent. There was no way to pretend Nicholson didn't matter. She had been here before, dealt with female cops who had to make every other female look bad in order for them to look good. "Out standing in the field," as her deceased husband, Johnny, would have said. There was a time when she would have gotten an adrenaline rush from the challenge. Problem was, she had gotten used to life without the Nicholsons of the world. Now she just resented being hassled.

The coroner's S.U.V. arrived just as Marti and Vik approached the vacant house. It was the last house on the west side of the street. The height of the windows made it difficult for anyone to see inside. Deer Woods began where the close-clipped lawn ended.

"Well, look who's here," Vik said. "And just when I was getting used to Gordon McIntosh, assistant coroner and major pain in the butt."

Marti was surprised to see Dr. Nilesh Mehta get out of the coroner's vehicle. Janet Petroski, who was not a physician, had retired October first, and Dr. Mehta had just been appointed to replace her. If she had given it much thought, Marti would have assumed that he would spend most of his time in his office, or comforting the bereaved, as Janet had for twenty-five years. Then again, Mehta was a doctor. Although the job was elective, someone had decided that the new coroner should have an M.D. and be a pathologist.

"Takes getting used to," she said.

Vik raised his eyebrows, as if he was about to ask a question. "Be interesting to see how things change around here," he said instead.

Marti felt a sadness that was both uncomfortable and familiar. She didn't like change, always had a hard time adjusting. Maybe that was part of her problem with Lieutenant Nicholson—too many new faces, too many new names, and very different personalities. Maybe Vik was right and things would settle down soon. She wished everything could have just stayed the same. A childish thought, something her eleven-year-old son, Theo, or her stepson, Mike, also eleven, would say, but true nevertheless.

It was almost an hour before they were allowed to see the most recent victim. The rooms were empty, and painted a neutral off-white with beige carpeting.

"Messy," Mehta said. He was East Indian, two inches shorter than Marti's five feet ten inches, with curly black hair and dark eyes. Unlike Dr. Cyprian, the medical examiner they usually worked with, whose expression was always calm and inscrutable, Dr. Mehta telegraphed many emotions. Tonight he seemed weary of death, but he also seemed eager . . . for what? Maybe, like her, he wanted the victims to tell him what had happened and point out who had done it.

Blood had pooled under and around the body and saturated the carpet, but was not spattered anywhere. There was one red streak, as if someone had slipped, and a palm print on the wall where he or she tried to regain his or her balance.

"Cause of death is manual strangulation, not the stab wounds," Mehta said. "Oh, and this one's not a woman."

"What?" Marti and Vik spoke in unison. The victim was wearing a skirt and had long dark hair.

"I'll know more when we get him to the morgue."

"Any guesses as to how long he's been dead?"

"There's early rigor in the neck. And it's warm enough in here to keep the pipes from freezing." Dr. Mehta shrugged. "Maybe five to ten hours."

"That's helpful as hell," Vik complained.

Mehta was already walking away. "That's it until the autopsy."

Marti squatted beside the body. The victim had been dead long enough to lose any semblance of ever having been alive. It was almost like looking at a mannequin. He was young, early twenties maybe, five feet six or seven. The long hair was a wig. He had acne and a few moles that might help with identification. The odor that came from not bathing was stronger than any other smell. Marti stood, looked down at the bruises on his neck, and wondered for a moment how he came to be here and who would mourn him. Then she got out her camera.

"Homeless," Vik said, "from the looks of him. Just like Fred. Maybe Fred thought he had picked up a female and got a surprise."

"Maybe."

"How likely are we to find two homeless people in such a nice part of town? And now that we have, what are the odds that they've never met?"

"Fred doesn't strike me as one for socializing."

Vik frowned. "Doesn't matter. Even if he is, odds are that once he talks with an attorney, his dreams won't be the only thing he can't remember."

While they waited for Dr. Mehta to examine the second body, they did a walk-through. There was no vandalism, no sign of anyone's living there.

"So far, we haven't found much," the female evidence tech told them. "This place is really clean, except maybe the rooms where the bodies are. Dr. Mehta hasn't allowed us in there yet."

"This one's ripe," Mehta said when he came up from the basement. "Swelling, gases, blisters."

"Male?" Marti asked.

"No, female."

"Great," Vik said. "If there's one thing I like in a case it's inconsistency."

Marti got the jar of Vicks VapoRub out of her purse, rubbed some on her upper lip, and gave it to Vik.

Again there was only a pool of blood, no spattering. This time all she could tell about the victim was that she had brown hair.

"I guess this means our killer doesn't have a fetish for blondes," Vik said.

Marti got out her camera again.

3

The sky was getting light when they went outside.

"About time for the dog to return from the woods," Vik said. "We might as well keep an eye out for him."

They headed for the campsite. At least a dozen uniforms were stationed among the trees.

"Must be a quiet night," Vik said.

"Either that or someone notified Nicholson."

Four animal-control specialists were waiting near the clearing where the tent was set up. They were wearing protective padding. One had a tranquilizer gun, two had poles with loops for catching the dog, and one had a leash and a muzzle.

Marti and Vik sat on a nearby log beneath a dense tangle of tree branches. Small birds began making one- and two-chirp predawn queries. A cardinal gave a few tentative calls.

"Too many people," Vik said. "They'll just scare him away."

Ten minutes later, Marti heard branches snapping. She turned to see a dog about three feet behind her. He was small, but muscular, white with brown spots and markings. She remained motionless. He came closer, stopped, sniffed, then, when neither Marti nor Vik moved, hunkered down on his front paws with his butt in the air, and looked from one of them to the other.

"Hey, Geronimo," Vik said in a quiet voice. Then, "Come here, boy."

"Geronimo," Marti said. "Good boy. Come on, it's okay."

The dog wagged his tail.

"Come on, Geronimo," Marti encouraged. "Come on."

Geronimo came closer. By the time he reached her, not only his tail but his entire behind, was wagging. He was wearing a pronged collar with several tags attached; one with the date of his rabies shot, another with the I.D. number of a microchip. Marti held out her hand. When he didn't shy away, she tried stroking his muzzle. He tensed, but didn't move. She began massaging him behind his ears, something her dogs enjoyed. He leaned into her hand and closed his eyes.

"Good boy," Vik said. "Unlike those other idiots, we come in peace."

"We need a leash," Marti told him. "And make sure they know he's not dangerous."

Vik got up slowly. Geronimo opened his eyes and watched as he walked away.

A few minutes later, Marti walked the dog into the campsite. Geronimo understood heel, sit, down, and stay. When she halted, he sat with his muzzle even with her left knee, calm but alert.

The animal-control specialists watched in silence.

"Ferocious, man-eating pit bull has been caught and subdued," Vik called out.

The uniforms came from behind the tree trunks. Two had their guns unholstered.

"Put the weapons away," Vik said.

"You've got a pit bull there."

"Does he look like he's about to attack anyone?"

"Good boy," Marti whispered. She reached down and patted him.

Geronimo licked her hand.

Sharon went to Lisa's room again. She couldn't sleep, couldn't stop checking to be sure Lisa was all right, even though the two of them were alone in the apartment. She checked the locks again, checked the windows, made sure the bar was in place that kept the patio door from being opened from the outside.

DeVonte had found her. He would get in if he wanted to, no matter what she did. Nothing would stop him, even though they lived on the third floor and the entrances to the building were locked. He had tried to kill her once. He could be planning to try again.

Maybe this was some kind of trick, or a game. He could have just told some woman to say she was Iris, told the child to speak to her. That didn't have to mean that they were in any danger. He could have paid them to do it. That woman couldn't have been Iris. Nobody knew where Iris was, what had happened to her, if she was even alive. Not even Marti knew that.

Whatever DeVonte was trying to do, this was her fault, all of it. If she hadn't told DeVonte about Iris, none of this would be happening. Who was that woman? That child? He wouldn't harm a child. Or would he? DeVonte Lutrell. Mr. Wonderful. And she was Sharon Lutrell, even though she never used his name. This was happening because of her. What was happening? What was he doing? And why? To get even with her? With Marti? Why had he called? What did he want? She knew what he would do to get it, but what in God's name did he want?

"So," Marti said. Geronimo trotted along between them as they walked to their cars. "They euthanize them after seven days at the pound."

"And you're not going to let that happen, are you?" Vik said. "You want to take him home. Well, maybe I've got a better idea. I heard Lieutenant Nicholson is going to get vice under her command. Cowboy's going to need a friend."

"Cowboy?"

"Why not?"

"Cowboy?" she said again. "He likes dogs?"

Cowboy and his partner, Slim, were vice cops. Marti and Vik shared office space with them.

"What's not to like about Geronimo? Besides, Cowboy's a Desert Storm vet, too."

"He is?" Marti wondered how Vik had found that out. She didn't even know where Cowboy lived. She followed Vik to an address on Fulton Street, and pulled in behind him when he parked in front of a brick two-flat.

Vik walked to her car. "Cowboy owns a couple of rental properties. He lives here, above the garage."

More surprises, Marti thought as she followed Vik to the garage, and up a flight of stairs that led to a deck.

"Damn, MacAlister, it's six fifteen. I bet he's up and dressed already. Then again, it is Saturday. Maybe vice had a long night and he's sleeping." He banged on the door. "Police! Open up!"

Half a minute later, Cowboy yelled, "Who is it?" Then said, "What the hell are you two doing here? Wait while I put on some clothes."

Several minutes passed before he admitted them. He was barefoot but wore a pair of jeans and a sleeveless T-shirt. His eyes were a clear icy blue. He ran his fingers through hair so blond it was almost white. "Whose dog?"

Geronimo cocked his head to one side as he looked up at Cowboy and gave a single wag of his tail, waited, then wagged his tail again.

"Wait until you see the full tail-and-butt wag," Marti said.

"I don't want to see shit," Cowboy said as they followed him into the kitchen. "Figuratively or literally." He looked down at the dog. "Got that, pal?"

"I think he's thirsty," Vik said.

It was a two-room apartment with a kitchen and dining area taking up half of the space. Chrome appliances looked like those a professional chef would use. There were shelves with small appliances, most of which Marti couldn't identify, and pots and pans with copper bottoms hung from a rod that extended the width of the ceiling.

Marti and Vik sat at a table for two. Bar stools and a breakfast nook provided extra seating.

"So, a red-nosed pit," Cowboy said as he reached into a cabinet, got a bowl, and filled it with water. "Good breed. Bad rep."

Marti unhooked Geronimo's leash. He rushed to the bowl and slurped until all the water was gone.

Cowboy gave him a refill. "What happened to the owner? In a body bag at the morgue?"

"County jail," Vik said. "The two of them were living in Deer Woods."

"What did he do, the owner? Kill somebody?"

"Maybe," Vik said.

Geronimo drank most of the refill, returned to Marti's side, and laid down with his head between his front paws and his eyes open.

"I don't suppose you two took him out for breakfast." Cowboy went to the refrigerator, took out half a wheel of cheese and cut a wedge, then cut a thick slice of roast beef. Geronimo sniffed the food and gave it a cautious lick before wolfing it down.

"Coffee?" Cowboy asked. He mixed a variety of beans, and poured them into the top of a Cuisinart grind-and-brew coffeemaker. "So," he said, "does his owner have any next of kin in the area?"

"Don't know," Vik said. "Man's a vet, Desert Storm. Had a decent setup in the woods, waterproof tent, down sleeping bags for him and the dog, a place to cook. Says he has a pension so it seems more like he doesn't want to be around people than like he's got no place to go."

"War does that to you sometimes," Cowboy said.

Marti thought of her first husband, Johnny, how quiet he was when he came back from Vietnam, how he hated to go anyplace where there were trees; the times that he stared into the distance and his expression changed—sometimes fear, sometimes anger. It was as if he was still seeing things that she couldn't even imagine. Things that were even worse than what they showed on television or printed in news magazines. She remembered the way he hugged her and their two children every time he came home or went out, as if he was afraid he would never see them again.

She never asked him about what had happened over there. He never told her. He never spoke of 'Nam at all. Now he couldn't. He died in a park in Chicago, his unmarked car idling in a grove of trees, killed in the line of duty.

While the coffeepot made perking noises and an exquisite aroma filled the kitchen, Geronimo reconnoitered the area, pausing to sniff the floor near the stove and the refrigerator.

"Sorry," Cowboy said as he poured coffee into mugs and brought them to the table. "I'm all out of biscotti." He sat on the stool and watched as Geronimo wandered into the other room.

"Friendly little guy," Vik said. "Got his shots and everything."

"Don't push it, Jessenovik," Cowboy warned.

Marti blew across the surface of the mug, took a sip, then looked at Cowboy, surprised. And she thought the coffee he made at the precinct was good.

After the dog had been gone for a few minutes, Cowboy went looking for him in the other room. From what Marti could see, it looked like a combination sleeping-sitting area with a wide-screen television and a stereo.

"Asleep," Cowboy said when he returned. "And he snores. I don't snore. I can't stand being anywhere near anyone who does."

When nobody responded, Cowboy went on. "Dogs need to have people around. I have to go to work every day."

Vik stirred his coffee.

Marti stared at the appliances on the shelves, trying to figure out what some of them were used for.

"No fence," Cowboy went on, "unpredictable hours. Hell. Is he even paper-trained?"

Geronimo wandered back into the room, went over to Cowboy's bare feet, licked his toes, then hit the floor with a thud and closed his eyes.

"He's a smart dog," Marti said. "Trained, well behaved. Who knows, maybe Fred worked with a canine unit while he was in the military."

"How long do you think this guy will be in jail?"

"Just for a few days," Marti told him.

"You expect me to believe that? This is about a homicide, right?"

"It's you or the pound," she said.

"You know, MacAlister, I'm only doing this because I feel sorry for you two, getting stuck with Nicholson and all."

Marti glanced at Vik. He came close to smiling, but didn't say anything about the rumor that vice might be transferred to her command.

"The woman might have a plan," Cowboy continued. "The new chief brought her in. Maybe she's got someone she wants to bring in."

"Could be," Vik agreed. "Politics, favoritism, nepotism; who knows?"

Marti had been exposed to things like that while she was on the force in Chicago. She hadn't been important enough for it to matter. Until now, politics had not concerned her.

"And, Big Mac," Cowboy said, "with your connections, you've found out something about Nicholson by now. What's the dirt?"

"She's a career desk cop. She steps on, around, or over people on an as-needed basis. She's been everything but a field boss until now. She got the nickname "The Slasher" a few years ago because she made so many personnel changes. She made so many enemies that she took a leave of absence to work for a computer company. She developed programs for police departments. And now she's ours."

"I mentioned these administrative changes in the department with my dad the other day," Cowboy said.

Marti knew that Cowboy's father had Alzheimer's, and that like Vik's dad, he was a veteran of the local force.

"That was the first thing I've said in a couple of weeks that got his attention."

Marti was more interested in the probability that Nicholson had an agenda and she was on the "to go" list. Maybe she was getting soft. A catfight didn't have the appeal it had when she was a young cop. She finished her coffee in two gulps and regretted not being able to stay long enough to have more. Geronimo lifted his head when she got up to leave. He looked at her, then Vik, his eyelids drooping, lowered his head, and went back to sleep.

"I didn't see one curtain move the entire time we were here," Marti said when they returned to Hemlock Street.

"Nobody came outside either," Vik agreed. "But there's no way they all slept through it, even if it was two in the morning. Somebody saw something."

There were eight houses on each side of the street. Vik took the odd numbers, Marti took the even. Before she was halfway down the block, she realized this was senior citizensville. Two men wore hearing aids, another was in a wheelchair. One woman used a walker with a green tennis ball at the tip of each leg. Although most of them admitted to knowing the police had been there during the night, everyone expected Marti to tell them what had happened. Nobody had noticed anything unusual in the past few weeks.

"It's the way the houses were built," one elderly man explained. "Gives us more privacy."

Marti had noticed that all of the houses sat back an equal distance from the street. And although the houses were not alike, they were more or less L-shaped, with the short end of the L an attached garage on the right. Because the length of the L extended toward the street and most of the entrances were near the garage, it was difficult to see anyone entering unless you were looking out a side window. Unfortunately, in addition to privacy, this had allowed someone to enter and exit one house unobserved.

At the fifth house she went to, a woman who looked to be about seventy came to the door. If that age estimate was correct, it would make the woman the youngest person Marti had spoke with thus far.

"Ma'am, I rang your bell and you opened the door," Marti said, not for the first time.

"Yes?" The woman seemed puzzled.

"Do you have a security chain, ma'am?"

"No. Why would I?"

"A dead bolt?"

"What's that?"

Marti showed the woman her identification and suggested that a little more security and some caution before opening the door might be a good idea.

"But I've lived here for over fifty years," the woman said. "And just about everyone else on this block has been here at least that long as well."

Feeling exasperated, Marti decided to get the beat cop out here and their alderman. Maybe they could convince these people of the need for more security. Hemlock Street was a crime wave waiting to happen.

She said, "So, you knew the family who owned the house at the end of the block? The house that's for sale?" According to the Realtor, it had been put up for sale by a Howard Atkins, who was out of town.

"Ed and Margie Atkins. Ed's been gone for thirty-four years now. Lung cancer at forty-nine. Margie died in her sleep August seventeenth. They had four children . . . three living. They lost one, a little girl . . . about the time Eisenhower was elected. We lost a few children back then. The Atkins . . . let's see . . . there's . . ."

Midway through a rambling genealogy, Marti interrupted. "And Howard put his grandmother's house up for sale. Has he been showing the house?"

"No. The real estate agent has brought a few people by, but there hasn't been a parade like there was when the Rands sold their place and moved to Tennessee. My guess is that Howie is asking too much."

"Has Howie had anyone out to make repairs or do routine maintenance?"

"Howie? Squeezes a nickel until the buffalo squeals, as my husband used to say."

"Have you seen anyone near the house?"

"Well, there was that man who came by and measured the windows."

"When was that?" Marti asked.

"Maybe last week, maybe . . . let's see . . . I'm not sure."

"Can you describe the man?"

"My sight's not what it used to be, even when I am wearing my glasses. Besides, he had his back to me."

"What was he wearing?"

"Clothes. I think his jacket might have been brown, or blue."

That was as much of a description as Marti could get.

"How do you know he was measuring the windows?"

"Why else would he have been standing by the window?"

"How did he get there? Did you see him walk by?"

"There was a car parked by the woods."

When pressed the woman thought the car was small and either black, brown, or dark green.

"Never drove one," she said when Marti asked what make and model.

"Did you see the license plate?"

The woman pointed to her eyes. "I wasn't wearing my glasses then either."

Marti looked toward the Atkins house. She couldn't see much of anything from where they were standing. The woman took her by the arm and led her down the walk until they were about twelve feet past the next door neighbor's garage.

"See?"

Marti looked where she pointed and could see two of the windows on the right side.

"Can you remember what time it was?"

"About six twenty, six twenty-one."

"Were you wearing a watch?"

"No. My daughter-in-law brings me my supper every night.

When I went outside to watch for her, she was nineteen minutes late."

Marti motioned Vik over and relayed the information to him. They returned to the houses they had already visited without being able to confirm what the woman had seen. Nobody else on the block had seen anything either. The people who lived across the street were not at home when the alleged sighting occurred. When they reached the Atkins house, a man was walking around the perimeter, staying clear of the yellow crime-scene tape.

"Sir?" Marti said.

"Are you the investigating officers?" the man asked. He was wearing a blue-and-orange Chicago Bears jacket and cap, looked to be in his mid-fifties. He was her height, bandy legged, and thin. His gray hair seemed just a little too long, almost curling at his neck, and he needed a shave. Marti thought his face seemed familiar, but couldn't place him.

"Wittenberg," he said. "Karl. Alderman." He held out his hand. "So, we've got a death investigation on our hands. A first for this neighborhood."

Marti didn't answer. Neither did Vik.

"We're all family here," he said. "I grew up knowing the Atkins, went to school with their kids. Good people. Too bad this had to happen at their place. You found the guy who did it in the woods, huh?"

"Sir . . . ," Marti began.

"I know. I know. Police investigation. Hush-hush. That's fine. I know you're just doing your job. I just wanted to check things out for myself."

He walked toward the woods before they could say anything.

Marti waited until he was too far away to hear her and said, "Who the hell . . . ?"

"Wittenberg's been alderman here for at least thirty years," Vik explained. "Always agrees with the mayor or the majority, never has an opinion, and gets what he wants for the people in his ward."

*   *   *

Karl Wittenberg walked through Deer Woods until he found a small clearing where the campsite had been. His father had forbidden him and his brother from playing in these woods when he was a child. There were herds of deer here then, quiet, shy creatures who peeked from behind trees and ran away when anyone tried to come near. The other children talked of seeing foxes and skunks, rabbits, muskrats, and raccoons.

He had envied those children, even sneaked here to play with them a few times. Then, the summer he turned seven, little Mary Atkins died. She was a pest who always got to tag along with her brother and he never did feel bad about not having her around anymore. Then, a couple of his school friends died that winter. One day they were there, the next day they weren't. At first he thought it was like sleeping, and he kept waiting for them, but they never came back. For a long time he wondered what they looked like, dead, and what it was like, being dead. Most of all, he wanted to know what had happened to them, if it was something that could happen to him, too. That was the scary part, not knowing.

Not long after one of the funerals, his father caught him coming out of the woods. Dad's face got so red it was scary. "I told you not to come here," he said. Then his dad slammed the palm of his hand into Karl's shoulder and walked away. His shoulder hurt all week. After that, he didn't come here until he was eleven or twelve, when he was old enough to help his father at work. They would dump drums filled with antifreeze and oil and other stuff that came from the cars that his father tuned up and repaired. Sometimes his father would set fire to it. The smoke would sting the inside of his nose. They buried the batteries here, too, hundreds of batteries.

This campsite wasn't more than twenty feet from where they buried two truckloads of batteries. Dad always buried them near the stream that ran through the center of the woods. The deliveries didn't stop until Dad was too sick to come here. He stopped coming then, too. The deer were gone; the kids grown up; their parents were getting old like his were.

As alderman, he made sure that Deer Woods stayed just as it was when he was a boy. No nature trails. No hikers. No camping. No cookouts. Until now. He looked around the campsite. Fred Reskov. Karl had paid a lawyer to bail him out. Reskov couldn't know this had been a dumping ground for Wittenberg Car Sales and Repairs. The police suspected him of committing two murders. Maybe he was smart enough just to cut and run.

Karl walked to the place where the batteries had been buried. He was taken aback by the pieces of metal casing that had made their way to the surface. Had Reskov been here? Had he noticed this? Did he know what they were?

Sharon watched from the window as Lisa climbed into Ben's S.U.V. She would spend the weekend with Marti's sixteen year old, Joanna. As soon as the S.U.V. pulled away, Sharon went into the kitchen and heated a cup of water in the microwave. She added instant coffee, then tried to sit at the table while it cooled. She got up, began pacing from one room to another, one window to another. DeVonte. Was he watching her? Could he see her now?

A van pulled up across the street. A man got out. She took a step back, clutched the drapery. Was it him? Was he here? Did he need a place to hide? No, this man was too tall to be DeVonte. His walk was different. He had a beard. Maybe DeVonte had a beard now. He must have changed the way he looked to keep from being caught. He could have walked past her while she was at the store yesterday. He could have followed her home.

She released the curtain, leaned against the wall, felt the light switch pressing into her back. He had found her. She had moved three times in less than a year. She had an unlisted phone number that she had changed twice. But he had found her anyway. He knew where she was. He would get in here whenever he wanted to. Even if he hadn't killed that woman, that child, he would kill her and Lisa.

Marti. She had to tell Marti. Now. She couldn't wait any longer. She couldn't take care of this without help. She went to the phone, surprised at how calm her voice sounded as she left a message for Marti to return her call.

4

The desk sergeant stopped them as they entered the precinct, and pointed in the direction of Lieutenant Nicholson's office.

"The queen is waiting for you," he said with a wink.

Vik cussed in Polish, then said, "It's Saturday. Doesn't she ever go home?"

When they reached Nicholson's office, Vik took a deep breath, raised his fist, hesitated, then knocked. "We await her majesty's call," he grumbled, and checked his watch. Even though Lieutenant Nicholson wanted to see them, it would be three minutes before she acknowledged that they were there. Marti found it insulting. When she mentioned it to her mother, Momma said, "Poor child. No home training."

As they stood waiting, a uniform in the cubicle across the hall called, "Surveillance?" and grinned.

"Maybe your sources exaggerated," Vik said.

Marti shook her head. "She's into power, Vik, and, worse, control." Playing power games could be amusing. Sometimes it was even a challenge to outmanipulate someone. But people who played control games worried her. She always wondered who they really needed to control, and why. They were the ones she thought of when she heard the expression "going postal."

"I wonder what the status is on this task force meeting Monday."

The lieutenant had mentioned it, but advised Marti and Vik that, although she had had a request that they attend, she had decided against it.

"Maybe she's going," Vik said. "It's still at the organizational stage."

"Be good to get in on the ground floor." Marti figured that was one of the reasons why Nicholson wanted them excluded. Power. All Marti had ever really wanted was participation. That was all she wanted now, inclusion.

Vik scowled and checked his watch again. He held up three fingers and mouthed a countdown—three, two . . . When he reached one, the uniform pointed to a wall clock, and then the lieutenant's door, just as Nicholson called, "Come in."

The first thing Marti noticed every time she came in was that Lieutenant Dirkowitz's defused grenade wasn't on the desk anymore. A large calendar covered the nicks and scratches it had made when Dirkowitz let it fall on the desk, a signal that their meetings were over.

Lieutenant Gail Nicholson was a petite woman in her midforties. She wore "the uniform"—a dark-colored suit, always with a skirt and a tailored white blouse. Delicate features in a heart-shaped face framed by naturally curly hair that would never need a perm suggested a European background. Nicholson could have passed for white were it not for her chestnut brown skin.

Looking at her, Marti thought of the extra ten pounds she had put on since September and the annual physical that was coming up, and for the first time in years felt uncomfortable with her size and unhappy about the weight gain. One hundred plus sixty-five pounds. She hadn't always been this heavy. There was a time, before she was a teenager, when she had been almost as slender as the lieutenant.

Nicholson avoided making eye contact. She picked up a folder instead and began paging through the forms and reports. Marti stood beside Vik, wondering if they would ever be invited to sit down. Vik gave a slight nod in the direction of the wall of photos. All were of Nicholson standing with one politician or another, most of them Republicans. The first time they left her office, Vik had said, "The wall of George. No way I can trust anybody who has had her picture taken with Daddy George Bush, King George W., and Governor George 'Driver's License' Ryan."

"At least the pictures prove she can smile."

"Or suck up," Vik had responded.

Now Marti wondered why there were no family photos. A quick look around confirmed that there wasn't anything that could be considered personal. Even the letter opener, paperweight, the clock, and pen set lined up above the desk blotter had the seals or insignia of civic groups or other organizations. Maybe that was part of the lieutenant's problem. No life. If so, too bad.

"Well," Nicholson said, "Detective MacAlister. I was hoping that after two weeks there would be some improvement in your investigative procedures." She took a manila folder out of a drawer. It had to be their most recent closed case. "So much for my expectations."

Marti refused to react.

"And this was just a domestic homicide. At least that's what it turned out to be. We all could have been embarrassed by this one. You made no effort whatsoever to determine if there was any possible suspect other than the boyfriend."

Marti considered suggesting that Nicholson pull the case up on her computer and read through the beat cops' reports of prior domestic violence, which included several hospitalizations. There was also the tape of the victim's sister calling it in. "Hurry! Please hurry!" she screamed. "Sammy is going to kill her this time." Instead, Marti said nothing.

This wasn't about procedure. This wasn't about one cop letting another cop know who was in charge, although that was part of it. Until now, Marti had been the only black female cop in this department with rank and visibility. Nicholson would be just another black female cop who outranked her unless she discredited or got rid of Marti, or gained her own rep, or both.

"And now," Nicholson said, "we have another homicide. We even have a suspect and quite possibly sufficient evidence to get an indictment. I expect you to be thorough this time, and follow correct police procedure." She leaned back and looked out at the narrow view of the lake the window provided. "Although I appreciate the dedication you bring to your work, MacAlister, and even though you have an adequate closure rate, I will be watching how you handle this current case. In order to continue in your present position, Detective MacAlister, you are going to have to significantly improve your job performance, specifically as it relates to using computer programs to access information and for filing reports. Nothing handwritten will be accepted under any circumstances. You will also have to follow correct police procedures without any deviations—"

"Ma'am," Vik said.

Nicholson was clearly annoyed by the interruption, but waited for Vik to speak.

"MacAlister and I are a team," he said. "We work together. We both sign off on everything except our individual reports. We both take responsibility for whatever we do."

Nicholson nodded toward him, then toward the door.

As they headed down the hall, Marti said, "Adequate? Ninety to ninety-five percent is adequate?"

"Well, it's not perfect," Vik said, then, "I guess you're right, MacAlister, she sees you as a threat. Either that or she's been sucking up to white male cops for so long she can't break the habit. Just for the record, we're partners. I don't need this and I'm damned close to telling her so."

"Thanks, partner, but I don't think she'd hear you. Or care." On a bigger force, this would be considered a personality conflict, and no big deal. But, maybe there wasn't enough room in Lincoln Prairie for two African-American female cops in positions of relative authority. This was the closest she had come to competition in the five years she had been here. She had become complacent. No, not complacent, content, which was equally dangerous in terms of job security.

"Male cops play the same games," Vik said.

"Yeah, but the teams are bigger. With females it's usually one-on-one."

"One-on-two," Vik reminded her.

"Men seem to have rules when they fight," Marti told him. "Women fight dirty." Then she asked, "You got any ideas on how we can get rid of her before she gets rid of us?"

"Death," Vik said without hesitation. "Hers." He popped a couple of antacid tablets, then added, "It's that or ulcers, insomnia, hypertension, or a heart attack. Ours."

His last comment worried her. His wife, Mildred, had multiple sclerosis and it wasn't getting any better. He had been taking a lot of antacid tablets lately. She was thinking about suggesting that he see a doctor. Maybe he *was* getting an ulcer.

Lieutenant Gail Nicholson waited until the door closed behind MacAlister and Jessenovik, then she pulled out a manila folder. Field command experience, the only thing she lacked, and she had to have these two working for her. She had received several job offers. Supervising sixteen detectives anchored by two competent, well-respected senior detectives with a solid arrest record had seemed the smart choice. At the time, she thought that would be the easiest way to get the experience she needed for further advancement. This was only a way station, after all.

Now that it was too late, she was beginning to understand why she would have been much better off accepting a position where the officers were less experienced and she could immediately take charge, demand improvements, hire and fire almost at will, a position where immediate improvements would demonstrate her leadership ability in a minimal amount of time. Come June, the heads of two departments smaller than Lincoln Prairie would be retiring. She intended to apply for both positions.

She opened the file folder, took out the reports and other documents relevant to the current homicides. She had gone through every case MacAlister and Jessenovik had worked in the last three years without coming up with anything that would even hint at human error, let alone incompetence. Lieutenant Dirkowitz had suggested that she "just leave them to it and they'll get the job done." That was not good enough. She did not approve of the way they did their jobs. She did not intend to tolerate the lack of respect evident in their attitudes. They would do things her way, or not at all.

As soon as they reached their office, Marti checked her voice mail. Nothing that couldn't wait, she decided. Fred was in a cell, still sleeping it off, but he had been identified through his fingerprints. Frederick Daniel Reskov had been a sergeant in the Marine Corps. He retired in 1996 with a disability and a full pension. The crime lab had determined that the handprint on the wall where the John Doe was found was Fred's and the blood type on Fred's fatigues matched the John Doe's. They had also found traces of John Doe's blood in the treads of the sole of Fred's boot.

"So, we've got a blood stain on his right knee, and traces of blood on the soles of his boots," Marti said. "But they've searched the woods without coming up with any other bloody clothing or a weapon. And there's nothing so far to connect him with Jane Doe."

"We can place him in the house and connect him with the most recent victim," Vik said. "That's enough to take to the state's attorney, although we'd have a stronger case if we could tie him to both."

Marti didn't feel good about doing that. Not yet. Maybe it was because of the dog. Not that she found it hard to believe that someone could be that attached to an animal and be a killer. There was just something about Fred, or maybe it was the memory of Johnny's finding and bringing home that scrawny mixed-breed puppy with legs that were too long and feet that were too big. What would her kids do, what would she do, without Bigfoot? What would it be like for Fred without Geronimo?

"This might be a good time to talk to him," she said.

The sheriff's deputy on duty at the county jail advised them that Fred was still "sleeping it off" in the infirmary.

"Wake him up," Marti suggested. "We'll be over in about twenty minutes."

When they went into the interview room at the county jail, Fred was slumped over the table, cradling his head on his arms. He moaned when Marti said his name. Vik shook his shoulder.

"Hey, man. My head."

"Hey, man," Vik said. "You've got problems. Right now you're charged with drunk and disorderly. The lady who called it in signed a complaint. Want to talk to us?"

"Want to sleep," Fred said. "Want a drink. Want my dog." He lifted his head. "My dog, man. Where's my dog?"

"He's staying with a friend of ours who's a Desert Storm vet, too. And a cop. I hope that's okay."

Fred looked at Vik for a long moment. "You didn't take him to the pound?"

"No need for that," Vik said. "He's a good dog."

Fred's eyes glistened. "I owe you," he said. "What do you want?"

"We want to know where you were last night."

"Wherever you found me."

"What do you remember doing last night?"

"Getting drunk."

Vik ran his fingers through his hair.

"What about the dream?" Marti asked.

Fred shook his head. "Just dreams. Crazy dreams. War dreams."

"You've had these dreams before?"

"Yeah."

"Was there anything different about this dream?"

He frowned, thought for a moment, then shook his head.

"You mentioned blood."

"Blood," he said. "There's always blood. And sometimes there's this kid in my platoon who got blown away. He wasn't more than ten feet away from me when they got him. Eighteen. Just a kid."

"Why did you go into that house?" Vik asked.

"What house?"

"How long have you been in this area?"

"The woods? Tuesday."

"Where were you before that?"

"We spent most of the summer in Arkansas and Missouri, just heading north now. We'll go up through Minnesota and into Montana for the winter. I've got a cabin there."

"That's a lot of moving around."

"Been on the road for six years now. Just keep moving until the snow comes."

Fred folded his arms on the table and put his head down again. "A house? Why are you asking about a house? I live in the woods."

Marti shook her head. Vik nodded in agreement. They wouldn't mention the blood on his pants and boot, or the palm print. Not yet anyway.

Fred laid down on the cot. Hard, solid, the way he liked a bed. He looked through the bars until the orange walls outside the cell hurt his eyes. Thank God for the bars. They kept him from feeling like he was locked in a box. Four walls would have made him itch all over, would have made his legs twitch, would have made him crazy.

He put his arm over his eyes. The light was making his headache worse. His mouth tasted like someone had shit in it. He had refused breakfast—something in a paper cup and a doughnut. He wanted a drink, or even just an aspirin. When they brought him back from seeing the cops, the nurse promised him more Tylenol in an hour.

Jail. Why was he here? What happened last night? Did he need a lawyer? The cops wanted to know about a house. What house? There were no houses in the woods. No houses, no people. Just him, his dog, and his dreams. Awake, if he thought about what had happened in Iraq, he remembered sand. But sleeping, he always remembered death. And blood. He saw that kid being blown away, and then the kid became Andy and he woke up.

Jail. Damn. He just wanted to leave everyone alone. He just wanted everyone to leave him alone. At least he had this cell to himself. As long as he didn't think about being locked in. As long as he could see through the bars. He opened his eyes. Blue ceiling. Blue, like the sky. He just wanted to live in the woods with Geronimo, think about the time before the war, the time when he slept without having nightmares, the time when life seemed good and he still had a wife and a kid. The time when he had Andy.

What had happened last night? What had he done? They wouldn't tell him. They would wait until he told them. But he didn't know. Not that he drank to forget. He drank so that he wouldn't think at all.

Sharon reached for the phone when it rang, but didn't pick up until the fourth ring. Her hand shook.

"Mother dear," Lisa said.

Sharon ignored the sarcasm. Four days ago Lisa wasn't speaking to her at all.

"Yes, my darling daughter."

Lisa laughed. There was no humor in it. "I just want you to know that I am going to Joanna's volleyball game. I will be meeting Eduardo there. We will be going to that little Mexican place near East Campus afterward with Joanna and Tony. Then we'll all go home. Eduardo and I will not be alone."

"Thanks for letting me know." She tried to focus on the fact that Lisa was keeping her end of their most recent agreement by telling her this and ignored the fact that Lisa still considered Marti's house her home.

"And you're staying the night."

"Yes, Mother dear. If that doesn't give you enough time with your current Mr. Wonderful I can stay over tomorrow night, too, and go to school from here on Monday."

Sharon didn't bother trying to tell her again that there was no

Mr. Wonderful. There hadn't been anyone since DeVonte. And now he was back.

"Why don't you stay over until Monday, Lisa?" She would be safe there. "Will Marti and Ben be home tonight?"

"Ben. Marti's working a case."

Which meant Marti might not get her message for hours, or might not take the time to call back since it didn't sound urgent. After Lisa hung up, Sharon called Marti again. Got her voice mail again. Asked her to call back. This time she added, "It's really important."

There were morgue photos of their John Doe when Marti got back to her desk. The crime lab was still processing whatever evidence they found on him and the Jane Doe. The autopsies were scheduled for tomorrow morning. She checked her messages. Sharon again. Important this time. Probably checking up on Lisa. She didn't have time for that now.

"He's young," she said, looking at the John Doe photos. In one, he looked just as he had when they found him. In the other, the wig had been removed. She placed the photos side by side. John Doe was neither pretty as a female nor handsome as a male. His features were delicate, narrow nose, thin lips, curly eyelashes. But there was the acne, and the scars from previous acne outbreaks, and his eyebrows were thick and not shaped.

"No match on his prints," she said.

Vik looked up from the report he was reading. "Well, he's definitely a male. No body-altering surgery, not even a padded bra. Just a cross-dresser from the looks of it. He was just wearing women's clothes and that wig."

Marti didn't have to guess what type of clientele he would have attracted on the street.

They turned on the computers and began looking for possible matches in missing persons. When a knock on the door interrupted their search, two hours had passed and they had come up empty.

"A Mr. Howard Atkins to see you," the uniform said.

Howie, Marti thought, looking up. He was short, fat, and smiling. "Mr. Atkins," she said.

He extended his hand as he entered the room. Vik got up and walked over to him. He pumped Vik's arm as they shook hands. Vik motioned him to the chair beside Marti's desk.

"How can I help you?" Howie asked. "Whoever they are, I'm sorry they got into the house and killed each other or committed suicide or whatever." He shook his head. "This, and the fact that it looks like development will start in the woods soon is sure going to make it damned difficult to sell the place. Sorry it took me so long to get here. Home appliance sales are booming. One of our shipments got sent to the wrong store."

Marti thought he talked as if he'd had sixteen cups of coffee.

"When's the last time you were in the house?" she asked.

"A week ago last Wednesday," he confirmed.

"And you went through the entire place," Marti said.

He nodded.

"Including the basement."

"No. I didn't go down there. I didn't check the garage either."

"Any unusual odors?" Vik asked.

"You don't mean . . . they were there? Where? I didn't see any bodies."

"The coroner hasn't yet determined how long they were there," Vik assured him.

"Odors." Sweat broke out on his forehead. "I have no idea. I didn't notice anything. Odors. A nurse found my mother. She had been . . . there . . . in bed . . . for two days."

"Sorry, sir," Vik said. "When did the repairman go to the house?"

"What? Who?"

"A repairman, sir."

"Why would I send a repairman? There was nothing wrong with the house. It's in excellent condition. Nothing needed to be fixed."

"Usually there's something," Vik said. "Did you change the locks, replace the screens?"

"No. Nothing," Howie said.

Vik asked him a few more questions.

After he left, Vik said, "I wish one other person had seen something. You think that old lady made it up?"

"Hard to say without collaboration."

"An old-model, dark-colored car. No description of the subject," Vik said. "And her eyesight's poor, even when she does wear her glasses."

"Well, if she did make it up, and we talk to her again . . ."

"It'll just reinforce it. She might even elaborate. If she wasn't so old, and wasn't half blind, she'd make a more reliable witness. A jury or a judge might even believe her."

As much as Marti hated to admit it, given the vagueness of the woman's recollections and her age, Vik was right.

Sharon spent the day sitting on the sofa waiting for the phone to ring. Night came. The curtains were pulled and the room was dark. There were three tiny red lights on the phone; one pulsed on and off. She wondered where DeVonte was, how close he was when he called. Was he standing outside now, or driving past, looking up at her darkened apartment? Should she turn on a light, let him know she was here? She wanted him to call, wanted to hear that woman's voice again, listen to the little girl again, know they were still all right. She wanted to know what he was up to, what he wanted from her. When the phone did ring, she jumped.

"So, Sharon, how have you been?" He spoke as if they were friends.

"Are they okay?"

"Why wouldn't they be?"

"Because they're with you."

He chuckled. "You know me too well."

"What do you want?"

"Oh, a lot of things. The question is, What do I want from you?"

She waited.

"I seem to remember a 401K account, a pension, a college fund for Lisa."

"Money? That's all you want? Money?"

"That's it, baby."

Her hands shook with relief.

"How soon can you have it?"

"I . . . I . . . don't know. I've never . . . I . . ."

"Monday," he said. "You call first thing Monday morning and find out. And it had better be fast."

He hung up. Sharon checked the caller I.D. Blocked call. She went to the window, pulled back the curtain just enough to peek outside. Three cars were parked across the street. They looked empty. There wasn't anyone loitering or walking by.

Her stomach rumbled and she realized she hadn't eaten all day. She felt suddenly nauseated, ran to the bathroom, and dry heaved.

Marti and Vik made the rounds of the Public Action to Deliver Shelter facilities together. At each, they gave a copy of John Doe's photos to the site manager. At each, the volunteers took time to study his face, then shook their heads. It was a struggle for Marti to go to one church basement after another and see not just men who were unkempt, unwashed, and hungry, but women as well, some with a child or children, and even families. At one there was a baby who was only six months old. One of the volunteers looked at her in mute appeal. Another said, "We shouldn't take them this young, but what else can we do?"

Marti called Denise Stevens. Denise was head of the juvenile probation department and Marti was reluctant to call the Department of Children and Family Services, for fear that the child would be taken from the mother. The child did not appear to be abused or neglected.

Denise was there in fifteen minutes. As usual, she was wearing a hat. This one was felt with a narrow brim and forest green with a pheasant feather at the base of the crown. Like Marti,

Denise was what black folk called healthy. She wasn't comfortable with her size. Marti thought about the weight she had gained and for the first time understood not just what Denise was doing, but how she felt. The hats were intended to draw attention away from Denise's hips and to her face, and those generous features God sometimes blessed African-American women with. Tonight, like Denise, Marti hoped nobody noticed the weight she had put on.

"The nearest shelter for women with children that has an opening right now is in McHenry," Denise told her. "I'll take them." Marti left her there, holding the baby and talking with the mother.

A cold wind hit them as they rounded the corner of the church and headed for their unmarked vehicle.

"Damn," Vik said. "Two more shelters to go."

By the time Marti got home it was after ten. She could hear music and laughter coming from the den, but she didn't go down to check on Joanna and Lisa and their boyfriends. Instead she grabbed a handful of chocolate chip cookies, went into the darkened living room, and sat down. She wanted to talk with someone, but Momma must have gone upstairs and Ben had duty tonight. She reminded herself that homelessness was worse in Chicago. Then she decided to talk with her pastor tomorrow to see what could be done about having separate facilities for women with children. That decided, she leaned back and closed her eyes. She awakened to the sound of her cell phone playing the theme from *Dragnet*. It was Sharon. She checked her watch. It was one fifteen A.M.

"Sorry I didn't get back to you. Lisa's here. Everything's all right."

"Nothing's all right," Sharon said. "DeVonte's back."

5

SUNDAY, NOVEMBER 9

By the time Marti got to Sharon's and got all of the details, it was three in the morning.

"You can't tell anyone, Marti. You can't play cop with this," Sharon insisted. "I don't need a cop. I need a friend."

When Marti didn't answer, she said, "Please, Marti. If he does have that woman, or that little girl, Lynn Ella, and anything happens to them . . ." She began to cry.

"Okay, Sharon, listen up," Marti said. They had been friends since before kindergarten. They had both done many silly, even foolish things. They had shared secrets nobody else would ever know. They didn't criticize each other. Sharon might deceive everyone else, but eventually she would tell Marti the truth.

"Sharon, we both know DeVonte. He's killed before, he'll kill again. We might not be able to save this woman, if there is one, or even the child, but we have to stop him."

"I don't want anyone else to die."

"Nobody wants that, Sharon. Now, Lisa's staying with me until this is straightened out. You'll be safe here for now. He needs your money. Sit tight, keep the doors locked, and answer the phone."

"Do you think he has Iris, that Iris has a little girl?"

"Anything's possible," Marti admitted, but she didn't think so. From the day Iris left home at seventeen, it was as if she had fallen off the face of the earth.

*   *   *

As much as she hated to, Marti called Lieutenant Nicholson. The possibility that Sharon could be telling the truth and that there could be repercussions was reason enough. After she explained the situation, Nicholson asked a few questions, then summed things up.

"So, MacAlister, your best friend married someone who has never been arrested, but who is wanted for questioning regarding at least one homicide. The subject has made several untraceable phone calls to her, suggesting that he has two individuals with him. One of them could be your sister-in-law. All communication has been oral. There has been no sighting of, and no physical contact with, the subject. He's requesting money. You don't know where he is, or if, in fact, he does have a woman and/or child with him, either voluntarily or involuntarily."

"That's correct," Marti agreed. Lieutenant Dirkowitz would have called Sharon and DeVonte by name and probably asked about Lisa. At least Nicholson hadn't complained about being awakened.

"We have no way of establishing jurisdiction here, or even of establishing the facts. Bypass the state police and call the FBI. And MacAlister, this is not your case, it's theirs. If they want it. Cooperate. Keep out of their way. I won't have any interference."

As soon as Marti hung up, Sharon said, "He'll know. And he'll kill them. He will kill them, Marti. Whoever they are, they're as good as dead."

"Sharon, he has to be stopped."

"And you really think you can catch him?"

"Not me, Sharon. The FBI."

"Oh, God," Sharon put her hands to her head. "Oh, my God. What have I done? He'll kill them."

Nicholson was wide awake when she hung up the phone. What in hell was going on? Why had MacAlister called her at this hour of the morning with what was, on the face of it, still a personal—perhaps even a nonexistent—problem? She didn't for a minute believe that MacAlister was finally acknowledging who was in charge. So, why had she called? To placate her friend?

She knew MacAlister had a life outside the cop shop. She had gone to her office one night, seen the pencil holder made with popsicle sticks, the picture of two boys with big grins holding up fish the size of minnows. She had read the framed newspaper article with the photo of MacAlister's daughter on the pitching mound. Occasionally she wondered what a life like MacAlister's might be like, then thought of her own childhood, growing up hungry and poor with eight siblings all lighter and brighter than she was, and no daddy. She had no regrets because she chose not to marry, no guilt because she preferred contraceptives to childbirth.

But who would have thought MacAlister's private life included a friend who might have married a murderer and a sister-in-law who had disappeared years ago? She would have liked to have asked questions, to have found out more details, but MacAlister might have misunderstood her interest, thought she gave a damn. How *would* having these problems affect how MacAlister did her job? Could her haphazard, I've-got-a-hunch methodology get any worse?

Marti stayed with Sharon until an FBI agent arrived a little before six in the morning. Mark Dobrzycki was a middle-aged man, medium height, with thinning brown hair. He was wearing running shoes and a jogging outfit, and carrying a tape recorder and headset. Sharon remained calm as she explained what had happened.

"DeVonte Lutrell is under suspicion for homicide," Dobrzycki explained. "We got involved because he crossed state lines. He is wanted for questioning, but we have no eye witnesses. No evidence, no outstanding warrant. This case, such as it is, is cold. And given what's going on in the country right now, it has zero priority."

"You can't help them?" Sharon said.

"We can't even substantiate that there is a 'them,'" Dobrzycki said.

"He called me. I talked to them."

"I understand that, but he could be playing some kind of con game. Until we have something more substantial, there's not much I can do. I am going to have someone come in this morning and play with your phones. Then, if he does call again, we might be able to do something."

Dobrzycki turned to Marti. "It's Sunday. Under the circumstances, there's not much we can do today unless we can verify a call from him. I will get busy trying to track down your sister-in-law and her child, if there is one. I'll get back to you on that as soon as I have something."

He gave both of them his card.

After the autopsies on John Doe and Jane Doe, Marti and Vik met with Dr. Mehta. The early morning events with Sharon and the FBI agent had been depressing enough. Now, meeting with Dr. Mehta in the office that had once belonged to Janet Petroski, Marti felt downright despondent. This was the first time she had been here since Janet retired. As soon as Marti looked at the conference table, she realized how much she would miss her. No matter what the season, there had always been a vase filled with fresh flowers on that table. Now everything of Janet's was gone.

Janet's serenity in the face of death, however senseless or brutal, had always strengthened Marti's determination to give closure to the living and bring justice to the dead. Change. Some people craved change, created change, seemed to thrive on it. Why did she always feel diminished by it?

One ornamental bamboo plant on the top shelf of the bookcase signaled Dr. Mehta's occupance. He had been looking out the window, but turned toward them as they entered the room.

"So," he said. "We begin."

These were their first homicides since he'd accepted the job.

He waved them to chairs, but remained standing. "We have two victims, killed approximately a week apart. Strangulation until unconscious, then a stab wound to the heart, which caused them to bleed out, followed by multiple postmortem stab wounds. Both victims had a dent in the top of the head made by a hammer."

"Ambivalence?" Marti asked. "First he gets close enough to touch them, then he gets angry."

"Exactly," Mehta agreed. "But that's not all. He does not stab them until they do not present any threat. He does not torture, maim, or rape. Just one blow to the skull when they are dead."

"A ritual," Marti said, then asked, "Trophies?"

"Not unless he takes something they are wearing. There are no missing body parts. He has not clipped their hair." Dr. Mehta thought for a moment. "He might have some aversion to physical contact. John Doe has no bruising and he was stabbed where he fell. Other than strangling him, he did not touch him with his hands. It's interesting that he didn't use a garrote of some kind."

"You're thinking serial killer," Vik said, then asked, "Are there any other similar deaths in the county?"

"Not that I'm aware of."

"The state?"

"I'll have to check."

"We've got morgue shots of John Doe," Vik said. "Anything useful you can tell us about Jane Doe?"

"You already have the generalities: height, weight, blood type. That's about it until we get DNA results."

"What about facial reconstruction?" Vik asked.

Mehta shook his head. "Both victims appear to be indigent. I can ask, but unless there's some compelling reason, or the state's attorney insists, I don't think the county will pay for it."

"And that's it?"

"We have trace evidence, Jessenovik, but nothing yet to compare it with."

They had not come up with a possible identification on John Doe yet, but at least they knew what he looked like. Now, having spent the better part of an hour behind a glass partition watching Mehta work on Jane Doe, Marti could close her eyes and see the decaying corpse on the stainless steel table. Brown hair, five feet one, missing teeth—no dental work—an ankle fracture severe enough to give her a permanent limp, broken ribs, a broken arm, none of which had ever been set. Marti wasn't optimistic about identifying her.

"I don't like your new boss," Mehta said. "And not just because she thinks she knows my job better than I do and has the right to tell me how to do it. Do you get along with her?"

"It's not like working for Lieutenant Dirkowitz," Marti admitted.

"She didn't want you to go to this task force meeting tomorrow, but I insisted."

Marti smiled. "Thank you." In Illinois, coroners were the only ones with the authority to arrest the sheriffs. That was often enough to make people cautious about disregarding their requests.

Just another depressing November day, Marti thought as they hurried back to the precinct. This was her least favorite time of year. Eight days of Indian summer had ended in mid-October. It seemed like the sun had been on hiatus ever since. There was nothing now but bare trees, gray skies, and a cold wind coming off the lake.

They drove over to the Sunrise Restaurant for breakfast: a three-egg Denver omelet oozing melted cheese for her, pancakes floating in syrup for Vik. While they ate, Marti filled in Vik on what had happened with Sharon.

"You really think that bastard's back?"

"That's what she says."

"No offense, Marti, but she wouldn't make this up, would she? You said Sharon and her daughter haven't been getting along. A little danger, real or imagined, and you get to keep the kid for a while, maybe Sharon even gets to leave town, go into hiding, whatever."

Something similar had occurred to her, at least the part about taking care of Lisa. Not because she didn't think Sharon wanted Lisa with her, but because she knew that their relationship had deteriorated. Marti had just negotiated another truce between them, and Lisa had told her then that she didn't want to be with her mother anymore. Marti knew that, like Joanna, Lisa needed someone to set boundaries for a few more years. Sharon couldn't seem to set limits for herself.

This business about DeVonte could be Sharon's way of asking for help. Her relationship with DeVonte, although brief, had changed her. She had become so indecisive that Marti had to help her with simple things, like where to take her car for repairs. And instead of teaching this year, Sharon had transferred to a desk job within the school system, which was little more than pushing papers and signing off on requisitions and didn't require any decision making at all. Maybe if she suggested to Sharon that Lisa spend the rest of the school quarter with her, this business with DeVonte would go away.

The desk sergeant smiled and shook his head when they arrived at the precinct. Lieutenant Nicholson wasn't there.

"Thank God," Vik said.

"Maybe, Jessenovik. Maybe." Mehta scheduled his autopsies early. It wasn't nine A.M. yet. "She hasn't taken a day off since she's been here."

They had missed first-shift roll call.

"I made sure everyone got copies of the John Doe morgue shots," the sergeant told them. "Beat cops will show them to the locals in the vicinities of the P.A.D.S. shelters."

"Good," Vik told him.

"Maybe we'll get lucky," Marti added.

Their best shot at identifying their John Doe was now. The faster they got the photos out, the more likely they were to run across someone who would remember seeing him. They had left copies at the bus station yesterday, but the Metra train station was closed on weekends. They would go there tomorrow.

* * *

"Mmm," Marti said. The aroma of freshly brewed coffee greeted them as soon as she opened the door to their office, but there was no sign of Cowboy or his partner, Slim. There was a box of doughnuts. She selected a chocolate filled and decided to drink the coffee black. She stared at her computer monitor while she waited for the coffee to cool.

Whenever she went through missing persons reports, she kept an eye out for anyone who could possibly be Iris. She also did that when she was checking wants. And now that the lieutenant was forcing her to, she could access programs she hadn't known existed. She was still amazed by the amount of information and the extent of the detail that could be retrieved. At first she was just trying to keep up with Vik, but now it had stopped being an unpleasant chore. She was almost beginning to look forward to spending time on-line. Sometimes it was almost fun. It was scary.

Nothing on Iris ever came up. If Iris was still alive, she didn't have a criminal record. She had not had a Social Security card issued in her name, nor had she showed up on a Chicago census. Iris, Johnny's big sister. Back when the department was still insisting that cocaine was not an inner-city problem, Iris discovered it. The funny thing was, when Iris, who was always so hyper she had trouble sitting still, became calmer, able to focus her attention on whoever was talking to her, everyone thought it was because she was getting older, not because she was getting high.

Then Iris dropped out of school, left home. Johnny, never the most talkative person, became quieter, seemed to withdraw, even from her. For a while he seldom spoke at all. Over time she got used to the silence, learned to interpret his cryptic one- or two-word commentaries. "Side one," he would say, and she knew he meant he was waiting for something else to happen. "Batter up" meant that he was expecting something to go wrong. Marti had never been close to Mrs. MacAlister after Iris went away. Johnny's mother had gone to her grave blaming him because she couldn't blame herself. And Johnny never shook off the guilt.

Now, when Marti thought about the day Iris left, she thought of a quilt her mother used to have. It was old and faded, but you could still make out most of the colors, until one day when it got tossed in with something that bled and it came out of the washing machine a dull uneven pink.

"A serial killer," she said. She tried not to think about the calories as she helped herself to another doughnut; doing that just made her eat more.

"Maybe, MacAlister. Maybe. Mehta said it looks that way."

"If it is, we might be one up on him, identifying it this fast." She had worked several cases involving serial killers while she was on the force in Chicago. Problem was, the city was so big and the victims seemed so random that they didn't realize who they were dealing with until the suspects were in custody.

She turned on her computer and began paging through the missing persons reports again. Vik did the same. This time they watched for brunettes and read the descriptions.

Marti came up with a couple of women who might be Jane Doe, but none of them seemed likely. "Nothing," she said. It sounded like a judgment. Or a prediction.

The door burst open.

"Son of a . . . ," Cowboy said. He stopped when he saw Marti and tossed his five gallon hat on his desk.

Slim, Cowboy's partner in the vice squad, came in right behind him and slammed the door. Slim was tall and lean with skin the color of caramel. He reeked of Obsession for Men, as always, but did not saunter over to Marti's desk and favor her with a dimpled, Cupid's-bow smile the way he usually did. Both men sat at their desks, arms folded.

"We haven't made any *real* arrests in six months," Cowboy muttered. "She needs to get off her ass and get out on the street. Going to tell me how to do my job? Like hell."

"Sounds like you two have met Lieutenant Nicholson," Vik said.

Marti suppressed a smile as she watched Vik struggle to keep a straight face.

"We're making too many misdemeanor arrests for prostitution," Slim said. "We don't have enough felony arrests for pandering."

Cowboy tilted his chair back until it hit the wall. "If the lady goes out on the street and finds her own johns, gives her man her money, and he knows how she got it, he's a pimp. And that's a misdemeanor. Period."

"Right," Slim agreed.

"She doesn't know anything about our clientele," Cowboy said. "Crack down on escort services? Give me a break. These guys want a quick blow job or maybe a threesome at a motel. Johns with any class hook up with one of those services that use bored suburban housewives."

Slim got a cup of coffee. "Woman's clueless," he said. "We're trying to talk to her about the increase in child molesting, getting LaCasa in to train new recruits on handling rape cases, supervising released sex offenders—"

"And," Cowboy interrupted, "underage kids getting turned out. Fastest growing population on the street—male and female—and all she wants to know is if we can nail the pimps for pandering. Like these kids are going to tell us that someone arranged for them to have sex."

"I take it she's your new boss," Vik said.

"Don't even go there, Jessenovik," Cowboy told him. "One man retires and in less than two months the whole department goes to hell. Someone needs to put out a hit on her." He turned to Slim. "You gonna cut back on the Obsession for Men?"

"What's this?" Marti asked.

"It clogs her sinuses," Slim said. He thought about that for a moment, gave Marti a slow, dimpled grin. "The better to stay away from you, my dear," he said. Marti could tell by the way he gave one short laugh that he was not amused.

Marti showed Slim and Cowboy the photos of their John Doe.

"Looks like a new face in town," Cowboy said.

"Nobody we've met up with," Slim agreed. "Or we're likely to meet. I take it he's dead."

Cowboy picked up a couple of the photographs. "We'll show him around."

When Lieutenant Nicholson sent for Marti and Vik, there were no snickers or smart remarks.

6

DeVonte hoisted his sports bag over his shoulder and got off the bus from Chicago. He was in a small town in downstate Illinois. In addition to wood-frame houses with porches and flagpoles, Main Street had one red brick building that looked as if it had been built at the turn of the century. It housed the police station, city hall, and the court. The fire department was in a newer red brick building, and had two engines, one ladder, and an ambulance. There was even a corner grocery store. Oranges were stacked in the window, along with apples, pears, and squash. A faded green-and-white striped awning was rolled out. At the far end of the street, DeVonte could see a white clapboard church with a steeple. He wondered how people could live in a place as quiet and ordinary and isolated as this.

It was a little after nine A.M. The bus should have pulled in at eight twenty, but now he would have less time to wait for Iris MacAlister O'Neill. The hospital for crazies that Iris was to be released from today was just outside the city limits. The bus passed it on the way in. Hospital patients were discharged every Sunday, which was also visiting day.

When DeVonte contacted the hospital and said he was Iris's brother Johnny, they told him that Iris never had visitors and, since nobody had made arrangements to pick her up, she would take the bus to Chicago. He thanked whoever it was and hung up before she could ask him any questions.

The bus station consisted of one room with pop, coffee, and

candy machines, and a public bathroom. It smelled of disinfectant. A man in a Greyhound Bus Lines uniform was sitting behind a desk reading a magazine.

DeVonte didn't want to call attention to himself, so he went outside. It was cold, and there was no sunshine, but there was no wind either. The sidewalk slanted toward the building. A rusting Cutlass Supreme was parked at the curb. The next bus to Chicago would leave at ten fifty A.M. He had over an hour to wait. He began walking.

The local shelter was a block away. DeVonte went to the next parallel street, walked down an alley, and stood where he could see what was going on without being noticed. It was just a storefront with a wide window and no curtains. People were sitting on couches and at card tables. One table, pushed against the wall, had a large coffee urn. A hand-printed sign announced: BAG LUNCH—NOON. Half a dozen men and a couple of women were standing outside smoking.

Farther down the block, there were a few street people standing in the doorway of a vacant store sharing a bottle in a paper bag. Most of the men were wearing jeans and jackets and watch caps, just as he was. So far, he had counted five blacks. He wouldn't stand out, at least not in this part of town.

DeVonte retraced his route as he headed back to the bus station, but kept walking until he found a diner a couple of blocks away. The waitress was talking on the phone. She kept talking as she doubled a heavy-duty paper cup and filled it with coffee, then put two muffins in a bag. She was still talking when he left. Back at the bus station, he ducked into a doorway across the street and waited. When the ten thirty bus came, nobody got off and nobody got on. There were four buses on the Sunday schedule, two the rest of the week. The next bus wasn't due until three fifteen P.M.

Vik had a new approach to dealing with Lieutenant Nicholson's three-minute response time. He took out a pocket-sized edition of a crossword puzzle book and a pencil. Marti wished she had learned how to crochet. She tapped her foot instead.

As soon as they stepped into her office, Nicholson said, "Sergeant Reskov has been released on bail."

"Bail? But who . . . ?" Marti asked. "There's no Sunday court. We could have held him until tomorrow."

"We were holding him for being drunk and disorderly. He's sober now."

"There's still a possibility that he could be charged with homicide. He has no address. And we let him go?"

"I don't tolerate insubordination," Nicholson said.

Marti chose to ignore the implication that asking questions was being insubordinate.

"Why weren't we notified right away?"

Instead of answering, Nicholson opened a folder and pulled out a typed report. "One little old lady might have seen someone at the window?"

"Reskov has the John Doe's blood on his shoe and his clothing."

"State's attorney didn't think that was enough to charge him. The area has been thoroughly searched, there's nothing else. Reskov's a drunk. He wandered into the house, got blood on himself, doesn't even remember doing it."

"So he says," Marti objected. "I can't believe this."

"He's a vet," Nicholson said. "Desert Storm. His kid just died over there. Friday was the kid's twenty-first birthday. He got drunk. Maybe he did wander into the house. So what?"

"And how do you know all of this?" Marti demanded.

"Maybe if you had asked the right questions . . ."

"Who did?"

"His attorney."

"He can't have a public defender. He hasn't been to court."

"Private," Nicholson said. "Retained."

"By whom?"

"I assume by Sergeant Reskov."

"Dumb call," Marti said. "A really dumb call. Who—"

Nicholson banged her fist on the desk. "Officer MacAlister! In this office, I make the decisions and I ask the questions."

"Yes, ma'am," Marti said. That was one rule the lieutenant was going to regret.

"And as for Dr. Mehta's suggestion that we might be dealing with a serial killer, anything is possible, but that doesn't mean it's likely. What you both need to understand is that nobody is going to give a damn about what happened to a woman who allowed herself to be battered for years, or a teenage transvestite, both of whom were indigent."

Marti thought of the years she and Johnny had spent looking for Iris. She wanted to say that might not be true, but didn't. She didn't think the lieutenant would hear her.

"With everything that has happened since nine-eleven," Nicholson went on, "and with ongoing military operations in Iraq, people *will* care about a decorated war veteran, especially one who served in Desert Storm *and* lost a son who was fighting in Enduring Freedom for Iraq. So, we will avoid using the words 'serial killer' in connection with this case, and when making any reference to Sergeant Reskov."

"We haven't determined that the victims were indigent, ma'am," Vik said.

"Oh? You think they dressed and lived like that on purpose? Or maybe they were out slumming?"

When Vik didn't answer she said, "What have you determined, Detective Jessenovik?"

"How they died," he said.

"That is a beginning."

In Marti's opinion, Nicholson was less hostile when she spoke to Vik. Of course, Vik was being careful to make statements and not ask questions.

"And what about family? Friends?"

"We're still checking that out, ma'am," Vik said.

"You can't even find a missing persons report on them. That should tell you something. Admit it. Their own families don't even care enough to look for them."

"Maybe when people read about it in the *News-Times*," Marti said, "and see a picture of the second victim—"

"There will be no picture in the newspaper," Nicholson told her.

"But if we don't—" Marti began.

"Detective MacAlister, I really don't need anyone to tell me how to run this department, or how to handle this case."

Marti felt as if she and Vik were playing good cop–bad cop, and she would be bad cop as long as Nicholson was their boss.

"There will be nothing in the newspaper that will call attention to these homicides. If these people are homeless, which I believe they are, there is no reason to alarm the public. They are not at risk. Should Sergeant Reskov become associated with or charged with their deaths, we'll keep it as low-key as possible."

"There could be additional victims," Vik said. "If—"

"Have we identified any within our jurisdiction?"

He shook his head. "No, ma'am."

"What happens outside of Lincoln Prairie is not our concern. And MacAlister, that includes that personal business we discussed earlier." Nicholson nodded toward the door and was reaching for the phone as they turned to leave.

Marti was mad as hell as she walked back to their office. First Nicholson gets on her for not following procedure, and then she does this. What was *with* that woman?

"Stupid, stupid, stupid," Marti said. "Dammit, Jessenovik, if she screws up this case, we will not take the blame."

Was that what Nicholson wanted? Would Nicholson allow a killer to go free because she didn't think anyone would care about the victims? Well, Nicholson had that one wrong. These victims had as much right to live as anyone else. And their killer would be found, and charged.

Neither Marti nor Vik spoke again until they reached their office.

"No questions!" Vik said as soon as he closed the door. "We can't ask her any questions! I didn't think she would shoot herself in the foot that fast. This is great!"

Everything was different now and she hated the way things had changed. "Maybe Cowboy is right, Vik, and our replacements are sitting there on the sidelines waiting for us to screw up."

"But we're not going to screw up, MacAlister."

"Wanna bet? These are throwaway people, Jessenovik. Reskov's a transient. If he goes away, and he did it, this case goes away. Then what? Whose ass is on the line if he is a serial killer and more bodies do turn up?"

Vik didn't answer.

"Look, Vik," she said. "The big cities have taken so much heat, they have so many people watching them, that they've got to clean up their act. Chicago has twelve thousand cops. We've got two hundred. Who's going to pay any attention to us? The only watchdogs we have are the people who live here. If they don't care . . . If two homeless people do not have the value of one drunken war vet, then we are expendable."

Vik took out a legal pad, picked up a pencil, and said, "Since we can't ask our boss any questions, what do we need to know?"

They wrote a list, but it was Sunday. Most of the people they needed to talk to weren't available.

"Mehta is proceeding with the inquiry on similar M.O.s statewide," Marti reported half an hour later. "Some counties are not cooperating. It is optional. And who knows if we'll get any information on Reskov from the military. Next of kin, maybe. And that might be all."

Vik swore in Polish and snapped a pencil in half. "Suppose we do find other victims. What if Reskov is our man?"

"Politics," Marti agreed. "Dirkowitz managed to stay above all of that, or at least keep us out of it. If it does come down to Reskov, he'll have to be arrested, if we can find him. The question might be how aggressively anyone prosecutes."

"Sounds like they'll negotiate something. I'm surprised he got a lawyer this fast. Makes you wonder why. Odds are he's already left town."

"His dog," Marti reminded him. "He doesn't know where his

dog is. He has to contact us sooner or later if he wants him back."

"If," Vik said.

The phone rang and Marti picked it up. It was a cop friend in Chicago.

"Hey girl, just thought I'd pass the word along about that new boss of yours. Watch your back."

"I've kind of figured that out."

"I actually got this from a guy, MacAlister."

"Got what?"

"Like I said, not much. No smoking guns. Lady plays it by the book. Got her degrees, looks good on paper."

"And?"

"She likes being the only double minority, and has gotten rid of other sisters—at least twice—by discrediting them. And Lincoln Prairie could be her stepping-off point for becoming a small-town head honcho. Meanwhile, my friend says you don't want her to think of you as the competition—for anything."

Marti thought it was a little late for that.

"Hyacinth," DeVonte said, "Is that your real name?"

"Real name? What's a real name? The one somebody gives you before you're born, or the name you give yourself when you find out who you are?"

She was wearing a pale-blue satin gown beneath a loose-fitting coat that hung just below her knees. The fake leopard fur swirled when she turned around, which she did often. The hem of the gown was torn in places and the fabric was stained.

"Hyacinth," he repeated. He didn't think she would let him call her Marti, like the others had.

His mother wouldn't have thought much of this one either. A tease, she would have said, someone looking for a little fun. But no spirit, boy. The woman has no spirit.

" ' "They called me the hyacinth girl," ' " she said in a singsong voice. "And what is your name, good sir?" Her gray hair looked as if someone had chopped off most of it. When she curtsied, DeVonte could see a few bare places.

"Just call me Eliot," he said, catching the poetic reference from "The Waste Land." "Or just T. S."

"Ah, a gentleman and a scholar." She sang that, too, and smiled up at him. Her teeth were crooked and yellow. Her breath smelled of onions and tobacco.

"You said you know a place where we can smoke a joint," he reminded her. "Without having to share it, my dear Hyacinth. I only have enough weed for two."

"I know many secret places."

"I bet you do."

"Oh, you agree, good sir."

"I think nobody had better see us go there."

She twirled around and the coat swung out again. " 'The dead tree gives no shelter,' but I will take you to the hyacinth garden."

This one might have had spirit years ago. She might even have a little spirit now.

He smiled, and thought, But soon she would know fear.

A white van with the seal of the state of Illinois pulled up in front of the bus station at ten minutes to three. Six men and a woman got out. They were each carrying a garbage bag. The men were wearing clothing that looked like it came from the Salvation Army. Two had on winter coats, the others were wearing light jackets. The woman was wearing green slacks. Her jacket was green, too, but they didn't match. She was wearing a red felt hat.

DeVonte watched from the corner. He had changed his clothes and stuffed them in the sports bag along with the hammer. He tossed that into a Dumpster not far from the abandoned building where he left Hyacinth.

He waited until the woman came out with a couple of the others to smoke a cigarette, then approached her. They all stood away from each other, taking long slow drags on their cigarettes.

"Mrs. O'Neill?" he asked. "Iris O'Neill?"

She looked up at him. "Missus. I haven't been called that in a while."

She was shorter than he expected, maybe five feet two, and even with a winter coat on he could see that she was thin. She had been pretty once. Her features were small and even. Her eyes were dark and almond shaped and slightly slanted, giving her face an odd, exotic look that was dissipated by the flatness of her expression.

"I'm Darrell Loomis," DeVonte said. "My wife and I are Lynn Ella's foster parents. She asks for you sometimes and we thought you might like to see her, too, but we didn't know how to get in touch with you. You know how the D.C.F.S. is. Then a case-worker let it slip that you were hospitalized."

Iris was looking at him as if she either didn't understand what he was saying or didn't believe him. Instead of explaining again, DeVonte took out the Polaroids he had taken of Lynn Ella yesterday. The child hadn't wanted to leave the house until he promised her a chocolate milk shake if she walked to the playground. He took several pictures inside first, and she had looked at herself and said, "No! It be in there."

When he tried to explained, she said, "No! No! It be in there. It catch me!"

She ran into the closet and slammed the door.

It took him half an hour of explaining that the camera was magic and magic was like being a seer or working root to get her to come out.

"Big Mama work root," she whispered.

She had to be talking about one of the women she had lived with in foster care.

"Did the mama who gave you to me work root?"

She shrugged. "Sometime she do."

"Can you?" he asked.

She nodded. It was his turn to be afraid. *I see,* she said. *I see.* She was a conjurer. She had been taught to work root. The mama who taught her to work root knew what he looked like. He would have to be careful with this one. Not let her know when he hurt her mother. Leave her some place afterward and get away from her, away from her magic.

Now Iris was staring at the photo that Lynn Ella had been afraid of. She reached out, touched it. When she didn't take it, DeVonte held it out. "Here. It's yours. This one, too."

"Lynn Ella," Iris whispered. "My baby." She shivered.

"You're cold," DeVonte said.

"What else is new?"

This one did have spirit. His mama might have liked her—for a few days anyway. "Then I'm cold," he said. "If you're not. Let's get some coffee."

As he motioned for her to walk ahead of him, he realized he was glad there would be someone in the apartment who might be able to get Lynn Ella to eat and maybe even sleep in a bed and play with dolls like a normal kid. Once they were in the apartment and she was with Lynn Ella, he would have to find out if Iris needed drugs or had prescriptions to be filled. She had left this child before. She would leave her again. He might be able to string her along for a few days by pretending to look for her older daughter, Kim, but only until he got the money from Sharon. When he held the door to the bus station open for her, Iris turned to look at him. She seemed puzzled. But unlike Hyacinth, she didn't seem crazy at all.

7

Fred sat on a log not far from where his campsite had been. They had his dog. They had his gear. The gear he could replace, but he missed Geronimo. He looked up, saw blue skies beyond the tree branches, breathed deeply. Fresh air, no human smells, no jail odors. He stood up, stretched, walked deeper into the woods. No bars, no walls, no barriers. Just trees. He listened. Sparrows arguing. The sudden flapping of crows' wings. Familiar sounds. Nobody calling for the nurse. No guards talking to the prisoners or laughing or talking to each other. Nobody watching him. He patted his pocket but did not take out Andy's letter.

He walked for a while, getting used to being free again. Eventually he went to the edge of the woods and found the place among the trees where he could look at the house without anyone seeing him. There was a for-sale sign out front and yellow police tape blocking off the front steps. Something had happened there, but what? He was drunk that night. Did he do something he shouldn't have?

He wouldn't have broken into the house. He had no reason to do that. He never wanted to be inside a house again. He didn't even sleep in the tent unless it was too cold or too wet outside. Until he found Geronimo, he had wanted to be alone. He didn't even want to hear the sound of his own voice until he began hanging out with that dog. And the only reason he talked to Geronimo was because a dog couldn't talk back.

He would have to find out what happened. If they thought he

did something, why did they let him go? Because they couldn't prove it? And, who sent that lawyer? He hadn't asked for one. Maybe they were trying to trick him. Maybe they released him to see if he would go into the house. Was there a cop watching the place, waiting for him? He felt trapped. He couldn't leave, not without Geronimo. He didn't think those cops were lying when they said Geronimo was with another cop, but he needed to be sure. He had to make sure Geronimo wasn't at the pound, wasn't going to be put down, he had to see if the cop would keep him for a few more days. Then he could decide what to do next.

He went back to the place where his tent had been, walked a bit farther to the nearest ravine. Dipped his hands into the water and drank. He was thirsty. The water had a brackish taste, but it was cold. There was something odd about this place. Birds came, but there were few nests in the bare trees. Geronimo had caught a rabbit with one hind leg and a little bump where its other leg should have been. Some of the squirrels had odd-shaped bare patches where no fur grew. Others had stumps where their tails should have been. And, even though it was close to winter and getting cold, foxes and raccoons and even skunks should still be foraging, but he hadn't seen one. But then he was used to forests, not little patches of woods in the middle of the city. Maybe the size of the place and the traffic and businesses close by made a difference.

Iris looked out the window on the bus and watched the trees go by. She hadn't seen this many trees in months. Mr. Loomis sat beside her. She did not like him.

"Lynn Ella was so excited when we told her you were coming," he said.

She wished he would shut up.

"Wait until you see the doll she got for Christmas. We ordered it special. It looks just like her."

He was talking about her baby, her Lynn Ella, as if he were the child's daddy. As if she stopped being a mother when the state took her daughters away from her.

"She loves burgers from Po' Boys and chocolate milk shakes."

She didn't know that. She didn't know Lynn Ella's favorite cartoon character, or favorite toy, or best friend. She didn't know what grade she was in or what school she went to. Lynn Ella was as much a stranger to her as she was to Lynn Ella. Why did he have to keep reminding her of that?

The pictures he had given her were in her pocket. She wanted to take them out, look at them again. Lynn Ella would have no pictures of her, no memories of her. Lynn Ella would not know who she was. She might even be afraid of her. What would she say to this little girl? She had not seen her or held her since she was three months old. She was not ready for this. She could not do this. Not yet. Not today.

"We should be stopping somewhere soon," he said. "Last stop before we get to Chicago."

When he patted her hand, she wanted to snatch her hand away. Mr. Loomis wasn't the kind of man she would ever want to be around. Too smooth, too slick, too uppity. He wasn't someone she would want her child to be around either. Maybe that was because he knew her little girl better than she did. Still, she couldn't stand being touched by him. His smile, the things he said, it all seemed phony. She wouldn't have believed anything he told her about Lynn Ella if he didn't have those pictures.

Were they really pictures of her child? Why did she think they were? This was a small, scrawny child. Her baby had been a big girl, chubby. This child did not look like the man who fathered her. Iris didn't think Lynn Ella looked like her either. Something was wrong. She knew that. She just didn't know what. Trust your instincts. The thought came to her so suddenly, and was so unexpected that she caught her breath.

"Are you okay?" Mr. Loomis asked.

She nodded. Johnny. Her brother Johnny used to tell her to trust herself. She had gone back once, to the two-flat where they grew up. The second-floor apartment was empty. The tenant on the first floor still lived there. An old woman, she peered out the window, then opened the door. "Iris! It really is you! How have you been? Come on in. You just come right on in."

She didn't go inside. She stood on the doorstep and asked where her mother was.

The woman shook her head. "You've been gone too long, Iris. She passed back in 'eighty-nine. Heart attack." She snapped her fingers. "Went just like that. And Johnny, he's gone, too. Got shot. Come in and sit awhile and I'll tell you everything that's happened since you left."

Gone. Johnny and Ma. They were both gone. She turned and went away. "Trust your instincts." How many times had Johnny told her that? She had refused to listen to him then. Maybe it was time that she did.

"When we get to Chicago," Mr. Loomis said, "we'll catch a cab to my place. I left my car at home. Lynn Ella knows you're coming. She'll be up waiting for you."

She could hear the Islands in his voice. "Are you from Jamaica?"

Instead of answering he said, "I live not too far from a cemetery. I hope that doesn't bother you."

"Can you see it from your house?"

"No."

"Then it won't bother me. I won't be staying there anyway. I have someplace to go. I think I should go there first, see Lynn Ella tomorrow."

"Oh, no, no," he said. "Lynn Ella is waiting. She is so excited. I can drive you wherever you need to go after you see her."

"How long have you had her?"

"Since she was two. Wait until you see the photo albums. She'll grow up right before your eyes."

She would be a stranger to that child. There would be no welcome there. If anything, Lynn Ella would be angry with her, or afraid that she would take her away from this man and his wife. They were her parents now. She was nobody. Trust your instincts. She did want to know her child. She did want to see her. But more than anything, she wanted what was best for her. Visiting at a halfway house, with a mother who had A.D.H.D., who was bipolar and a recovering crack addict, would not be what was best for any child. Not after living in a real home with the same family for six years.

"Do you have other children?"

He hesitated, then said, "No. My wife could not have children."

"Then you must want to adopt her. She's been with you for as long as she can remember."

"We want her to know her birth mother."

That might not be a good thing, Iris thought. She did not say that aloud.

The bus pulled off the highway, made a couple of turns and pulled into a truck stop. The driver parked near the gas pumps. There were fast-food places on both sides of the street.

"Food," Mr. Loomis said. "I'm hungry enough to eat anything. How about you?"

"I have money," she said. She had fifty-three dollars.

He followed her off the bus and took her by the arm. When they went into the filling station it was like a small store.

"Hot dogs, doughnuts," he said. "Not much, but it will do. My wife will have supper waiting."

"I need to use it."

"Me too." He hesitated. "You go first."

"There are men waiting ahead of you," she said, "but no women standing around."

A woman was walking toward them.

Iris spoke loud enough for the woman to hear. "I promise I won't get lost, Mr. Loomis. And I know you won't let the bus leave without me."

The woman stopped. "Oh," she said. "I remember you from the hospital." She looked at Mr. Loomis. "I'm going to Chicago, too. She can come to the restroom with me."

He hesitated.

"We'll only be here for another ten or fifteen minutes," the woman said. "You'd better hurry up, unless you want to use the bathroom on the bus. She'll be safe with me. Now go."

He went.

Iris let the woman take her by the arm. As soon as they were in the bathroom the woman said, "You looked like you were in trouble. I go to that hospital every week to see my daughter. I see the men waiting at that bus station to see if any women are released, watch them getting friendly. Some of them even have cars. Predators, all of them."

"I don't know him," Iris said. "I don't believe what he's telling me."

"Then you get away from him. There will be another bus coming through in two hours."

As Iris turned to go, the woman said, "Wait. Give me your hat."

The men's bathroom was crowded. When DeVonte came out, the woman was waiting for him, but not Iris.

"I made sure she got on the bus," she told him.

"Thanks."

"She got herself some food. You want something, you'd better hurry up. The bus will be leaving in a few minutes. Oh, and she's sitting in the back with me, keeping me company."

DeVonte didn't like that at all. But he would be near the front. Iris would have to walk past him to get off. When he got on the bus, he looked for Iris in the back, saw her red hat. The woman smiled and waved at him, then leaned down to talk to Iris. As soon as he sat down, the bus pulled out.

Marti and Vik were getting ready to order something to eat when the phone rang.

"How's Geronimo?"

"Fred?" Marti asked. Vik raised his eyebrows. He checked the number on the caller I.D. and picked up his phone. Marti nodded. He was getting Fred's location.

"Yeah, man. I don't know what the hell is going on here, but I want to know if my dog's okay."

"Wait a minute. I'll let you speak with the cop who has him." She passed the phone to Cowboy.

"Yeah, Fred. What's up?" Cowboy said, then, "He's more than welcome to stay with me as long as you want, but I think he misses you."

He listened for a moment.

"No, I haven't been feeding him that brand. He eats though. I'll stop and get him some on the way home. Anything else I need to know?" He listened again. "Bones. Sure thing. He's a good dog, man. But I don't think he's too crazy about being inside so much. I take him out two, three times a day, but that's not like being in the great outdoors. He does sleep a lot. Huh? . . ." He listened. "No, man, he's real good. He hasn't chewed up anything. I'm just not you. He's *waiting* for you, man. How can I help you so you can get him back?" He waited again.

"No, no. Geronimo isn't going anywhere until you come and get him or I bring him to you. You don't have anything to worry about. Just figure out what I need to do to get you two together. Here, I'll give you my cell phone number. Got a pencil?" Cowboy gave him the number, repeated it, then said, "Hey, look, man, I'm a Desert Storm vet, too. Army." Cowboy told him his division, brigade, and battalion. He listened, then said, "You were a jarhead at Khafji! First Marine Expeditionary Forces! Damn! You guys were awesome. We didn't come in until after the Eighteenth Airborne did their thing." He laughed again, listened. "Yeah, been there. Look, man, anything happens, you got a friend. Just call me. Anytime. And don't worry about Geronimo. Anything I can do, anything, you let me know. Hell, you might be why I'm still alive."

When Cowboy hung up he just sat there for a few minutes. Marti didn't intrude. He pushed his hat back, sucked in his breath, finally said, "That takes me back a long way. Marines went in first at Khafji, then Airborne. We went in last. If it hadn't been for the Marines, we might not have gone in. Or, worse, not come out."

"He didn't ask any questions about Friday night?" Marti asked. "About being arrested?"

"Nope."

"He didn't ask about his gear, did he? The evidence techs aren't finished with it yet."

"He just wanted to know about his dog."

"Good." Marti turned to Vik. "You get a fix on where he is?"

"Called from a pay phone four blocks from the Deer Woods. Looks like he went home."

Marti looked at Cowboy. He was staring out the window. His face was expressionless. Johnny had done that, hiding whatever he was reliving, whatever he felt, just like Cowboy was. What was it about war that did this to them? She had assumed it was the killing, the destruction. But looking at Cowboy, thinking about Fred, and remembering Johnny, she knew it was more than that. Whatever it was, it reached into their souls.

"Do you think he killed those two people?" Cowboy asked.

"Don't know," Vik said.

"Got enough to charge him for it?"

"No. Not yet."

"Cowboy," Marti said, "my gut feeling is that Fred didn't do it. Our killer is very methodical, very angry, has rituals. When we get more information about Fred, I'll have a better feel for it; but right now, being a loner, being a vet, going through God knows what in Iraq, doesn't make him a killer. Listen, I know, I married two Vietnam vets. Johnny was a cop. Ben is a fireman paramedic."

"Yeah," Cowboy said. "And I'd trust you and Jessenovik with my life. This one's personal though. Real personal. And we've got this loose-cannon lieutenant now . . ."

"Oh," Vik said, "don't worry about her. As far as she's concerned, it's hands off with Fred. He's a vet. Our victims are indigent. Who gives a damn about them?"

"You serious?" Cowboy said. "That's good. For Fred. At least I think so. I want to go with you if you bring him in."

Marti looked at him. Vik spoke. "Are you sure?"

"I owe him that."

"We'll remember," Marti promised. God, she hoped the killer wasn't Fred.

"I need to help you with this," Cowboy told them. "But I don't know what I can do."

"Let him talk to you," Marti said. "Try to keep in touch."

"And be a cop," Cowboy said. "Be a good cop."

Marti didn't like the way he said that. She thought she knew Cowboy well enough to expect him to do what he had to, but she also knew there were things about men and war that she would never understand.

Marti got out the file she had put together on DeVonte Lutrell. He had no arrest record, no prints or photos on file, but she had located his birth certificate. He was born in the West Indies on Grand Bahama Island. The information on the birth certificate matched what he entered when he applied for a license to marry Sharon. Marti hadn't traced back much further than that. He had no siblings and both of his parents were deceased. Their deaths were the only oddity. His mother had killed his father in self-defense when DeVonte was nine years old. Eight years later, the mother was killed by an unknown assailant. DeVonte left the island after her death. He completed his undergraduate studies in Florida and Georgia, had been a graduate student at Cornell University. He left without receiving his degree, and Marti had lost the trail at that point. But as far as missing persons went, Iris was the real enigma. After Johnny's death, Marti had found the file he kept, the searches he made, the records he checked. Johnny had not been able to come up with anything either.

When Lynn Ella woke up, DeVonte was still gone. He made her go outside yesterday, Big Mama and Mama Dee never let her do that. She was afraid, but he held her hand. They walked to the place that had toys to play on, but there were children there and Big Mama never let her go near the children.

"School?" she asked.

"No. This is a park with a playground. The other children won't hurt you."

He had a box that he pointed at her and when the paper came out she was on it. When Big Mama saw them do that on television, she said the devil was in the box trying to catch them.

"It be in there," she said.

"This is your picture," he told her. "It's magic, like working root."

She backed away. She didn't want nobody working root on her. And she didn't want the devil to catch her.

"I'm going to show this to your mama so she can see what you look like."

"A new mama?"

"No. Your real mama."

"Real?"

"Yes, like me. I'm real."

"Daddy?"

"No," he said. "I'm not your daddy."

She put her hands over her ears and cried.

DeVonte wasn't her daddy. He didn't want to be her daddy. And he was gone. Maybe he wouldn't come back. Maybe she would be here all alone, or maybe another mama would come and take her away. She liked it here. She liked DeVonte. She wished he was her daddy.

It was day when he left, but now it was night. That was a long time to be gone. Maybe he was gone away, the way all the mamas went away. He had to come back. He couldn't leave her. Who would take care of her?

When it had been quiet for a long time, her stomach told her it was hungry. She didn't want any food, but her stomach said she should eat anyway. She tiptoed to the kitchen. He had left a bag of food on the table. It wasn't McDonald's, but something round and wrapped in paper was inside. When she opened it, it was a sandwich. Bread. Meat. Ketchup. A leaf. She put the leaf into the bag and squeezed the bag until the leaf was dead. Then she ate the sandwich. There was a milk shake, too. It wasn't cold anymore and it didn't taste good, but she drank it. Then she went back to the closet. Would he come back? Would he bring another mama? Would she have to leave? She curled up on the blanket, put her head on the pillow, and waited.

It was dark when the bus pulled in at Ninety-fifth Street in Chicago. DeVonte didn't know that it stopped there. He looked behind him and saw Iris's red hat. When they reached the terminal on Randolph, he would get off, wait for her right by the door, make sure she didn't leave his side again. They would walk outside together. He would hustle her into a cab and take her to his apartment.

He was looking out the window when he saw the red hat go by. He turned again. Both women were gone. He jumped up, got off. He could see the red hat on the other side of Ninety-fifth, but the woman wearing it had on a black coat, not a green jacket. What the hell . . . ? He didn't see the woman who had helped Iris anywhere.

Brakes squealed as he crossed the street. Car horns blared. A man yelled curses. He kept going until he caught up with the red hat.

"Where is she?"

The woman snatched her arm away. "Don't you put your hands on me, young man."

"Where is she?"

"Where are your manners?"

"Where is she?"

"Where's who?"

"The woman who was wearing that hat."

"This hat? Woman sitting beside me gave me this hat. Gave me ten dollars not to take it off. Nice hat; warm, too."

"Who was she?"

"Who was who?"

"The woman sitting beside you."

"I don't know. I never saw her before. We were both visiting family at the hospital."

DeVonte turned away. Too many people could identify him. This woman would remember him. The other woman who had spoken with Iris would remember him. That bum in Lincoln Prairie had seen him at the house where the women were found. He was running out of time.

8

Iris got off the Greyhound at Ninety-fifth Street at three minutes after twelve in the morning. It was a well-lit area, an overpass built above the expressway. Traffic was heavy, but moving fast on the Dan Ryan. Even though she was on the south side and far from the Loop, she felt safer than she would have if she had gone to the Greyhound terminal near downtown Chicago. The streets were dark there, and all but deserted except for the winos and junkies and the homeless. And she thought Mr. Loomis would be more likely to wait for her there. She didn't know why, but she didn't trust Mr. Loomis. She put her hand in her pocket, touched the Polaroid snapshot he had given her. If this was her little girl . . . No, seeing Lynn Ella again was not a good idea. They had already said their good-byes.

A bus came, then another. The third bus was hers. Two transfers later and she was a block and half from Miss Lottie's house. That wasn't where they told her to go when she left the hospital, but Mr. Loomis wouldn't be able to find her there. If Miss Lottie let her come in. The last time she was here, close to two years ago, she had left with Miss Lottie's money.

Iris looked at the small brick bungalow for a few minutes, then held on to a wrought iron railing as she walked up the steps to the front door. L. Hodge. The name on the mailbox hadn't changed. It was several more minutes before Miss Lottie came to the door.

"Who is it?" she called without opening the door. "What do you want?"

"It's me, Miss Lottie, Iris O'Neill."

"Who's with you?"

"Nobody. It's just me."

There was no answer. A few moments later she said, "Are you really alone, Iris?"

"Yes, ma'am."

"Why are you here this time of night?"

"I don't have anyplace else to go."

"What makes you think you've got a place here?"

"Nothing, ma'am. I've just got no place else to go."

"You come on in, then, Iris. It's too late to be walking the streets."

Iris followed Miss Lottie down the hall to the kitchen. The rooms were small, the kitchen little more than an oversized pantry. The refrigerator and stove were olive green. The orange linoleum was worn down to the wood floor in places. There was a small Formica table by the window, with two mismatched wooden chairs. The curtains looked new. White with yellow and orange butterflies.

Lottie Hodge was a tiny, dark-skinned woman with caring eyes and a smile that made Iris feel welcome. She reminded Iris of her second grade teacher, a gentle, quiet woman who never scolded.

"Where are you coming from?" Miss Lottie asked as she opened the refrigerator door.

"State hospital. Got out today."

Miss Lottie was a retired social worker and a volunteer at a soup kitchen. Somehow, they had become friends.

"They said I'm bipolar with attention deficit disorder."

"You think so?" Miss Lottie assembled bread, cheese, and lunch meat on the table.

"The medicine they give me for it works."

"And the cocaine?" She added a small jar of mayonnaise and a squeeze bottle of mustard.

"I've been clean for eleven months and six days."

"Craving?"

Iris wondered about that as she put ham and cheese on a slice of bread. "No," she said. She hadn't thought about doing drugs in a while. It was an odd kind of freedom, not wanting drugs; it took getting used to. "I feel different with the medication. I'm not always jumpy and on the move. I can sit awhile, read a book. I can even think about one thing at a time."

"You've been diagnosed with half a dozen things. Maybe they got it right this time."

"Yeah, Miss Lottie," she said. "Maybe they did." She took a bite out of the sandwich.

"Coffee, tea, or Kool-Aid?"

"Red Kool-Aid?"

"If that's what you want."

Miss Lottie got a plastic pitcher down from the shelf.

"I've got your money," Iris told her.

"We can talk about that."

Twenty dollars. Miss Lottie let her in that night, told her she could sleep in the spare room, and while the old woman warmed up some gumbo, she stole twenty dollars and left. Today, she found it hard to believe she had done that; but back then, it was no big deal.

"We need to talk about my baby."

"Lynn Ella?"

Iris showed her the Polaroid snapshots and told her what had happened. "I can't even say for sure that she's mine. It's been so long I don't know what either one of my girls looks like."

Lottie looked at the pictures. "How old is she now?"

"Eight in September."

"But you're not sure this is her?"

"If I could see her, I think I'd know. But that's not going to happen."

"If nothing else, it would put your mind at ease to know both of your girls are okay. Want me to see what I can find out?"

Iris nodded. "Foster care," she said. "Sometimes they're not put in good foster homes."

Fred woke up to silence. He reached out for Geronimo, remembered the dog wasn't there, and sat up. Trees. Cold. It was still dark. Darkness. Something had happened Friday night, but what? Whatever it was, it was hidden in his brain and he couldn't remember. Thirsty. He went to the ravine, scooped up some water, and drank it. He shivered, relieved himself, went back to his sleeping bag.

Alcohol. No matter how bad it tasted, it promised at least the possibility of a few hours without dreams. Now he wished he hadn't got drunk that night, the night of Andy's birthday. He did not understand this absence of memories, or even fragments of memories of what had happened.

Marti called Denise Stevens at home as soon as she woke up. She explained what was going on with Sharon.

"You want to try to find this little girl?" Denise said. "Lynn Ella; last name, MacAlister?"

"I assume so. If she exists."

"I know," Denise agreed. "Sharon could be crying wolf. Unfortunately, even if she is, we still have to check it out. Worst case, we all look like fools. That's a lot better than, worse case, somebody is dead."

"Thanks," Marti said. The possibility of DeVonte Lutrell's having a child with him was scary. She didn't believe for a minute that he would let a woman live, or a child. Assuming he wasn't alone, whoever was with him was dead as soon as he got Sharon's money. If not sooner. People like DeVonte enjoyed killing, and they didn't leave witnesses, at least not on purpose. This was one time when she hoped Sharon was lying. God help them all if she was telling the truth.

*   *   *

Lieutenant Nicholson sent for Marti and Vik right after roll call. Vik popped a couple of antacid tablets as they headed for her office.

"How's Mildred?" Marti asked. He was still grumpy, which wasn't that unusual, but several times while the sergeant was talking, Vik was staring into space.

"She's going to physical therapy for her leg muscles, has to use a cane or a walker. The hallway is narrow and the rooms aren't that big. I think I'm going to have to sell the house, find a place where she can get around a little easier. It's that or get rid of most of the furniture."

He didn't take out his crossword puzzle book as they waited the proscribed three minutes before being admitted to Nicholson's office. When they did go in, Lupe Torres, Marti's favorite beat cop, and a male uniform new to the department were sitting there. Although Marti didn't react, she did resent their being allowed to sit when she and Vik were always required to stand.

"I've assigned Officers Torres and Holmberg to you for training, effective immediately," Nicholson said, without preamble. "It will take a couple of days to get your office rearranged."

Marti resisted an impulse to put her hands over her ears. She didn't want to hear this. She wanted to turn and walk away. Change. Again. There wasn't enough room in their office for six cops. Cowboy and Slim would be relocated. She didn't think she could handle many more of these abrupt, unexpected changes. She felt hot, then got a chill. Cowboy had been right. Nicholson did intend to get rid of her and Vik. She was looking at their replacements. Lupe was a good cop, had a good rep, was female and a minority, and had worked with them before. But Holmberg? Why had Holmberg been chosen?

Marti approached their office reluctantly, wondering what else had changed, expecting Cowboy and Slim to have moved out while they were with Nicholson. By the time she opened the door, she was sweating. She looked in, then exhaled slowly.

Everything was the same. For now, she cautioned herself, but not for long.

Cowboy and Slim had been in court all morning. They had three rape cases scheduled and Marti expected them to be there all day. If either of them knew this was going to happen, he would have told her. She wrote a quick note: "Lupe and new uniform now working with us and sharing office. Don't know what's happening next." She gave it to the sergeant to have delivered to them.

"You know how to make coffee?" Vik asked Holmberg.

"No, sir."

"Well, you'd better learn—fast."

"Yes, sir." Holmberg was close to six feet in height. He had brown hair and brown eyes. He looked good in a uniform and seemed at ease with everyone.

Lupe had worked with them often enough to make herself at home. Marti looked at her now and saw a few gray hairs mixed in her black hair. There were creases at the corners of her dark eyes, too. Marti didn't think it was from smiling. Right from the start, Lupe had been a good cop. Focused, determined, assertive without becoming aggressive. She took to neighborhood policing like she was born street-smart, and even though she was barely five feet four and had to look up at half the people she encountered, she got immediate respect.

"So," Lupe said. She took the chair by Marti's desk and waved Holmberg over to the chair by Vik. "What's up? I don't trust that woman as far as I can spit. She blindsided us on this one. No advance notice. Word is, she's got it in for you, Marti."

Marti shrugged. "Been there before."

"Well, I haven't been there," Lupe said. "Until now. And I don't appreciate it. Whatever this is, you've got a friend."

"Thanks." Marti leaned back and looked at Holmberg.

"Criminal justice degree," he said. "Minor in computer science. Northwestern. I interned with the Cook County Sheriff's Department. Are you two shorthanded?"

"We get twelve to twenty homicides a year, on average," Marti told him. "This has been a big year for homicide-suicides. Vik and I handle all death investigations and work on about two dozen cold cases when we have the time. When we have a lot going on, Lupe helps out."

"So, we're not here because you've got too much to do."

"No. We average a ninety- to ninety-five–percent arrest rate."

Holmberg whistled. "I didn't think I'd find the same politics here as there was in the Sheriff's Department."

"The only place where you can get away from politics is in a casket," Vik said. "And I'm not sure about that."

"I just want to be a cop. And I grew up here. And this department has a good reputation."

"And it should," Vik said. "My dad was a cop here. How many homicides have you worked?"

"Two. Canvassing, mostly. And they let me watch interrogations."

"Well," Marti said, "you might not do much more than that now. We'll bring you up to speed on the case we're working on. You're going to go through all of the reports. Then, we'll see."

"And it's not busy work," Lupe told him. "It's the only way you learn. And although there are no quizzes, these two will expect you to know as much as they do about what's going on."

Holmberg smiled. "Sounds good."

Marti liked him. He wasn't arrogant like some rookies who had a new gun and a shiny badge. "How good are you with computers?" she asked.

He shrugged. "They're just another tool. Make life easier. Usually."

She exchanged looks with Vik. This might not be too bad. However, as soon as this case was wrapped up, she was going to have to start looking for another job. She thought about the task force meeting. Word was that it was really an interview. Maybe that was why Nicholson wanted to go.

*   *   *

Dr. Mehta called before Marti and Vik could leave for the task force meeting, which was scheduled for ten A.M. When they came to the coroner's facility, Marti had to remind herself that Mehta was not sitting behind Janet's desk. It was his desk now. But she couldn't help looking at the conference table and wishing for a vase of flowers.

Dr. Mehta looked tired. "I thought you would want to see this right away." He pushed several fax sheets toward them. "These two women have also been found dead since the shelters opened at the end of October. Both were homeless, both found in Cook County. Manual strangulation with a dent in the skull."

Marti looked through the reports, waited while Vik read them twice, then admitted, "Fred could have done this. Minimum, he's not likely to have an alibi."

"You have a suspect?" Mehta asked.

"More or less," Vik told him. "Maybe."

"Meaning?"

"Sorry, we can't explain."

Mehta frowned.

Marti looked at him and decided she could trust him. "Fred is a Desert Storm vet. His son joined the Marines, too, and died in Iraq earlier this year. Our victims are just . . ." She shrugged.

Dr. Mehta nodded.

The task force meeting wasn't what Marti expected. They met with Frank Winans in a small office in the County Building. Marti only knew of Winans by reputation. He had retired from the Sheriff's Department as chief of detectives with the rank of captain. Word was that he was a cop's cop. Winans was a tall man with a burly chest and the build of a man who worked out regularly. His hair was receding, but clipped short. He had a white handlebar moustache and greeted them with a serious expression that gave way to a smile.

"This is an idea," Winans began. "And I'm asking for your input. For the next few weeks I'm going to be meeting with detectives who work throughout northern Illinois and have experience in five areas: organized crime, vice, gangs and narcotics, violent crimes, and homicide. The questions of the day are: Can we be more effective if we apply your expertise on a countywide, rather than just a departmental, basis? And since the criminals don't confine their activities to one jurisdiction, should we continue to conduct our investigations as a city or town, or on a regional basis?"

They discussed those questions for about two hours. Marti liked the idea of a county or regional operation for major crimes. Vik wasn't opposed, but he did have concerns about the effect on community policing.

"What do you think?" Marti asked, later, as she drove back to Lincoln Prairie.

"You heard my questions," Vik said. "Would all departments be required to cooperate? How would we interact with other departments? Who would have ultimate jurisdiction? Sounds great in theory. But, hell, we can't even get all of the counties in this area to check for victims that fit our subject's M.O."

"I know," Marti agreed. "But it's an interesting idea, isn't it?"

"Especially given our current job situation," Vik agreed.

"If offered would you . . . ?"

"I don't know," Vik admitted, voice gruff. "I really don't know."

Marti heard the sadness as he spoke, knew how much pride he took in being a cop in his hometown, just like his father had been.

"Change," she said. "Even when it's good, it's not. Even when it's necessary, I hate it."

The next meeting was scheduled for Wednesday. Marti wasn't sure how she felt about it, or if she wanted to attend.

By noon, Fred had gotten a haircut and a shave. He also bought a pair of jeans and a down jacket. That done, he went to the pound. He didn't think he looked that different, but if the animal control people had been asked to watch for someone who looked like he did in his mug shot, they might be less likely to make the connection. He asked if they had picked up a pit bull, then checked out all seven caged dogs. Geronimo was not among them.

He walked downtown, picked up a *News-Times,* and sat on a park bench. He went through the newspaper twice before he found what he was looking for.

"Bingo," he said aloud.

This had to be it. Two people found dead. Possible suicide. But the only unusual deaths this weekend. They thought he killed two people. But they hadn't charged him with it. And they let him out. Did that mean he was in the clear? Or that they just didn't have enough evidence to hold him? And they hadn't just released him, someone had bonded him out. But who? And why? The lawyer wouldn't say. What had happened Friday night that he couldn't remember? And what was going on now? All he had to do was get the hell away from here. No, they could track him down through his military records. Running would only make things worse. Besides, he couldn't just up and leave his dog. Bad enough he had left his wife and his kid. No, he couldn't run, not again. Not because he didn't want to, but because everything he ran from so far had found a way to catch up with him.

When the call came in from the bus station, Lupe and Holmberg were out canvassing. Marti was at her computer, working her way through half a dozen report forms. A driver had just come in, looked at John Doe's picture, and remembered him. The bus was due to leave for Chicago in ten minutes. Marti agreed to talk with the driver on the phone now, but explained that they might have to meet later.

"He got on in Milwaukee," a woman said. "Friday morning. He was dressed like a girl, but I could tell right off he was a guy. He was too young to be doing things like that. Way too young, but none of my business."

That was all the driver remembered.

"John Doe," Marti said when she hung up. "He arrived about this time Friday, came here from Milwaukee."

"How many vagrants you think they've got there?"

"Maybe there's a want on him."

"For prostitution, most likely," Vik agreed. "Let's clear it with the lieutenant and go up there."

"Great idea. As soon as I finish entering this. These new programs are okay." They were much easier to use and she liked being able to look up information instead of requesting it from someone else. She supposed she had Lieutenant Nicholson to thank for that, but she would never tell her.

"They grow on you," Vik said.

"Milwaukee," she said. "I wonder if they have C.H.R.I.S., or something similar." The Criminal History Records Information System, the *Who's Who* of convicted criminals. She liked the idea of checking out another department's programs and comparing them to her own. She was more than a little interested in who she might find. "We should check out their shelters and soup kitchens, too, while we're there."

Vik gave her a look that suggested that was the last thing he wanted to do.

When everything was entered, she made a few corrections, then reached for the *News-Times,* looking for anything on the two homicides. "Section three," she told Vik. "Page seven, lower corner. Right next to the ads for funeral homes." She read it aloud. "'Murder-Suicide Suspected. A man and woman were found dead Saturday morning. Their relationship is not known at this time. Identification is being withheld pending notification of the families.'"

"Not only is that inaccurate," she said, "but we've had so many murder-suicides this year that nobody will pay much attention."

"Well," Vik said, "nobody lied."

"Come on, Jessenovik, suicide? Notifying the family?"

"We don't know when this was released. We didn't know what happened until the autopsies."

"This is misleading at best."

"The victims most probably *are* indigent, Marti."

"And? It doesn't matter how they died or who killed them?"

"No, but the lieutenant was right on a couple of points. We don't have enough to prove this subject is a serial killer. We don't know if he's killed before or if he'll kill again. And, realistically, except for the do-gooders, how many people are going to care about our victims? Given the situation in Iraq, the fact that Fred's son died there, that Fred fought there in Desert Storm . . . The defense would probably claim post-combat stress syndrome, or whatever they're calling it, and everyone would be rooting for him to get off. Other than the satisfaction of finding the killer, this could be a no-win situation."

"Everybody who goes to war does not come home homicidal."

"I'm not saying that."

No, he wasn't. "I hear you," she said. She wasn't sure what her stake was in Fred's guilt or innocence. But she wasn't ready to concede that his life was more important than the victims'.

Instead of returning to his apartment, DeVonte got off the C.T.A. bus near where he had parked his car and drove to Lincoln Prairie. He parked in a strip mall near a grocery store and walked from there to the woods. It was getting late. Only a few houses on the nearby streets had lights on. He kept to the curb to avoid setting off sensor lights. Even though the moon was hidden behind the clouds and there were few streetlights, he felt exposed. When he reached the house on Hemlock Street, yellow police tape warned him away.

He went to the tree where he had seen the man standing, and walked into the woods. There was no trail that he could see, but he could see where bushes had been trampled. Not far from that he found a place with the blackened, partially burned limbs from a tree, and, nearby, a stream. The man who had seen him might not have set up camp here, but, then again, maybe he had.

9

DeVonte pushed the shopping cart through the store, pausing to watch a woman just ahead of him who was talking on a cell phone. He looked away and studied the labels on different brands of tomato paste. When she stopped talking and moved on, he followed, but stayed well behind her. When he caught up with her in the produce department, she had put her purse in the shopping cart and had her back to him as she squeezed heads of lettuce. As he walked past her, he reached into her open purse and took the phone.

Back in his car, he called the number he had written on an envelope. The woman who answered the phone repeated the name he gave her, then said, "Sorry, he doesn't work here anymore."

Even though he thought it was futile, DeVonte asked for his contact's new extension.

"He's no longer employed by the State of Illinois," the woman told him.

DeVonte clicked off. Damn. He had paid good money to get this guy to find out who was on record as having custody of Lynn Ella, and then locate her mother. The guy had promised to find out what out-patient mental health facility Iris was to report to for her medication, but at the time, DeVonte hadn't expected to need that information.

Luck was not with him now the way it had always been in the past. It must be because of the child. What was *it*? What could she see that he could not? She was scared to death when he took her outside, but she did not fear him. Why not? Because she could work root on him? Because she could conjure spirits who would protect her? If she did have the eye and could see, then why couldn't she also see that he intended to harm her?

Sharon began making phone calls at nine o'clock. The news wasn't good. She could not access Lisa's college fund unless her ex-husband agreed. There was a penalty for making withdrawals from her 401K account in addition to a hefty up-front tax payment to the IRS. The bank in Chicago that managed her pension fund said she couldn't touch that until she retired—unless she was fired or quit her job. To make things even worse, when she told DeVonte about the money before they were married, she had lied and doubled all of the amounts.

She felt like bolting from the apartment when the phone rang. The caller I.D. said cell phone and gave a number. She hesitated. Maybe it wasn't DeVonte. She didn't know how the FBI equipment worked. That meant she couldn't disable it. She had thought about doing that. She didn't want them involved. She didn't want them to track down DeVonte. She just wanted to get Iris and that little girl away from him. Now she didn't know how that would be possible. Nor did she believe DeVonte would allow either of them to live. And he would probably come after her and Lisa, too. There was no way they could get away from him. He would kill them all.

"Hi, babe," DeVonte said when she picked up.

Her stomach lurched. She could taste the coffee she drank an hour earlier. The number he was calling from had a Chicago area code. Maybe he wasn't nearby. She swallowed hard, then said, "I'm trying."

"Which means?"

She gave him the information she had, but didn't mention dollar amounts.

"So, you'll be quitting your job today. How long will it take to get that money?"

"I didn't ask."

"Well, maybe you'd better do that, like, right now. I'll call back."

Had their conversation been recorded? Was someone listening? What was she going to do? She couldn't call Marti. Marti would tell her not to give him anything. The FBI would set up some kind of trap. They didn't know DeVonte like she did. They hadn't seen the expression in his eyes when he decided to kill her. They had been on their honeymoon on Grand Bahama Island. When the hurricane hit, a storm surge had flooded his condo and given her the opportunity to get away.

Sharon knew she didn't like the people she worked with, but she didn't realize how much she detested her job until she called in to quit. She never really wanted to be a teacher. She had always wanted to be a lawyer, but there wasn't enough money for that. Not that she didn't like children. When she began teaching, she got along with them better than with most adults. It was the adults, not the children, who disappointed her.

The first time she went into a classroom, she felt proud. The congregation had stood and applauded when the pastor announced she had her degree. Her mother, who never believed she could do anything, had actually told some of the neighbors. Even her first husband, who had suggested she consider something less demanding, like becoming a secretary, had seemed impressed. Now she never wanted to enter a school or a classroom again.

Having quit her job, she called to request the cash value of her pension. The results of this transaction would be between her and DeVonte. She would have to figure out a way to get him to free Iris and the child before she gave him the money.

"So much for going to Milwaukee now," Vik said. "Maybe tonight. We'd better talk to whoever is working these Chicago cases first and take a closer look at Fred."

They had decided to skip lunch. A fine drizzle fell as they

walked back to the precinct, contributing to the gloominess of the day and Marti's less than cheerful mood.

"One victim found near Midway Airport," he added. "Another in Morgan Park. Public transportation. He wouldn't need a car."

Lupe and Holmberg—"their replacements," as Marti tagged them—were back at the office, grumbling about old people with lousy memories.

"Looks like we've got something else for you two to do," Marti told them. The two victims in Chicago had not been identified either.

Marti took the Morgan Park case and called Area Two in Chicago. Vik took the other case. According to the detectives they spoke with, both victims had been found in abandoned buildings. The Morgan Park victim was found three weeks ago, the body near Midway Airport was found two weeks ago. There were no witnesses, no leads, little more than trace evidence, and, so far, no next of kin. The Chicago detectives agreed to copy them, as soon as possible, on the available reports, and Marti and Vik advised them that Fred Reskov was a possible suspect.

"Both cases are cold, Jessenovik," Marti said.

"So are ours. What else is new?" He ordered pizza.

Once the reports from Chicago were faxed in, Marti made copies for Lupe and Holmberg. They went over everything they had on all four cases.

"They didn't find any bloody clothing either," Marti said. "I wonder what he does with it."

"Stabbing them when they're in a prone position and unconscious doesn't make that much of a mess," Vik reminded her.

"You're right, Jessenovik. And, that could be why he kills them the way he does."

Vik looked at Holmberg. "Serial killer, maybe," he admitted. "Looks that way right now. Sometimes they're opportunists. Sometimes they want to outsmart us. This guy is totally consistent. He just wants to kill."

"Why does he hit them in the head with a hammer after

they're dead?" Marti wondered aloud as she read through the autopsy reports again. "Well, look at this. The hammer he used on the Morgan Park victim was half a centimeter smaller than the one he used on the victim near Midway."

Marti checked that against their John Doe and Jane Doe indentations. Again, there were minor variations. "It can't be a copycat. There hasn't been anything in the newspapers. It's got to be the same subject. He's just not using the same hammer. Must throw them away. He's smart enough now to know that we can find trace evidence on just about everything."

"He could toss it almost anywhere once he was away from where he killed them," Lupe said. "Nobody would ever make the connection."

"So, if it is Fred Reskov . . . ," Holmberg said. He pointed to the pictures of their crime scene. "If he hadn't slipped here, and touched this wall . . . Look at the shot of the victim in the basement. Nothing. Victim bled out onto the carpet."

"We're checking Fred's clothes for trace evidence," Marti told him. "But there's not much to check. The only clothes they found were dirty and in a mesh laundry bag."

"Doesn't the fact that our subject doesn't make a mess when he kills them mean something?" Holmberg asked.

"Maybe," Marti said. "He could have some kind of fetish, be obsessive-compulsive."

"Or, like Fred Reskov, be orderly, like a soldier."

"Sometimes," Marti said, ignoring Holmberg's implication, "when they clean up the crime scene or try to keep it clean, not touching them any more than they have to . . . Sometimes that's an indication that they know the victim, but here I don't think he does."

"These are the kinds of things we figure out backward," Vik explained. "You get the right subject, and it falls into place."

"What if he's associating the person with someone he knows?" Holmberg asked.

"Like his mother?" Vik asked. "Maybe. It's usually not that simple."

"But it's a smart way to think," Marti added. "As long as you remember two things have to come together here: the victim and the killer. The victim and the crime scene tell us what happened. The 'why' questions are harder. It can take both to get you to whoever did it. You have to be methodical. The mechanics of how you work a case have to become a habit, leaves you free to think."

Vik waved at the work on his desk. "Now, you two are going to continue going through the missing persons files. Add these two victims to the search. Marti and I are going to find out what we can about Fred Reskov, then take a trip to Milwaukee. Sorry we don't have more for you to do right now. Sorry this is grunt work. But we're somewhere between a standstill and a break-through and that's a tricky place to divvy up an investigation."

It took several phone calls and the intervention of the state's attorney's office and their congressman to get authorization for limited access to Fred's military records. Marti checked the information the Department of Defense had provided, dialed the phone number again that was listed for next of kin, Fred's sister, got the same message again, not in service, and hung up.

"Well, Vik, Sophia Reskov Connolly doesn't live here anymore."

She turned to her computer, typed in the Web site for the white pages, and printed out all of the Connellys who lived in Hanging Limb, Kentucky. There were eleven.

Vik complained as she gave him half of the list. He wasn't as grumpy today, but when he wasn't busy, he looked worried. She knew it had something to do with Mildred. She also knew it wasn't anything urgent. Whatever it was, he would tell her when he needed someone to talk to.

Marti reached for the phone. Three calls and she located Sophia's sister-in-law.

"Nothing's happened to him, has it?"

"What makes you think that?"

"Well, according to his ex-wife, Fred hasn't been any better than okay since Desert Storm, and he's been worse than that since their boy died."

"When did she say that?"

"Last month."

"When did their son die?"

"Andy got killed right about the time I broke my hip."

"Killed?"

"In Iraq. He was a Marine, like his father and his grandfather."

"When did he die?"

"February sixteenth. Fred came to the funeral. He didn't say more than three words to anybody. Nobody's heard from him since he walked out of the graveyard after he watched them bury Andy. Nothing's happened to him, has it?"

"Like what, ma'am?"

"Like his trying to harm himself. He tried that once after he came home from the war."

Fred's ex-wife had remarried and moved, but she still lived in Hanging Limb. Marti got her name, address, and phone number from Fred's sister-in-law.

"I haven't seen Fred since our boy's funeral," the ex-wife confirmed. "I've been worried about him ever since. Nothing's happened to him, has it?"

"What makes you ask?"

"Fred was prone to nightmares and depressions when he came home from Iraq. He didn't want Andy to enlist. Didn't want him to go to Iraq. Tried to get him to use some law about the only son, about being exempt from military service."

"If you had to guess, where do you think Fred could be now?"

"Anyplace where he could be alone. I didn't think being alone was good for him, but that's what he did after Desert Storm, kept to himself."

"Is there anyplace that was important to him?"

"His daddy had a cabin up in the woods, but that's been torn down for years now."

"What kind of job did Fred have?"

"Oh, Fred went to college, for a while anyway. He wanted to be a veterinarian. He has a healing touch with animals."

"Does he have any formal training?"

"He worked with the local vet from the time he was twelve. Loved animals." She sniffled, then said, "I tried to tell him to come home." She sniffled again. "He said he didn't have a home anymore."

After Marti hung up, she shared what she had found out. Vik had been talking with Fred's last commanding officer.

"There was some mix-up in communications while Fred was in Iraq," Vik said. "His division didn't move out when they were supposed to, got caught in enemy fire. The mix-up didn't have anything to do with Fred's responsibilities, but a guy right in front of him went down. His commander said that sometimes things like that keep you playing mind games—like 'why' and 'what if.' He also said Fred was awarded several medals for bravery and had to see a doctor for post-traumatic stress disorder."

Marti thought about that for a couple of moments. "Wasn't there something not too long ago about a lot of domestic violence at some military installation that they thought was caused by this stress disorder?"

"Could have been."

She put in another call to the ex-wife, and asked if there had been any spousal abuse "He didn't hit her," she told Vik, "but he came back with a hair-trigger temper and would break things when he got upset, punched holes in the walls. She said there were times when she was afraid of him."

"Doesn't look good," Vik said.

"Mehta thinks the killer is someone in control, not an angry drunk."

"State's attorney might not see it that way."

"Circumstantial," she countered.

"Right now," Vik admitted. "We don't have the forensic reports yet, nothing to tie him with the first victim. But, Marti, bad guys like dogs, too."

Marti heard the underlying message: Don't let your emotions get in the way. This was one time she couldn't argue with that.

Fred hid behind some trees as he looked at the house. He wanted to go inside. Maybe that would help him remember. But if a cop was watching, or the neighbors . . . He didn't look like a vagrant. He was still wearing the clothes he bought this morning. But if anyone noticed him, he would still be a stranger. Maybe when it got dark . . .

He stayed among the trees as he walked the length of the house. There was a Cyclone fence, four feet high, along the side by the woods. The back of the yard and the other side of the house had a six-foot privacy fence. If he waited until tonight, he could scale the Cyclone fence without being seen. Then he would have to get inside. And there was a streetlight. He would have to stay away from the windows. There was a rear door, a patio with a sliding door out back, but no rear windows. There were two windows on the side nearest the woods. If the house was alarmed, or if an alarm had been disabled or turned off when those people died . . . He didn't know anything about alarms.

He returned to his campsite, where he had stowed his sleeping gear under a pile of leaves. He looked at the tree branch where he had hung the flag that had been draped over Andy's casket. He could not believe he would do anything as awful as killing two people on the anniversary of Andy's birth. But he did have a temper. He did get angry. That was part of the reason why he was alone. And he had learned how to kill in Iraq.

Iris sat in Lottie's living room and looked out the window. It was quiet here, but a few blocks away there were gangs and drugs and excitement. Not wanting to be a part of that was a new feeling. She had been in the hospital or in jail many times since she ran away from home. This time things had been different. The doctor told her she was self-medicating with street drugs, that if she stayed in the hospital long enough they could find out what was really wrong and give her the right medication. She didn't believe him, not then, but times were hard when they picked her up and had her committed. She needed to be someplace for a while. Having bad food was better than having no food. Getting drugs without having to work for them was nice, too.

Now, even though she had not believed that life would ever be any different, this was better than it had been, at least for today. Last night, she didn't want to go back to the street. She wanted to go to the halfway house, but she wanted to get away from Darrell Loomis even more. If he had found out where she was and when she was getting out, he must have found out where she was supposed to be going. So, she came here instead. Not that she could impose on Lottie for long.

Sometimes, while she was in the hospital, she had wondered what it would be like to have her daughters with her again. Those thoughts were scary. She didn't even know how she would take care of herself. She remembered Lynn Ella, little and helpless and cute. She remembered Kim, always wanting something, clothes, food, a toy, things that she had not always been able to give her.

Then there were the things she wished she could forget: how the sounds of Lynn Ella's crying and Kim's talking and the television playing became all jumbled up in her mind, and trying to figure out what to do next became impossible.

She remembered enough to know that having them again wouldn't be like anything she saw on television or in the movies. There was no daddy, no job, no money. Maybe, where they were now they had that, had more than public aid, more than clothes bought at Goodwill, and food that came from churches. The only thing she could do for her daughters now was keep out of their lives, and make a life for herself.

If she could do that, then maybe someday, when they were grown, she could at least let them know that even though she made a mess of her life, almost made a mess of theirs, she had learned how to be a survivor. When Lottie returned, she would know for certain that both of her girls were okay. She was hungry to see them again, hold them. But she knew she could not. Knowing they were all right would have to be enough.

10

It took Marti forty minutes to drive to Milwaukee. They stopped at police headquarters first, spent an hour going through the state of Wisconsin missing persons files, then focused on the Milwaukee area, and came up empty.

"Same problems, different place," Vik said as he consulted a list of facilities for the homeless, then checked out a map of the city. They let the sergeant know they were carrying and gave him a list of the shelters they planned to go to so he could alert the beat cops.

St. Ambrose Center was an older building with a wraparound porch. Fire escapes had been added. It had been converted into a halfway house for mentally ill men. A few of the guests thought they recognized the morgue shot of John Doe, but were vague about where or when they might have met him. Most of them shook their head. One man waved his hand in the air as he spoke to them. Another turned away, yelled at someone only he could see, and went upstairs, muttering.

"Well, that was a waste of time," Vik said as he stood on the front porch. "This whole trip has been a waste of time."

Marti didn't say anything. She knew he wanted to be with Mildred.

"Halfway house. These guys are about half a hallucination from a mental institution. Fifteen men and I don't think three of them had a clue as to what we were asking them. They probably think he's a rock star."

"I think they could tell he's dead, Vik." Her stomach rumbled. Lasagna was on tonight's menu at the halfway house and the aroma was enough to remind her that she hadn't eaten in a while.

"Morgue slab, no clothes, taken from shoulders up while in prone position with eyes closed."

"Maybe," Vik conceded.

A patrol car was approaching as they reached the sidewalk. It was an urban area, looked like a downscaled version of a blighted Chicago street. Fewer people, fewer houses, lots of garbage, beaters parked at the curb, some with broken windows, one without tires. The usual, Marti thought.

"Some things stay the same," Vik commented, as he stepped over a pile of dog shit.

The police vehicle pulled over to the curb. Two officers got out and walked over to them. The older one was tall with a gut. The younger one was blond, and same height as his partner and at least fifty pounds lighter.

"You two got business here?"

"Police," Marti said.

They showed their I.D.s.

"Lincoln Prairie," the younger cop said. "Homicide, huh?"

Marti and Vik followed the squad to a sub shop with seating for eight, which served a full-bodied cup of coffee and sandwiches with thick layers of Italian cold cuts and provolone.

"You might want to leave a couple of those photos with us," the older cop suggested. "There are a few people you're not likely to run into who might know who he is."

"What happened to him?" the younger cop asked.

Vik filled him in on the M.O. and both cops said they would keep an eye out for similar victims.

Trouble, the German shepherd who guarded their property, was patrolling the perimeters of the yard when Marti got home. The sensor light came on as soon as she pulled into the driveway.

Trouble looked her way, but continued walking. By the time Marti parked in the garage, outside rounds were over.

"Good girl," Marti said. She rubbed the dog behind her ears, then gave her a treat. It was after eleven P.M. Ben's S.U.V. was here, a few lights were on in the house. From the looks of it, everyone was home. "Ready to come in? Come on."

As she passed the gardening tools hanging in the garage, she thought of Johnny's irises. He had planted the rhizomes years ago in front of their house in Chicago. She had transplanted them twice. Every time she dug them up and replanted them, she worried, afraid that, like Iris, she would not see them again. This year the irises had bloomed in front of this house. Somehow seeing those purple and yellow flowers year after year gave her hope. But if Iris was alive, why hadn't they been able to find her?

Inside, Trouble paused at her water dish, then went off to make inside rounds, which she did faithfully every four hours all night. Marti had no idea what internal clock guided the dog, but those few times when she woke up to a cold nose nudging her, she felt reassured, and safe.

Now she switched on the alarm system, bypassed the kitchen, and went downstairs. There was no sign of Bigfoot, the dog of many breeds that Johnny had brought home from the pound as a pup. Bigfoot considered the boys, Mike and Theo, his puppies and could be found wherever they were, which now would be in bed.

She heard the violin solo on a Yanni CD and followed the sound of the music. Ben was sitting on the couch in the den, dozing. He was a big man, muscular, and aware of his strength, always gentle. He woke up when she flopped down beside him.

"Where's Joanna?" Marti asked. "And Lisa?"

"They're in." He yawned, sounded sleepy. "Joanna's new boyfriend came over. Tony. Seems okay."

At sixteen, sensible best described Joanna. That and practical. And bossy. Marti didn't think she had to worry about her, but she did anyway.

"Lisa's in no hurry to go home. I took her over to get more

clothes, and Momma Lydia made sure she did her homework. What's going on with her and Sharon now?"

"According to Sharon, DeVonte's back."

"What?" he asked, wide awake now. "Do you believe her?"

"That is the question, isn't it? I've alerted the FBI. He's totally off their screen. No priority." She filled him in on what Sharon had told her about Iris and a little girl named Lynn Ella. "Denise is trying to track down the child—if she exists—find out where she is."

Ben shook his head. "Well, Lisa will have to stay here. Do you think it's safe to let her go to school? This isn't going to do anything to improve her opinion of her mother. What are you going to tell her?"

"I don't know," Marti admitted, "but I'll have to talk with her in the morning."

She settled against his chest, felt his hand stroking her. "What is it about men and war?" she asked.

"No kiss?" he asked. "Nothing?"

They embraced and she resettled against him, put her head on his shoulder. It felt good to have someone to lean on.

"Sorry, I'm just . . . Our only suspect served in Desert Storm. His only son died in Iraq nine months ago." She told him about Geronimo, too.

"Are you worried about this guy because he's a vet or because he owns a dog?" Ben asked.

"Cowboy's a vet," she said.

"And so was Johnny. And so am I."

"It was different for you."

"Maybe," he agreed. "But I wasn't really a soldier. I was a medic. That was where I decided to be a nurse instead of a doctor."

"Why?"

"It cost less money, for one thing. And took less time."

"And . . . ?"

"I worked triage. Had to decide who got help first, who could survive, who wasn't going to make it no matter what we did. That's a lot different from shooting people, blowing them up, letting them burn to death, or waiting for them to do that to you. I wasn't part of that. I wasn't responsible for the deaths and injuries I saw. I wasn't protecting and defending my country by killing people in another country."

"And that's what made the difference?"

"Maybe and . . . some guys believe in war, some guys even enjoy it, at least if they win. Some believe in good and evil, good guys and bad guys, right and wrong. For some of them, that makes it okay."

She thought about that. "You think so?"

"I don't know, not for sure. I do know that, in our society at least, killing people isn't the norm. I think that some people are able to rationalize it somehow. Then there are those who can't. My dad was in World War Two. When he came back he would wake up at night talking, screaming. Mom says he still does, and, now that he can't get around like he used to, he seems to brood sometimes. She's trying to get him to take antidepressants."

"War's a bitch and then you live," Marti said.

"Something like that. None of us knew there wouldn't be any parades. We did what we had to, what we were told or trained to do."

"And you were trained to heal."

"To do no harm. But probably for every soldier who's like your suspect, there are dozens who will tell you, 'I did the right thing.' And they believe that, and get on with their lives."

"Do you think you did the right thing?"

"I tried to save lives, not take them. There's a difference."

"Do you have dreams?" she asked. "Cowboy does."

"Sometimes. Not often. And when I do the patient lives. For a couple years after I came back, though, I had this same dream over and over. I would be out with a field unit. It would be hotter than hell. We'd come across these dead bodies, and I would say, 'We can bring them back to life,' and then I'd wake up."

"Fred said his dream is always the same. He was with the first troops to go in."

"Then you add fear to carnage."

"Isn't everyone afraid?"

"Sure, but the first ones in have no idea what to expect." He pulled her closer, stroked her hair, kissed her. "I can't tell you how Johnny felt, or what he thought, or why. He loved you. He loved his children. He was a good man. Most of your memories of him are good. Sometimes that has to be enough."

Marti snuggled against him. This wasn't just about Fred, or Cowboy, or Ben, or even war. This was about Johnny, about the way he changed, about her inability to understand, to do something that would help. If only . . . Even now that thought would sometimes cross her mind. There were nights when Johnny would let her hold him, caress him, and it was almost as if she were holding a child. Then there were the nights when he turned away from her. Either way, she could not reach his pain.

"I love you," she said. "And thanks."

Miss Lottie's house was quiet most of the time, but especially at night. Iris couldn't remember ever just sitting and watching the stars and moon above the rooftops, until now. She was following the blinking lights of an airplane when Miss Lottie came in.

"Pretty, isn't it?" Iris said. "It makes you wonder how all those stars got there, what keeps them up there."

Miss Lottie patted her hand. "I've got something to tell you, child. The news isn't good."

"Lynn Ella." She knew as soon as she saw Mr. Loomis that she didn't want her baby to be with him.

"Yes."

"She's not dead?"

"No. It's nothing like that."

"That's not her in the picture, is it?"

"It could be."

Lottie's eyes told her even more than her voice did. She was sad. Worried, too.

"She looks malnourished, Lottie. Probably how she'd look if she was staying with me."

"Now don't you put yourself down, girl. You never gave yourself a chance to be her mother."

"Is she okay?"

Lottie hesitated. "There's nothing but to say it. The foster parent Lynn Ella was placed with was seventy-four years old. She died six months ago. There's no record of her sending Lynn Ella to school. Nobody knows where the child is now."

"But the state . . ."

"The state of Illinois doesn't know anything. They say they'll start talking with the neighbors first thing tomorrow. Might even put her picture in the paper if they have to."

"But they took her away from me so that she would get the right care, be safe." She stopped talking. The way she was when they took Lynn Ella, she might have lost the child herself. "She's just . . . gone?" She thought of Mr. Loomis. "Is she with that man?"

"They don't know. Have no idea. Don't even know who that man is. You've got to go to the police station tomorrow, see if you can find his picture. See if you can describe him. I'll go with you."

"But what do I do now? What if—"

"You've got to be strong, girl, and pray hard, and try not to even think about any of those ifs."

Tears stung her eyes. She blinked them back. She would not cry. This was her fault. She would have to do what she could to make amends. "How's Kim?"

"This real nice black family has adopted her. They live in a fancy house and she goes to a good school. And she's smart. Real smart. Gets good grades."

Everything Lottie said made her feel good and feel bad at the same time. Kim would never want to know someone like her.

"Does she know she's adopted?"

"They've told her. Point is, nobody thinks it's a good time to . . ."

"Tell her about me. Or let her meet me."

"When she's older," Lottie said.

"No, not even then. Let her be. It's good one of them will make it. But Lynn Ella, she's my baby." As bad as she felt, she would not cry. That wouldn't do anybody any good now.

* * *

It was close to midnight when Fred returned to the vacant house. He was wearing woolen gloves. When he climbed the Cyclone fence, it rattled. No sensor light went off when he landed in the yard. When he touched the kitchen window, no alarms went off. The window wasn't even locked. He wondered why not, but opened it anyway. It was too late to do anything else.

Inside, he went through the downstairs rooms. There was nothing. He went upstairs. The first two rooms were as clean and as empty as those below. In the third pieces of the rug were missing and a square had been cut out of the wall. He stood there and looked, seeing nothing more than what was there, remembering nothing. Then he left the way he had come in and trudged back through the woods.

Later, he woke up crying. He did that sometimes, but not often. When he did he could always remember what he had dreamed. This time he had dreamed of a woman. She was in the house on the floor. She was African-American. She had long hair. She was dead. He did not think he had killed her. He remembered killing in Iraq, details that he could never forget. The way a body looked when there was only a bullet wound or two. The way a body looked when it was blown apart. He could remember the smells of death, the sounds of death. If he had killed her, even drunk, he would never forget, but could he somehow bury it for a while, the way he had to bury what he saw, what he did, while he was a part of Desert Storm? Months from now, would he remember?

Sharon was dozing on the couch when the phone rang. She reached for it and said "Hello," before she woke up enough to wonder who it was.

"Hey, baby. You got everything taken care of?"

"DeVonte!" She sat up, swung her legs to the floor. "I called. Thursday. I'll have it Thursday." She thought about telling him exactly how much it would be, decided against it. She would have to deal with that when the time came. She couldn't risk making him angry now.

"Good girl. But I really called to ask about that pretty little daughter of yours, Lisa."

"DeVonte! Please! I'm doing what you want! Please!"

"Sharon, you overreact. I was simply inquiring as to how she's doing these days."

The last thing she heard was his laughter. Her hands were shaking so badly it took three tries before she punched in Marti's number.

"He threatened to hurt Lisa," she said when the answering machine picked up. "Please, please keep her safe." She disconnected before Marti could answer and waited. There was no return call. Marti had to believe her. She had to.

DeVonte took a long walk around the perimeter of the cemetery, from Sheridan Road, west on South Boulevard. South on Chicago Avenue, then east on Juneway until he reached Sheridan again and could look at the lake. Coming here made him think of the Islands. The lake seemed to go on forever until it met the sky. Moonlight glittered on its surface. Waves broke against the rocks sending up sprays of water. The lake. It's moods changed faster than the ocean's. But it was always so alive. It seemed strange to him that someone would think to bury the dead here.

He found a bench and watched the lake's choppy surface. Iris had gotten away from him. If he ever saw that woman who helped her, he would kill her as surely as he was going to find Iris and kill her. He could hear his mother's laughter, reaching across the years and from beyond death, to mock him. "My son, smart you are, huh? Smarter than this?" And she would hit him. "Or this." And he would be hit again. "How many times have I told you about these young girls you sneak out to meet? You think I don't know?" His mother's hands went around his neck, squeezing until he almost passed out. When she released him, he vomited. His mother laughed. "You are weak, just like your father was weak. You will die at the hands of a woman. And me—I'll throw dirt on your coffin and laugh." He could almost hear her laughing now.

Iris had gotten away. He had no way to find her, but he had to try. She could identify him. Maybe she had already. Maybe the police were looking for him now. She had Lynn Ella's picture, but that wouldn't do her any good. Not as long as the child remained inside.

Sharon would not give him the money until Thursday. And even then, it would only be a small amount of what she had. Sharon. She had gotten away from him, too, as had her daughter. But that was when they were on the island and the storm came. They would not get away from him this time.

Marti MacAlister would not get away either. She was too smart, that one. Or she thought she was. She was the one who guessed right about the women he invited to his condo, but sent to the bottom of the ocean instead. She was the one who told the island police, and the Fort Lauderdale police, what she thought he was doing when he took those half-day cruises to the island. She was the reason why he went to California and began riding the cruise ships to Hawaii. But the Pacific cruise took longer, several days, not a few hours. He could not go on board with a woman. He had to meet the women there. And always they were with someone else. He couldn't kill them and toss them overboard and leave the ship before they were reported missing.

The money the East Coast women had given him dried up. It wasn't that West Coast women were not as generous. They wore minks and had diamonds. Their homes were spacious. Their husbands were inattentive. He had filled many of their needs. He just couldn't kill them and get away with it, and killing them gave him a special kind of pleasure.

Soon he would have Sharon's money, and be able to kill Sharon and that cop. Again he heard his mother speak. "My son, the man. You can't even outsmart a woman." His mother would laugh now if she could. She would throw back her head, toss her hair from side to side, and laugh, just as she had laughed at him the last time he saw her alive.

Unlike the others, MacAlister would die the way his mother had died. Unlike the others, she would not be dead when he stabbed her again and again. He would stab her in places that would not kill her, would not let her lose enough blood to become unconscious. He would listen to her screams of pain just as he had listened to his mother's. It would be his turn to laugh.

Waves buffeted the rocks. DeVonte took off his shoes, rolled up his pant legs, and walked toward the lake. He entered the water, felt its sudden coldness as it swirled about his ankles. The lake overcame sand and rock and gravity and was master of all that it touched. Its waters yielded only to the demands of the moon. He, too, was like the lake, but even stronger. Unlike the water, he would not yield to anything, or anyone.

Fred heard the footsteps coming toward him. The footsteps were close. If he made a run for it, and whoever it was had a gun, he was dead. He lay still. His arms were inside the sleeping bag. He eased them to his sides. The zipper was not all the way up. He was on his back, legs straight. His head was exposed, vulnerable to attack. He was beneath a tree, not far from the trunk. There was a heavy branch beside him. The footsteps came closer. He heard heavy breathing. A man with a gun wouldn't have to come this close. Fred kept his eyes closed and waited.

When the footsteps were a few feet behind him, he freed his arms as he rolled away. He felt the branch before he touched the tree. Grasped it. A man was on him. He could not swing the branch. He swung his feet up instead. The man was propelled over his head. He heard a bump, then a moan. The man slumped on him. Fred pushed him away. Standing, Fred looked down at him. Nothing major. A nap, then a headache, and he'd be fine.

A brick that had not been there before was on the ground near where he had been sleeping. Fred searched the man for other weapons but didn't find anything. He kept the man's wallet. Fred lifted him, hoisted him over his shoulder. The man wasn't that heavy, maybe 160 pounds. He had carried heavier men to safety while under fire. He had carried his gear for miles through the heat and shifting sands of Iraq. Hell, he was a Marine. He carried this man three blocks to a place where a street created a boundary. A place where the man would be seen.

When he returned to his campsite he knew he had to leave here soon. He looked at the brick but didn't touch it. That man who attacked him must have wanted him dead, but why? When it was light he would check out the wallet. Then he would decide what to do. He sat with his back against the rough bark of the tree, afraid to go back to sleep, but not because he had been attacked. Going into the house had caused new nightmares. He didn't remember seeing the woman he dreamed about, but he knew he was not imagining her. All of his dreams were about something real, something he had seen or been a part of. Some were fragments. They were always about death, but they were real. He *had* gone into that house while he was drunk. He *had* seen that woman. The question was, had he killed her?

A shaft of sunlight almost blinded him when he woke up. For a moment, he wondered where he was. The gloom was gone. Then he realized the sun wasn't really that bright. Maybe it just seemed that way after so many days of clouds and gray skies. He blinked, rubbed his eyes. It came to him all at once. A man and a woman, getting out of a car, going into that house. They were black. The woman was short, with straight dark hair that hung to her shoulders.

11

Hey, wake up! What's the problem here?"

Karl Wittenberg heard the voice, felt someone grab him, shake him by the shoulders. The pounding in his head made him wince. Everything hurt.

"I . . . I . . ."

"Okay mister, what happened here?"

Except for the flashlight, it was dark.

"Police. What are you doing here?"

"Ohhh." The bright light made his head hurt worse.

"I . . . I . . . ," he whispered and closed his eyes.

The officer called for an ambulance, then asked, "What's your name?"

"Huh?" He tried to think, then said, "Wit . . ."

"Your name, sir?"

"Wit . . . Wit . . . Wittenberg."

"Did you see who did this?"

"Nooo."

"You know what time it happened?"

"Uh . . ."

His mouth was dry. He was suddenly thirsty, and he realized his pants were wet at his crotch.

Marti sat at the kitchen table with Ben and Momma. Lisa and Joanna sat across from them. Even though they were best friends, they could not have been less alike. Joanna liked sports.

Lisa liked boys. Joanna was six feet tall and still growing, Lisa barely five feet five. Joanna had light skin, Lisa's was darker. Lisa's hair was dark brown, short, and curly. Joanna wore her almost waist-length auburn hair in a braid.

Ben and Momma already knew what Sharon had said about DeVonte. Marti told them that he could be in the area, that the FBI was involved. Marti didn't mention that this had no priority with the FBI. Silently, she wondered if she should be more aggressive about that.

"And all of this is based on what my mother has told you?" Lisa said. "I never believe anything my mother tells me. She lies too much."

In Marti's opinion, that was a typical adolescent exaggeration. "I don't know what's going on with Sharon," she admitted. "I don't think this is something she would lie about. But she's been going through a lot of changes lately. That's the only reason I'm wondering if she's telling the truth." That was the root of the problem. "So, for now, we will assume that she is. You're going to have to stay home from school for a few days."

"Home? A few days? Not today. I *have* to go to school today." Lisa was close to tears. "I have to go to school today," she repeated. "She's doing this on purpose. She's always doing something to ruin my life."

Marti took a deep breath. Lisa regarded her mother and most adults in positions of authority as the enemy. That was one reason Marti had asked Joanna to join them.

"Why does she always do this to me?" Lisa asked. "Why me? Why is it always me?"

"I'm sorry." Even as Marti said it, she wondered why adults had this tendency to apologize to children for things they couldn't control. She decided not to go through the "your mother loves you" scenario again. She'd done that at least three times in the last two weeks and it had just made things worse.

"Lisa, we can't take the risk. Your mother might be making up things about DeVonte, but he is out there somewhere. He did convince you to meet him and Sharon on Grand Bahama Island. And when he tried to kill her, he tried to kill you, too."

Lisa shuddered. She put her hands to her face. "He pushed me in that lake," she said, "and the wind, the storm . . ." She shuddered again. "Is it always going to be like this? Even if she is lying now, isn't he ever going to go away?"

Joanna put her arms around her. "If he is out there, Ma will get him," she said.

"He drowned," Lisa said. "He drowned."

Marti didn't remind her that after the hurricane was over his body had never washed ashore. Lisa had gone through months of therapy to get over what she'd been through.

"I just need a couple of days, Lisa. I'm working a case now, but I'm doing the best I can to find out what's really going on. Until we know for sure, I don't think it's wise to take any chances. Everyone I've spoken with has agreed that we have to take your mother seriously. It's just too risky not to."

"Take *my* mother seriously?" Lisa said. "You've got to be kidding. She'll just pull this same thing again."

"You only get to cry wolf once or twice," Marti told her.

"Right. With my luck, the third time she'll finally be telling the truth."

When Marti left for work, Ben was flipping saucer-sized pancakes, Momma had gone upstairs to check on the boys, and Lisa and Joanna were still sitting at the table talking. Sensible, bossy Joanna, Marti thought. Sometimes that got on her nerves. Today it was a blessing.

Marti and Vik stood outside Lieutenant Nicholson's office for the required three minutes. Vik seemed to find it amusing. Marti found it annoying.

"It she wants us to bring Lupe and Holmberg along she'll have to tell us." She checked her watch. "We'll be late for roll call and that will be my fault, too."

Vik shrugged it off. "Women," he said. "She'll get over it."

When Nicholson called to them to come in he glanced at the wall clock and said, "See? Only two minutes and fifty-four seconds. What did I tell you?"

Nicholson was standing by the window. She was so petite and so impeccably dressed in a navy blue suit and pale-blue silk blouse that Marti felt dowdy and fat just looking at her. She had gained another two pounds, twelve in all since September. Most of it was in her butt and her gut, but she was either going to have to lose it soon or buy a few outfits in a larger size.

"So," Nicholson said. "Alderman Wittenberg was mugged last night."

Marti exchanged looks with Vik. This was the first they had heard of it.

"How well do you know him?" the lieutenant asked.

Marti assumed Nicholson had called them in because their double homicide happened in his ward. "Is he at home or still at the hospital?" she asked, as if she already knew what was going on.

Nicholson raised her eyebrows, but didn't answer. Maybe it was because Marti had asked her a question. She decided to compound her insubordination. "Has he identified his attacker yet?"

"What do you know about Wittenberg, Jessenovik?" Nicholson asked, ignoring her.

"There's not much to know. He's just an alderman. There are twelve of them."

"Do you think this was random, or could he have been a target?"

"Hard to say until we talk with him."

The lieutenant's jaws tightened, but she didn't say anything. Instead she looked at Marti.

"I don't have yesterday's reports yet."

"Geez, they're in there. Maybe I forgot to send them. Busy day."

"Send them as soon as you get to your desk."

120

"Yes, ma'am."

"If learning how to use these programs is too difficult, I'm sure Officer Holmberg can show you how."

"Difficult?" Marti said. "Piece of cake."

The way Nicholson raised her eyebrows and the slight upturn of her mouth suggested that she didn't believe her, but she didn't say anything. Instead, she turned to Vik. "Torres and Holmberg aren't clerks or gofers. This is an interesting investigation because we have so little information. Great for training purposes. I want them fully involved."

"We're keeping them briefed," Vik said.

"I want them on the street with you."

Vik didn't answer right away. When he did, he said, "Two officers can be intimidating. Four is a crowd."

"Not to mention the fact that Holmberg doesn't have much experience," Marti added. "I'd rather have a smart cop than a dead one."

"I'm sure Jessenovik can handle that," Nicholson said. "This isn't Chicago. And, Jessenovik, follow up on Wittenberg. The Hemlock Street homicides did happen in his ward." She turned her back to them and looked out the window.

As they walked back to their office, Vik said, "She didn't even ask about the task force meeting."

Of course not, Marti thought. Now that Nicholson's decision not to allow her and Vik to attend had been vetoed by Dr. Mehta, she'll act as if it wasn't happening as far as they were concerned and get her information from someone else.

As soon as Marti sat down, she turned on the computer. She checked the sent-mail file and found an entry indicating she had sent her reports to Nicholson yesterday. Sighing, she sent them again. Lupe and Holmberg were meeting with one of the deputy coroners to discuss the results of the John Doe and Jane Doe autopsies. She called to let them know about Wittenberg so they could canvass in the area where he had been found. And sometime today, Lupe and Holmberg were also going to have a follow-up interview with Howie Atkins.

"Do you think Nicholson paid any attention to what you were saying about four being a crowd?" she asked.

"Probably not. I get the impression that she's made a career of being attached to that desk and a computer. Maybe we'll get lucky and she'll find something in a manual somewhere about investigative procedures."

"If she still reads books."

"Maybe there's something on the Internet."

Marti thought for a moment, then said, "What if they are our replacements?"

"I'll take early retirement and you'll get hired by another department."

"What about this task force? What if they offered you a job?"

Vik thought about that for a moment. "It would beat the hell out of retiring, but I was talking with the desk sergeant before roll call. He heard they've got five more teams coming in next week from northern Illinois, and then the week after they'll be talking to five teams from the south and west Chicago suburbs."

"So," Marti said. "They're serious about getting this up and running, and we have competition, assuming we want the jobs."

Vik looked at her, then looked away.

Ben knew what was going on. But she had just mentioned the possibility of finding another job to Momma last night.

"When the time comes," Momma had said, "if the time comes, you'll know the right thing to do. And if things change . . ." Momma had shrugged. "That's happened before, child. Many times. It just takes getting used to."

Marti had sat in the kitchen long after Momma went to bed, wondering what she wanted to do, and if she would have to do anything, hoping she wouldn't.

Now she said, "Vik, suppose Nicholson . . . does something to discredit us."

"MacAlister, there's no way one case could do that, not even if we did screw up. Our record stands."

Marti didn't feel reassured. She wanted to believe that Nicholson just wanted to get rid of them, but if there was more to it than that . . .

Marti checked her voice mail. There was nothing from the FBI agent, Dobrzycki, so there must not have been any phone calls from DeVonte. She didn't think anyone at the Bureau would have bothered to run a want on the man. She had—again, but didn't turn up anything. She thought about calling Sharon, decided to wait. If she was putting Lisa through this for no reason . . . They had agreed that Lisa would stay with Marti indefinitely; she was still hoping that would be the end of it.

The real problem might be that DeVonte was still out there. Or at least there was no record of his death. It was one thing for Sharon to make up a story because she needed help with Lisa, another if someday Sharon's scenario came true. In a way, she was glad Sharon had done this. Alive, DeVonte would always be a threat to someone. She hadn't thought about him in a long time, and he was a dangerous man to forget. The next time she spoke with Dobrzycki, maybe she could convince him to give finding DeVonte a higher priority.

Marti started to call Denise Stevens, but changed her mind. Neither she nor Johnny had been able to locate Iris. There was no way Denise would find Iris's daughter, assuming she had one. If Sharon had made up this story about DeVonte, then she had invented everything else, too. In a way, Marti was glad about that as well. Maybe, with her, Denise, and the FBI involved, they would finally find out what *had* happened to Iris.

"Nothing, huh?" Vik said,

Marti turned to him. It took her a moment to focus on what he was asking. "No, nothing on DeVonte," she said. "And Lisa's with me." The more she thought about it, the more convinced she was that the only place that any of this existed was in

Sharon's mind. "But, we might not have heard the last of it yet. Sharon called last night and said DeVonte was after Lisa. The good news is, if Sharon is making this up, she can't pull this again. The bad news is, if there is a next time, and she is telling the truth, then nobody will believe her."

After Marti called the hospital for an update on Wittenberg's condition, she spoke with the beat cop who had found him.

"Wittenberg was discovered sitting under a tree a little before three this morning," she told Vik. "The doctor didn't think he was out there that long. He wasn't in shock, no hypothermia symptoms. Mild concussion. A headache. They haven't released him yet, but they'll let him go five, six o'clock tonight if he hasn't had any other symptoms by then. And," she added, "the uniform who found him is copying me on his report."

When the paperwork on Wittenberg arrived via e-mail, there wasn't anything on it that Marti didn't already know.

"How important do you think this is, Jessenovik?"

"Not very. My guess is the lieutenant wants us to follow up because she has no idea of how unimportant he is. She's probably angling to get a picture of the two of them to hang in her office."

"There is the possibility that this could have something to do with our two homicides, since it happened in the same part of town. I don't have a good feel for where he was found, though, in relationship to Deer Woods or the Atkins house."

Vik drew her a map, which didn't help much, gave up, and said, "Okay, MacAlister, let's go take a look. Anything to keep Nicholson happy."

That wasn't why she was doing this. Or was it?

Before she left, she gave the computer the perimeters of the subdivision and asked for data on muggings, robberies, and home invasions. There was nothing listed for the past five years.

"So," Marti said as she pulled out of the precinct parking lot. "Wittenberg has been in politics for about thirty years, but hasn't done anything important."

"That says it all."

"Is there anything else I should know about him?"

"Not really. My father always said the Wittenbergs opened their first car dealership and repair shop the day after Ford invented the Model T. They own United Motors now."

"Isn't that the dealership that runs that 'God bless America' commercial with Spandex Woman wearing the Stars and Stripes Forever?"

"Yeah. Before this one it was the commercial with the eagle laying an egg in the parking lot. I doubt that Karl had anything to with that, though. It's more like something his younger brother, Klaus, would think up. Klaus is the kind of guy who always makes an ass of himself after three beers."

Marti drove to the corner where the beat cop had found Wittenberg.

"Nothing here but trees and bushes," she said. "No houses, nothing."

"On the other hand," Vik said, "he was left in plain sight, propped against a tree."

"Just another random act of kindness, Jessenovik."

"Right. A thief with a heart of gold. But," he considered, "whoever it was didn't try to hide him, which means he might not have wanted to kill him. That seems to leave robbery, which has nothing to do with the homicides at the Atkins house."

Marti looked around. There were woods on both sides of the street where they were standing and the road sloped down. She couldn't see any houses. "We're, what, two blocks from there?" she guessed.

"Two blocks north, four blocks west."

"And Wittenberg lives . . . ?"

"He's four blocks north, three blocks east of here."

She took out her notebook, drew the configurations. She had been to this subdivision several times for routine deaths from illness or natural causes, but wasn't that familiar with the area. "When we saw Wittenberg checking out the Atkins place, from the way he talked, I thought he lived a lot closer. And he left damned fast when we showed up."

"The question is, Why was he out walking alone so late at night?"

"Especially here."

"He grew up here, MacAlister. A lot of people feel safe close to home."

"Too many," Marti agreed. But the circumstances did seem unusual.

"A lot of the locals wouldn't agree with me," Vik said, "but I'm glad they've finally decided to develop this place."

"Doesn't it belong to the Forest Preserve?"

"No. It's just vacant land. About ten years ago some big retailer wanted to come in, but Wittenberg circulated a petition and got the city council to turn them down. You can see what's happened since then. Nothing. The city totally ignores it."

"Are we going to check on Wittenberg at the hospital?" Marti asked.

"Nah. Not unless they don't let him out later today."

Marti took a look around and found a narrow, overgrown path.

"Oh, come on, Marti," Vik said when she began following it.

"You come on." She wanted to see where it went.

"Damn," Vik said after a few minutes.

"What?" She turned. He was rubbing his ankle.

"Nothing. Hit something. Looks like an old battery case."

"Are you bleeding?" She tried not to smile or say "Poor baby," but he caught on.

"Well, surprise, surprise," she said when the path ended near the place where Fred's camp had been. "Fred could have come to ground here, caught Wittenberg snooping around, and whacked him."

"But that's not what Wittenberg said. According to the report he was mugged near where he was found."

"And why would he lie?"

Vik shrugged. "He's an old guy, Fred's young. Pride maybe. Mugging sounds better. Then again, even in a small pond appearances are important if enough people know who you are."

There was a brick lying on the ground near the base of a tree. A brick, not a rock. Marti walked sixteen paces from the brick, then circled around.

"One brick," she said. "The only brick in the immediate vicinity."

They both took a closer look at it.

"No blood," Vik said. "No hairs. Not a weapon. Maybe Fred brought it here for protection."

"Or maybe someone else did."

"Wittenberg? But why?"

"Almost enough to make your nose twitch, isn't it?" Marti said. "You sure you want to wait until he's released from the hospital and pay him a visit at home?"

Vik thought for a moment, then said, "Yeah. We don't want him to get the idea that we think there's anything more to this than he's told us. Not yet anyway. Let's keep this routine. But when we do talk with him, let's show him Fred's mug shot."

Marti returned to the car and got her camera. When they went back to the precinct, they took the brick with them.

12

Sharon huddled on the couch, still in her bathrobe, with a blanket pulled around her. She had turned the thermostat to ninety degrees and she was still cold. She had to get up, get dressed, move. Yesterday, she signed her termination papers and faxed them to the company that handled the union's pension fund. Now there was nothing do but wait. She stared at the phone. Why didn't he call? He knew this was making her crazy.

When the phone did ring, she jumped. The last call had been from the assistant superintendent, wanting to know why she had resigned. Not that they cared. The phone rang again.

She hesitated, then picked up.

"Hi, baby. How's it going?"

"Where are they? I want to talk to them again."

"You do what you're supposed to and I'll think about it."

"No money, DeVonte, not until I know."

"You've got until Thursday, Sharon. And make sure you or your cop friend take good care of Lisa."

The line went dead. She looked at the phone in her hand. What if he was lying? What if he didn't have Iris or Iris's daughter? Even if he didn't, he had someone. She knew him too well to believe that he would just have some stranger call her. As soon as any woman got that close to him, she was as good as dead. She punched in Marti's number.

"Detective MacAlister."

When she heard Marti's voice, she hung up. Why would anyone believe her? That FBI agent didn't. Marti was going through the motions, just in case. But Marti knew her better than anyone else. And she knew Marti better than anyone else. Marti did not believe her either.

She was trying to convince herself that making a cup of coffee and eating a piece of toast was a good idea when the phone rang again.

"Thank you, *Mother dear*."

Great. Just what she needed.

"What did I do now, Lisa?"

"Oh, nothing. Just kept me from going to school on the most important day of the year. This is the worst week of my life."

"You're not in school?"

"Of course not, *Mother*. Because of you. You made up this damned story about that ass, DeVonte, just so I'd miss the school rally for the football team! You'll do anything to ruin my life! And I just called to say thank you! Thanks for everything!"

There was a loud bang as Lisa slammed down the phone.

"Damn, damn, damn!" Sharon threw a pillow across the room. "Everything is my fault! Everything! It's always my fault! Damn!" She wanted to scream. Instead she cried.

Fred sat at a picnic table and looked out at the lake. He was in a park near the beach. The water was a wintry slate-gray. Far beyond the curve of the breakwater a freighter headed toward the horizon. Here, waves barely broke the surface, then lapped against the shore. Seagulls cried as they rushed back and forth across the sand. The wind whipped at the evergreens. He pulled his watch cap over his ears. The parka he bought yesterday kept him warm.

He thought about the wallet in his pocket. The wallet he had taken from the man who attacked him. According to the driver's license, it belonged to a Karl Wittenberg. He couldn't place the man in the photo, or recall ever seeing him. There were also five credit cards. Wittenberg wasn't a street person wandering through the woods looking for a place to sleep.

He didn't know why anyone would want to kill him, or how Wittenberg found out enough about him to look for him in the woods—unless it had something to do with what happened in the house on Hemlock Street. This morning he checked the telephone directory first. Then a map of the city. Wittenberg didn't live on Hemlock Street, but he did live a few blocks away.

Now all he had to do was go to the police, give them the wallet, tell them what happened, and get locked up for assaulting Wittenberg and accused of the two murders. He had gone into that house, dreamed about seeing a woman with long hair lying on the floor. If only he could remember what the man had looked like, what kind of car it was.

Fred walked back downtown, found a pay phone, and called the cop's cell phone.

"Cowboy, partner, what can I do you for?"

Fred hesitated, then said, "It's Fred Reskov. How's Geronimo?"

"Sleeps a lot, doesn't he? Gets restless at night though. How are you?"

"Is it okay if he stays with you for a couple more days?"

"No problem. What's with you?"

"I'm okay." This Cowboy was a cop. He would have to be careful.

"Is there anything we can talk about?"

"Not yet," Fred said. "I haven't figured things out yet. Just give me a few days."

"Look man, you need me, I'm here."

"Just take care of my dog. Please."

"He's fine. I'm more worried about you. Anything happens, just give them my name. Make them call me. I'm here for you. I mean that. I owe you."

"Yeah, I, well . . ." He hung up.

Desert Storm happened a long time ago. The battles were brief, the memories indelible. Listening to Cowboy made it come back. Not the fighting. Not the dying. The guy next to him. The guy whose ass he would save, or who would save his ass. The young kid just ahead of him who spent half the night talking about his girlfriend and took a bullet the next day. Long after he forgot the heat, forgot the sand, he would remember standing together, fighting together, dying together, and then trying to figure out how to live alone.

"Fred," Marti said when Cowboy hung up.

"Yeah?"

"He called from a pay phone," Vik said

"What's your take on him now?" Marti asked.

"I'm not sure. He said he had to figure things out and it would take a few days."

"Where is he at right now? Where's his head?"

Cowboy thought about that. "In Iraq. You're always there. It never goes away. It's a . . . I don't know . . . You measure things by what happened there, you compare things to the way it was then. Everything is either before Desert Storm or after."

"Do you think he knows what happened in that house?"

Cowboy hesitated. "I don't know. You said he told you he had dreams, nightmares, that there was blood . . ." He was silent again, then said, "When you've been there, it's like . . . a filter. If he was drunk and did something or saw something, and it became part of those dreams, he'd know the differences, what was new. He might not understand it. It would be mixed in with everything else."

"Do you have dreams?" Marti asked.

Cowboy looked down at his hands, then he looked at her, his eyes a clear, frigid blue. "Sometimes," he said. "Sometimes." His eyes held hers for a moment, then he looked away.

Denise called almost as soon as Marti and Vik got back from a late lunch. They had taken Lupe and Holmberg with them and spent almost an hour talking about their current cases.

"Nothing, Marti. I can't find anything on your sister-in-law,"

Denise said. "It's almost as if Iris MacAlister never existed. Can you tell me anything else about her? Do you have an old photo?"

"She was sixteen when that picture was taken," Marti told her. "She's forty-two now."

"Did she marry?"

"If she did, she didn't invite any of us to the wedding."

Marriage. A different name. She wondered about that sometimes. If everything, Social Security numbers, a child's birth, was under another name, she had no idea of how to get from MacAlister to whatever that name was.

"What about boyfriends, Marti? Who was she dating when she left?"

Marti thought about that. "Sorry, I was too busy paying attention to Johnny to notice."

"Well, let me know if you think of anything. I don't know what else to do. There is no Lynn Ella MacAlister in the system. There are quite a few Lynns, a few Ellas, and even some Lynn Ellens and Ellen Lynns. I'm having checks run on them."

Marti felt sad when she hung up. She wasn't sure why, if it was because she wanted to know where Iris was, what had happened to her, or if it had more to do with Johnny. The changes after Iris left were subtle. Johnny had always been slow to speak, and soft-spoken when he did. He just said less. He still loved to dance, just didn't want to go dancing as often. He still smiled, laughed with her, but both all but disappeared when they were with anyone else.

She put in a call to a woman she had met who belonged to the genealogical group at Woodson Library in Chicago.

"Marriage records," the woman suggested. "The application, not the license. And you'll have to know what county."

Where would she begin, Marti wondered, after she hung up. Iris had walked out the door one day and never called, wrote, or came back. If she had gotten married, she could have been living anywhere. She could begin with Cook County, but if there was no record of Iris there, she had no idea of where to search next.

The phone interrupted her thoughts. Lieutenant Nicholson wanted to see her and Vik. Now what? Change. She hated it.

Fred couldn't remember the last time he had been inside a library. He liked to read. Back home, the library was small and the stacks narrow. It smelled of books the way old churches smelled of incense, and had odd corners and places under stairwells where you could read unnoticed for hours. He could remember checking out *Treasure Island* when he was about nine. The plastic that covered the jacket was cracked, the pages were a dull tan and worn. Most of the books he read had been that way. Now when he wanted to read, he found a second hand store with books pretty much in the same condition.

When he stopped at the desk and explained what he wanted, he was directed to the research librarian. She was friendly and helpful and suggested a computerized index on local forest preserves and also told him which ones had newsletters. Within an hour, he knew a lot about the preserves, but there was little to nothing about Deer Woods. The lure of the history contained in fifty- to eighty-year-old newspapers and newsletters was as strong as it had been when he studied history in high school and college. So he kept reading. The first reference he found to Deer Woods was in 1933.

"There are deer in abundance," the article read.

In a 1939 newspaper, there was a photograph of a doe with two fawns.

He began reading more closely because most of the comments were buried within articles about other preserves. Over the years, a picture emerged. The decreases in wildlife were laid to the fact that Deer Woods was not officially a preserve and therefore not under that umbrella of protection. Homes were built too close to the preserves. The children who played there scared the wildlife away. By 1962, there was a small headline in a newsletter that read, "Where Have All the Deer Gone?" The description of the woods was much the same as someone would describe the place now.

Fred consulted with the librarian again. This time she suggested maps of the area that would show how and when it was developed. She also brought him several books on the history of Lincoln Prairie. Fred went to an area with tables and chairs and studied the copies of the maps. Deer Woods had been part of a much larger parcel of land. Over the years, the area to the west and east of the woods, along Bellflower Street, had been commercially developed. To the south were the houses that were there now.

Fred's stomach grumbled. He wished he had a cup of coffee and a hot meal, but didn't want to take a break yet. Nearby, teenagers worked quietly, but he noticed that they stayed away from the homeless people who were sitting with a book or newspaper or magazine open on a table. One woman caught his eye. She was small and blond and dirty. Her pink jacket had a cartoon character on it and was too small. Something about her, perhaps her size—she was tiny—made him think of the picture of the doe.

He fingered the wallet in his pocket. Wittenberg. Then he took today's *News-Times* and *Chicago Tribune* off the newspaper rack and began searching through them to see if there was any mention of what had happened. He found out that Wittenberg was an alderman. His family owned United Motors, which used to be Wittenberg Automotive on Bellflower Street. Fred thought about that. He thought of the lack of wildlife, those few deformed animals he had seen, the water in the steam, cold but brackish. And he thought of the old battery cases he had found while digging a hole to bury garbage. There were a lot of them, now that he thought about it. At the time, he wasn't going to be here long enough for anything like that to be important. But now . . . he might need a place to stay until he could get Geronimo back. There was another place farther downstream that was even worse. He didn't know much about ground and water contamination, but he did know more than he wanted to about chemical warfare.

And he knew what must have happened at Deer Woods. Did whoever it was just bury batteries there? Or did they bury other automotive waste as well? Then he thought about his dog. Geronimo roamed those woods all night. What if he killed small animals filled with that poison? What effect would that brackish water have on him? He drank a lot of water. And he only weighed seventy pounds. He wasn't a big dog. No, Geronimo was all right. He had to be. They hadn't been in the woods long enough for either of them to get sick. But nothing he thought of convinced him it was okay.

On his way out he stopped by the woman in the pink jacket. It was the cartoon character, the little bear with his hand in the honey jar that got his attention and made him think of Andy. She looked up at him, seemed startled. He gave her a twenty dollar bill and walked away.

He couldn't find the card with Cowboy's cell phone number. He searched through his pockets twice, then called the police nonemergency number. The officer who answered put him through to Cowboy's voice mail. His heart began racing as Cowboy's voice instructed him to leave a message. He knew he was overreacting, but if anything happened to Geronimo . . . He couldn't lose anything else. Not again.

After the beep he said, "Get Geronimo to a vet, please, right away. Have him checked for lead and mercury poisoning. I just found out he's been exposed. Make them check for any kind of environmental water or ground poisoning they can come up with. Please, right away. Please don't let anything happen to him."

He didn't have the card the attorney who bailed him out gave him, but he did remember the man's last name.

"Fred Reskov," he said when the secretary asked. She explained that the attorney was not available today, but did give him an appointment to see the man tomorrow afternoon.

"And what is this in reference to, Mr. Reskov?"

"Just tell him I have to talk to him about what happened in that house on Hemlock Street, and about what's happening in Deer Woods."

Cowboy stood by the window looking down at the long, narrow space between the house and the garage that he occasionally referred to as "the yard." A six-foot chain-link fence had just been installed. So far, Geronimo did not seem to be adjusting to being confined. He wasn't barking, but he kept circling around, either looking for a way to get out or just making sure that was all the space there was. Not that he planned to have the dog that long, or intended to keep him outside. But if he couldn't make it home to walk him, a dog run was a safe place. The tenants would see that he went out.

Satisfied that Geronimo was at least getting used to his present situation, Cowboy picked up the phone, dialed his voice mail, and listened to Fred's message again. He looked down at Geronimo. He was a good dog, quiet—unless he was out of water or needed to go out. It was easy to understand how Fred had become so attached to him. He didn't complain, or bitch about the way he and Slim did their job the way a certain lieutenant did. He didn't have a clue as to why Fred was worrying about environmental poisoning. The dog could have gotten into something he shouldn't have, but how would Fred know? As he watched Geronimo sniffing blades of grass and lifting his leg to mark various places along the fence, the dog didn't seem sick at all.

Instead of calling a vet, he called the coroner's office and got the name of a forensic veterinarian.

"Does he seem sick?" the doctor asked.

"No. He's fine."

She asked a series of questions. Each time Cowboy answered no he felt reassured. Geronimo was okay. "No symptoms," the vet agreed. Then she suggested he get Geronimo to the coroner's lab anyway, and have a vet who handled emergency calls meet them there.

"Why?"

"Just a precaution."

Cowboy tensed, felt the fear rising, and began counting to ten as he took slow, deep breaths. If anything was wrong with Geronimo, how was he going to tell Fred?

Vik burst into the emergency room and rushed over to the desk.

"Sir, you're not allowed—"

"Mildred Jessenovik," he said. "Where is she?"

"X ray." The nurse nodded toward a cubicle. "You can wait in there."

Instead of going where the nurse indicated, Vik rushed out the double doors. Mildred was being wheeled out of the X-ray room when he got there.

"Are you okay?"

"I just fell again, that's all."

"You just fell? Again?" Mildred was on tranquilizers. He was not. "Where's Helen?" Mildred's sister should not have left her alone.

"She needs to get out every once in a while, Matthew. I thought it would be good for her to have a little time with a friend."

"You should have called. I would have come home."

"But I thought I would be all right."

He bit back the words "You'll never be all right. Never again." Instead he said, "How did you fall? When? Why didn't you call me then?"

Mildred looked away. She was crying.

"Tell me," he said. "What is it? What's broken?"

"Nothing, nothing. I'm fine now. I'm fine."

She didn't look fine. She looked small and frightened. At least she wasn't alone.

"Then what?" he asked.

"Nothing," she insisted. "Nothing. My side hurts where I fell. That's all. They'll give me something for that."

That wasn't all. But that was all Mildred would tell him. The doctor told him the rest.

"Your wife was alone when she fell, Officer Jessenovik. She couldn't get up. It took her half an hour to crawl to a phone, pull it down by the cord, and dial nine-one-one."

Vik said nothing. Helen never should have left Mildred in the house by herself. Their daughter, Krista, could have come over. He could have come home early from work. Or even on time. He didn't dare say any of that for fear of upsetting Mildred even more than she was.

"I'll take care of everything," he told the doctor. "She won't be in the house alone again."

"We're going to keep her overnight," the doctor advised them.

When Mildred objected, Vik said, "You will stay. I'll be here with you."

"No, Matthew. You will get back to work. This is not a good time to be away. I don't want anyone else to die, certainly not while you're sitting here with me when you should be out finding the one who did it."

They compromised. She would stay in the hospital. He would stay with her until Krista arrived then he would go back to work.

By the time Mildred was settled in a hospital room, she looked exhausted. He sat with her and held her hand as she drifted off to sleep. She had agreed to have someone come in to give Helen time off, but he was still worried. He knew how much it would cost her to give up those few hours of independence, that little window of freedom when she could be completely alone. He also knew that he could never again be called by dispatch and told his wife had been taken to the hospital, only to find out that she had hurt herself while home alone. She had laid on the floor helpless for half an hour. *"Moje serce,"* he whispered. My heart. My heart. What was he going to do now?

13

Mildred was all right when you left?" Marti said as they drove over to see Wittenberg.

"They're just keeping her for observation and running more tests. And Krista's there. She's like an angel with her mother. Always calm. Sometimes I can't believe she's the same kid who panics at the sight of blood."

"And Stephen?"

"He was on his way when I left, had to pick up Helen. He's the one who gets emotional about his mother."

Marti didn't say it, but she thought, Everyone will be there but you. At times like this, having Lupe and Holmberg as backup wasn't a bad idea. But she reminded herself, in all probability they were her and Vik's replacements.

Vik directed her to a street several blocks from Hemlock, but in the same subdivision.

"Wittenberg's father built this house," he said when she pulled up in front of a sprawling brick ranch with half a dozen tall pine trees growing out front. "He lives here alone. His wife died a few years ago."

When they rang the bell, Wittenberg came to the door. He had two black eyes. The left side of his head had a bandage. Stitches, Marti guessed. His left arm was in a sling. He limped as he led them down a short hall and into what looked to be a small den.

Marti felt claustrophobic. It was like entering a cave. Dark paneling, forest green walls, brown carpet, green velvet draperies that were closed. There were only two chairs. Vik stood. Marti sat, then glanced around. Half a dozen coffee cups and a lamp were on the table beside the chair where Wittenberg sat. Two stuffed cockatoos, one white and one pink, were perched on a bookcase. There were no books, just one shelf of magazines and two shelves filled with yellowing newspapers. The room smelled of the old paper.

"Feeling all right?" Vik asked.

Wittenberg shrugged.

"Did you see who did this to you?"

He started to shake his head, then winced.

"Can you tell me what happened?"

"I was just walking," Wittenberg said.

"Do you walk there often at night?"

"Only when I can't get to sleep."

"How did this happen?" Vik asked. Marti could tell by his tone of voice that he was getting impatient.

"Someone came up behind me, hit me. Took my wallet."

"You were sitting against a tree," Vik reminded him.

"I don't remember anything else."

"No idea of how you got there?"

"No."

Vik took Fred's photo out of his pocket. "Recognize him?" he asked.

Wittenberg's eyes widened, then, without looking at them, he shook his head. His hand trembled as he handed back the picture.

"What do you think?" Marti asked. Outside, the gray November day seemed bright, almost sunny, after being in Wittenberg's den.

"Is your nose twitching?" Vik countered.

"Yeah."

"Mine too. Why is Wittenberg lying? He recognized Fred from that photo."

Marti turned on the ignition, pulled out. As she turned the corner, Vik said, "The question is, Is Wittenberg just embarrassed, or is he hiding something?"

"He could be the one who took that brick into the woods. But why?"

Marti thought about the Atkins house. Two people had died there. She thought about the woods. Fred was living there. Was there any connection other than the obvious, that Fred had killed the two victims? "I wonder where Fred is," she wondered aloud.

"Somewhere between here and someplace else if he's got any sense," Vik said. "Or if he's guilty."

Was Fred guilty? Marti wondered. And, if he was, why didn't she think so?

After the detectives left, Karl Wittenberg sat in the darkened room. Was he the only one still alive who remembered loading the used batteries on the pickup truck, along with the barrels of solvent and used oil and paint cans? They brought in a backhoe to dig the holes to bury the batteries. The barrels were emptied and used again. He was twelve when he began helping. Klaus was what? Six? Seven? Klaus never helped out. Maybe he was the only one left who knew. He didn't know if there were rules for getting rid of that stuff back then. He didn't think the EPA existed.

He thought that when Klaus moved the business to Gurnee that would be the end of it. The land was sold and the buildings torn down. An oil-stained concrete slab remained there for a while. Then the contractors came. A family-owned restaurant and a couple of fast-food places were built there.

Now Frederick Reskov, the man who lived in the woods near where the batteries had been buried, had *his* wallet and knew who he was. And based on what he was going to tell the attorney *he* hired to help him, he must know about the car dealership as well.

DeVonte parked a block from the building where Sharon lived. He didn't know where her apartment was, but that should be easy to find out. He took the stolen cell phone out of his pocket and punched in her number. When she answered, he said, "Hi babe. I'm right out front."

A few seconds later a curtain on the third floor moved. He waved. "Just wanted you to know I'm in town for a few hours. How's Lisa? Staying at that cop's house on Brook Lane?"

"DeVonte!"

"Take care of business like you're supposed to and I promise not to come back."

"I—"

He clicked off before she could say anything else, waved toward the window, and walked back the way he had come.

Sharon's hands were shaking so badly she dropped the phone. If she called the police right now, maybe they could catch him. No, by the time they got here he would be gone. And if he saw them as he was leaving, and managed to get away, he would be angry. She couldn't risk making him mad. He knew where Lisa was. She was safe with Marti, but he knew. She picked up the phone, dialed. Ben answered.

"Where's Marti?'

"At work."

"He knows where I live," she said. "He was standing outside. And he knows where Lisa is, where you live. Don't let her leave the house." She hung up before Ben could say anything.

It was getting dark and Iris was getting impatient as the bus, crowded with tired workers and loudmouthed teenagers and cranky children, stopped and started and stopped again. She couldn't remember coming to this part of town before. Lottie told her it was called the Juneway Jungle. She didn't know exactly where she was going, but Lottie had suggested she get off near the cemetery and use that as a landmark so she wouldn't get lost.

She had spent three hours at the police station looking at pictures on a computer without finding Darrell Loomis. Then she had worked with a police sketch artist until the man drew someone who looked like him. And she had talked with a soft-spoken black woman from the state's attorney's office, who helped her recall things she hadn't even thought about while she was with him. The sound of the Islands when he spoke. A place where he bought hamburgers, Po' Boys.

The woman she was talking to smiled when she mentioned Po' Boys. "Juneway Terrace," she said. "That neighborhood has nothing but people from the Islands. And, Po' Boys, that little hole-in-the-wall has a major reputation. It's been there for years. Black folk visiting from out of town go there like it was the Sheraton." She picked up the phone and relayed that information to whoever was on the other end, said "Yesterday," and hung up. She brushed back dreadlocks as she leaned forward.

"Finding Lynn Ella has a very high priority, Mrs. O'Neill. The D.C.F.S. has no idea of where she is, and they are very anxious to find her. The composite picture of the man you know as Darrell Loomis is being distributed as we speak, along with copies of the photo of Lynn Ella that you gave us. Every police officer in that district will be looking for them around the clock."

"None of this makes any sense," Iris said. "Why does he have her? How did he get her? Why did he come to get me?"

The woman hesitated, then said, "Is it possible that this has something to do with your past?"

They went through the jail time, the hospital time, the people she had been involved with back then.

"But I can't remember anybody who looked like him," Iris told the woman. "I can't remember anyone named Loomis. I can't even remember talking about my girls." Other women talked about theirs. She had always felt too ashamed. She had been a willful child and must have broken her mother's heart many times. She could not tell the lie that her mother did anything to deserve that. Her mother was strict, and she couldn't remember many hugs or much praise, but she never doubted that her mother loved her. She could not tell anyone what a terrible mother *she* had been, and she couldn't blame anyone for that but herself.

She was exhausted by the time she returned to Miss Lottie's house.

"I knew I should have gone with you. What did they tell you? Were you able to identify him?"

Iris shook her head. "I didn't see anyone who looked anything like him. I had to look at all of the sex offenders who liked little girls her age. Thank God he wasn't among them." She told Miss Lottie about the picture they had drawn and about everyone looking for Lynn Ella.

"You have had quite a day. Just sit there and let me make you some Ovaltine. I drink it to calm my nerves." When she brought the cup of chocolate to the table she said, "Drink this and take yourself upstairs. You need a nap. I've got to run to the store while there's still some daylight. It's risky going out after dark around here."

"No place is safe anymore."

"You're right about that. I won't be gone long. You just rest. They'll find her."

As soon as Miss Lottie went out Iris wrote her a note and promised she would be back some time tonight. She left it on the table with a twenty dollar bill just in case she didn't make it back. Then she walked to the corner and caught the next bus. She knew the streets in ways that the police did not. Loomis knew the streets, too. He knew how to hide in a crowd and keep people from noticing him. He was smart enough to keep Lynn Ella inside where nobody would see her. And he knew how and when the police patrolled his neighborhood just as if they had given him a schedule. He would have to know things like that to survive.

When she got off the bus that went past the cemetery she put on the red hat she had bought at a secondhand store. It wasn't exactly the same as the hat she was wearing on Sunday, but that didn't matter. It would catch his eye. There was no way she could find one little girl. This place was too big. There were too many apartment buildings, too many people. But maybe, if she walked long enough, he would find her and take her to her baby—if Lynn Ella was her child. Who that little girl was didn't matter anymore. She was a small child with a strange man and in God only knew what kind of danger.

DeVonte headed for the south side of Lincoln Prairie. It was an area he usually avoided, but it was cold tonight and there weren't any stragglers near the local shelters. At first he was annoyed that the nice brick house was no longer available. But when he checked the real estate ads, he found another one in a quiet neighborhood near a school. It was closer to Marti MacAlister's house than the other house had been. He liked that, too. The only problem was that the house was on a corner. It was also closer than he liked to the sidewalk and to the houses on either side. He had waited until dark to force open a side door and go inside. As he expected, there was heat and water and electricity, not that he would turn on the lights. He closed all of the vertical blinds before he left.

He was driving through the downtown business district when he saw her. She walked as if her feet hurt. He slowed down and rolled down the window. He wasn't far from the lake and the wind blew strong. The night air was cold.

"It's late," he said. "And too cold to be out."

The woman gave him a look that was without hope and hobbled on.

"Are you looking for shelter?" he asked. She didn't answer, but he said, "There is a place, you know, a Unitarian church not far from here. My church. They'll let you in if I ask them to."

As he drove alongside her, he could see that she was not pretty, not even young, unless living on the street had taken her youth. She had that slump to her shoulders, that look about her of a woman who life had already defeated. An easy woman, his mother would have said, not worth his time or attention.

"Come," he urged. "It's warm in here. And I'll make sure they give you some food."

She looked in his direction. There was a mole above her eye that was big enough to be seen in the moonlight. Blond hair hung in a shaggy cut around the edges of a floppy knit hat. She was wearing a pink jacket that was too small. The sleeves stopped above her wrists.

"Come on. Last chance." He held up the medicine bottle filled with aspirin. "I have to take this prescription to my mother."

She hesitated, then walked toward the car. DeVonte smiled and reached across the seat to open the door. "It's cold for this time of year. You would think it was winter already."

She looked at him with bright blue eyes as she settled herself in the seat beside him.

"There is no winter where I come from," he said. "Just sun and warm breezes and pretty flowers all year round."

"Here they complain of the cold without knowing what cold is."

She spoke with an accent he couldn't identify. "You were not born in this country either."

"I came here three years ago from Serbia. There, Kosova, the wind of winter brings much snow and such cold that what they call winter here seems like spring."

Few of the women he picked up spoke to him. Most of them were fearful. He wondered if she was more talkative because, like him, she came here from another place.

"You came here because of the fighting there?"

"I wanted to come to a place of peace, yes. But there is no peace, not anywhere. I should have stayed where I was." She sat with her hands clasped in her lap, looking straight ahead and blinking rapidly.

He held up the medicine bottle. "My mother's house is right on our way."

She leaned back with her head touching the headrest and closed her eyes.

"If you wait in the car for a few minutes, I'll see if I can find a coat for you. My mother is eighty-seven. She fell and broke her hip last summer and still has a hard time getting around. She used to be a big woman, or so I thought. Now, like you, she is small."

When there was no response, he added, "I'll just pull into the driveway and leave the car running. It won't take more than a few minutes."

The woman gave a small nod.

"What's your name?"

"Jelena." She pronounced the J like a Y.

"Want a cigarette?"

When she nodded again, he reached into his pocket and gave her a pack that was already open and a lighter. Leaning back, she sucked in the smoke and blew it out through her nose. He hated the smell of tobacco, but smoking seemed to relax them, lower their guard. She had smoked half a dozen cigarettes by the time he pulled into the driveway. As he had hoped, it was late and, except for the blue light from a television a few houses down, the neighborhood was dark and quiet. He expected her to become afraid when he pulled out the fake gun. Instead she sighed, almost as if she had been expecting this.

"Come with me," he said. "Come inside and keep me company for a little while and I'll take you back to where I found you."

Once again, she nodded.

Before he returned to Chicago, DeVonte decided to check out those woods by the house on Hemlock Street again. Someone had seen him with that woman and was still alive to identify him. Once, on one of the boats that made the trip between Fort Lauderdale and Grand Bahama Island, one of the stewards had realized that a woman who disappeared while on board had been with him. That man tried to get money from him. That man was dead. Like him, this man could become a problem, too. Like him, this man should be dead.

He didn't think the man in the army fatigues would urinate in public if he lived there. And there was that place in the woods where someone had been staying. He pulled into the supermarket parking lot again, but parked where the woods began just across the street. The parking lot was almost empty. Traffic was light.

He walked among the trees, moving deeper into the woods when he got near Hemlock. When he reached a place where he could see the house, the neighborhood was quiet. Curtains were drawn, lights were out, except for the house at the far corner where all of the lights were on. There were a lot of cars parked at that end to the street, too. Maybe someone had died. He fingered the knife in his pocket and smiled. Unlike the other women, Jelena had shown no fear, just resignation. Maybe someone else would die tonight.

14

Fred sat in the dark and leaned against the trunk of a burr oak. Earlier, he had cleared a spot on the ground about forty feet from his old campsite. He had taken a nap, woke up a little past sunset, and got a couple of burgers at the fast-food place up the street, had them fill a thermos with coffee. He was wide awake now, thinking. After he saw that lawyer tomorrow he was going to have to go to Cowboy and, no matter how crazy it sounded, tell him what had happened with Wittenberg and who he remembered seeing at that house.

He didn't know if Cowboy would believe him, but Cowboy had kept his word about taking care of Geronimo. Surely he would keep his word about doing what he could to help him. Even though Cowboy was a cop, he was also a vet. War was something you never forgot, and Cowboy remembered it well, Fred heard that every time they talked. Maybe, by some miracle, he would get Geronimo back, get to leave here and go to Montana. There was something about missing that dog, about not being able to leave him . . . If only he wasn't out on bail. If he packed up and left it would only prove to everyone that he was guilty.

He had left everything when he came back from Iraq. Even his boy. Andy. They had kept in touch. He had written him dozens of letters, tried to explain why he couldn't stay there. But he didn't understand that himself. He just couldn't be around people anymore. At least Andy knew that he loved him. He felt that last letter in his pocket, thought about him and his dad and his son trading war stories. *"There is no time here."* Andy was in a place now where there was no time—no sand, no heat, no war, no more dying. He didn't take out the letter, or look at Andy's picture. He couldn't, not tonight. Tonight he would watch, and wait, and stay alert. He had no place else to go right now. And he wasn't safe here anymore.

When he heard the crackling and snapping of the underbrush he knew it wasn't an animal, too noisy. It had to be someone not used to walking through the woods, especially not at night. He sat still, but moved his head until he homed in on the direction the noise was coming from. Someone was coming toward him. Even if the person tripped over him, he'd have the advantage. He might not be armed, but he could kick ass if he had to.

Even though there was some cloud cover, the light from a quarter moon seemed suddenly bright. Fred crawled behind the tree, crouched there where he couldn't be seen. The footsteps came closer, then veered away. Fred saw the man moving among the trees and kept behind him, walking at the same pace. Then he moved deeper into the shadows and walked faster. He had almost reached the man undetected when the man tripped over a branch. Before he could get up, Fred was on him. It was the same black man he had seen at the house.

The man grunted as they wrestled. Fred gave him a short, hard punch to the gut and smelled the man's breath as he cursed. Onions. He punched him again. The man was gasping for breath. Fred sat on him. A punch to the chest and he was coughing.

"Who are you?"

Blood oozed from a corner of the man's mouth. He coughed again, didn't answer.

"Who the hell are you?" Fred repeated.

This time when there was no reply, Fred jabbed him in the ribs. He didn't want to hurt him too bad. Not yet anyway.

The man sucked in his breath. "Ahhh." Then yelled, "Help! Police! Help!"

"Shut up!" Fred didn't think anyone could hear them, but he slapped him anyway. "Shut the hell up."

The man yelled again.

"I said shut up. You want to say something, tell me your name."

The man coughed up blood. Opened his mouth.

"You yell again and I'll choke the shit out of you." He put one hand on the man's throat, and squeezed.

"Bitch," the man said. "You bitch." The man heaved himself up, and threw him off. Fred staggered back as the man pulled a knife from his pocket. Fred rushed him before he could open it and grabbed his arm, slamming it against a tree. The knife fell. The man took off running, yelling as he ran. Fred snatched up the knife, then stayed close enough to catch him, but far enough behind to get away if he had to.

When Fred reached the clearing near the house, three men were running toward the woods. Fred stayed out of sight, but kept moving in the same direction as the man. He kept to the underbrush, and when he thought it was safe, began closing in. The man reached the corner first. Traffic wasn't heavy, but there were a few cars passing by. The man was holding his side as he jogged into the street. A car swerved, just missing him.

As Fred approached the sidewalk, he saw the flashing lights of a police car and moved back into the shadows. He waited. The car slowed as if the driver was trying to decide whether to turn in to the subdivision or in to the parking lot where the supermarket was. The man dropped his arm, walked to a car, and got in. Fred kept out of sight. The officer chose the subdivision and turned in that direction. By the time Fred crossed the street, the man was driving away. As the car passed a streetlight, Fred memorized the license plate number. Then he went to a pay phone. Cowboy's voice mail picked up. Fred gave him the plate number and the address on Hemlock. Explanations would have to wait until tomorrow.

*   *   *

Momma was rolling out pie dough when Marti got home. It was a little after nine, just past the boys' bedtime and Ben was on duty at the fire station.

"Everything okay?" she asked, pausing long enough to give Momma a hug.

"Theo and Mike are just finishing up their homework. They don't play at this new school they're going to. No late assignments. This one is due tomorrow."

Marti frowned. Theo and Mike, both eleven, had transferred from the local public middle school with over six hundred students in grades six to eight, to a private school K through eight, with four hundred students. The academic requirements at their new school were significantly higher.

"Hungry?" Momma asked.

"I'll be back in a few minutes." They lived in a quad level. She went up to what the boys called the "middle place." Library books were scattered on a card table. Theo was on the computer. Mike was looking from an open textbook to a notebook and writing something. Both boys were in their pajamas.

Marti hesitated. Theo, her son, could get downright compulsive about homework and grades. Mike, Ben's son, was less organized and tended to get overwhelmed.

"You guys okay?"

"We're doing Egypt," Mike said. "It's great! I'm writing my life's story in hieroglyphs."

"You've got to come to open house," Theo told her.

"Yes!" Mike agreed. "We're making a tomb and a pyramid and we're going to dress up like gods. I'm Bes."

Theo laughed. "He even looks like Bes. Short and chubby."

Marti smiled. Mike was going to be big, like his dad. Next growth spurt and his height might catch up with his weight. Meanwhile, the word fat was a no-no.

"I protect children from evil spirits," Mike said.

Marti thought of a little girl who might be with a killer, then focused on the boys again. Mike was excited, Theo seemed relaxed. They both seemed okay.

"Bedtime," she reminded them.

"Five more minutes?" Mike said. "Please?"

Marti laughed. Last year he would have been in bed already. Anything to avoid studying. Even so, she felt anxious. They were too old to be tucked in, but not too old for hugs.

"Five minutes," she reminded them as she left.

"Nice, isn't it, the way they've adjusted?" Momma said when Marti returned to the kitchen.

"Surprising."

"There's a bowl of Joanna's special vegetable soup warming up in the microwave and she baked a couple of loaves of bread. There's ham in the fridge."

"How's Lisa?"

"Scared, mad, worried. You name it."

"Can't blame her." The microwave dinged. Marti put the soup on the table, then got the ham. Momma cut thick slices of bread.

"Remember when you were in second grade?" Momma asked.

"No. Not really."

"That's the year your daddy died."

Marti didn't answer. She avoided thinking about that. The only thing she could recall about the funeral was Momma holding her hand.

"I had to sell the house. We moved a couple blocks away. Instead of going to Miss Ruth's after school, you had to walk past our old house, past Miss Ruth's, and bring your little brother to an empty apartment and take care of him until I got home from work."

Marti looked down at the vegetables floating in a tomato broth. She didn't want to talk about any of this. And she wasn't hungry anymore either.

Momma came over and sat across from her. "Change, baby. Everything changes sooner or later. Past time you got used to that."

Marti shook her head. It wasn't any easier for her now than it had been then.

* * *

Vik hated hospitals. He had been born at home and never spent a night in one in his life. At nine o clock, the lights were dimmed. Mildred dozed, but the bed wasn't comfortable and she kept waking. The chair he was sitting in wasn't comfortable either. Each time Mildred opened her eyes, he held her hand. She had a rosary in her other hand and the beads would move slowly through her fingers until she slept again.

They wouldn't know the results of the tests the doctor had ordered until tomorrow. But their family doctor had come, and unlike the emergency room doctor, he was not reassuring. Mildred's M.S. was progressing—slowly, but relentlessly. She was not to be left alone again. Unlike Vik, he didn't care if Mildred needed time alone or some sense of independence. Like Vik, he wanted her to be safe. And that was the dilemma. Krista suggested a cleaning woman a couple of times a week so that her Aunt Helen could have some time for herself. Vik agreed. He didn't know what else to do.

"Matthew?"

"I'm here."

"You should be working."

"No. Everything's okay for tonight."

She sighed, patted his hand. "Good."

"Are you all right?"

She didn't answer right away, then she said, "Yes. I think I am."

"I'm not."

Again she was silent for a time. "Things are the way they're supposed to be, Matthew. We have each other. We have the children, our families. That has always been enough. That will be enough now."

As he looked at her, he could see her hair, not cut short and graying the way it was now, but the way it looked when it was long and blond and blown by the wind. He could remember the times when they danced the polka, the times when Krista and their son, Stephen, were babies in her arms, the day they were married.

"*Moje serce*," he said. My heart. "I always see you young. And always beautiful."

Mildred turned to him, squeezed his hand, closed her eyes, and smiled. "*Moje serce*," she whispered.

My heart, he thought. One day you'll die. As she reached up and touched his face, he hoped she couldn't see that he was afraid.

Fred fingered the knife in his pocket. He wanted to throw it away, but he knew he should give it to Cowboy. The street where he was standing dead-ended at Deer Woods. There was no traffic. It was quiet. He looked at the house where Wittenberg lived, at the window on the side where the light was on. He wasn't sure why he had come here. Something about confronting that man in the woods made him want to confront Wittenberg, too. Hitting that man hadn't felt good, but there was something different about seeing him face-to-face, talking to him. It was the first time in a long time that he hadn't walked away, or run away. Even so, what had happened in a town he never planned to come to and never expected to see again was not his concern. None of this should matter to him. But it did.

Most of the animals who once lived in those woods weren't there anymore. Some of those that were had something wrong with them. Whatever was there was in the vegetation, in the soil, in the water. He did care about that. He was a bum, a drifter, unemployed, a part-time drunk, and, he thought, maybe even a little crazy, but he had grown up in the hills of Kentucky, and his family had farmed there for close to 200 years. His father, his grandfather, his great-grandfather had fought for this land. His son had died for this land. And what was happening in Deer Woods was wrong.

The room was dark when Karl Wittenberg woke up. It took him a moment to remember where he was. He had drunk too much at old Edith's party. Old Edith was ninety-two today. She had outlived three of her children. The other four, along with their families, had gathered to celebrate. Karl didn't think there was much about getting old that was worth celebrating. Old Edith sat there in her wheelchair, more confused than bemused. Her hair looked like blue cotton candy, a dowager's hump bent her over. She was hard of hearing, going blind, and her hands and voice shook with tremors.

His parents died before they were sixty, sparing him all of that. Mom had a brain tumor, but died of a stroke. It took Dad a few years to die. He got lung cancer, even though he never smoked.

He wished he hadn't gone to the party. Despite the balloons and the flowers and the food, it had seemed to him more like a wake. And all the talk was of the Deer Woods development.

"Just think," Edith's oldest son, Lee, said. "An affordable assisted-living facility right in the old neighborhood. Mom won't have to move more than two blocks from here. The grandkids will have a pond where they can fish, the great-grands a playground. Best of all, us oldsters will still be able to go to the ravine and dangle our feet in the stream."

There had been talk, even plans for development, for about ten years now. This time he couldn't get enough nay votes to stop it. His family had done a lot of good in this community. His grandfather helped build the church they attended as children. His father collected Toys for Tots. Klaus collected coats and warm clothing for children every winter. As soon as the EPA came in and tested the soil and the water, the good they had done would be forgotten. Only the harm they had done would remain.

He turned on the lamp beside his chair. The two stuffed cockatoos seemed to stare at him from their perches on the bookcase. His head hurt. His shoulder ached. His mouth was dry. He poured brandy into a glass and sipped it. As its warmth filled his stomach, he realized how cold the house was. Instead of turning up the heat, he reached for the afghan folded over the back of the chair.

The house was quiet. No children. He and Hedda had both wanted them, but it never happened. Instead there had always been cockatoos. Sometimes he missed their chatter, but he had gotten used to the silence. This quiet, tonight, was empty. There had been so much going on at the hospital. Nurses and technicians in and out. The old man in the other bed had visitors all day long. The man's wife came, his brothers and sisters, his children and grandchildren. They all spoke in Spanish. Then there was Edith's party—four generations laughing and eating, retelling old stories about good times. As soon as he came home and walked through the door it hit him. Alone. He had been alone since Hedda died. He would be alone until he died. He poured more brandy, gulped it down.

He had never told Hedda what he had done in Deer Woods. He had thought about telling her, but never did. Sometimes when she cried because another month had gone by and there would be no child, he thought that was his punishment. Tonight he knew it was not. But this was: an empty house. An empty life. A different kind of dying—always to be alone. Except that he had reached a decision today. He knew what he was going to do about what had happened in Deer Woods. He opened the table drawer, got the gun, took out all but one of the bullets. He took his time, had another brandy. Then he put the gun to his temple. Click. He closed one eye, looked down the barrel. Not yet. But soon. One thing he didn't have to worry about was going to hell. This was hell. Two stuffed birds and an empty house. When the doorbell rang, he shoved the gun between the chair and the cushion.

"Who's there?" he called as he walked to the door. "Who is it?" There was no answer, but the bell rang again.

Fred leaned on the doorbell until Wittenberg opened the door. The man swayed as he stood there looking at him and Fred realized he had been drinking.

"You," Wittenberg said.

Fred pushed his way inside and closed the door.

"Me," he agreed. "We need to talk."

Wittenberg grunted, then turned and led the way down the hall. Fred followed him into a small, dimly lit room with two dead birds perched on a bookcase. Tropical birds with clipped wings. Birds who never foraged for food or built a nest or laid eggs or cared for their young. Pampered birds who spoke human words they couldn't understand and who never sang.

Wittenberg swayed again as he waved toward one of two chairs in the room, then sat in the chair near the window.

Fred sat, too. The chair was hard with a straight, uncomfortable back. "We need to talk," he said again. Even as he spoke, he looked at Wittenberg's bloodshot eyes, saw the half-empty liquor bottle on the table, and wondered if he should bother saying anything at all.

"Deer Woods," Wittenberg answered. "You know."

Fred thought of Geronimo. "My dog might be sick or dying because of you."

"And? What are you going to do about it?"

"Me? I don't live here. Don't belong here. I'm going to get my dog and head for Montana. What are you going to do?"

Wittenberg slumped in the chair. "Good question."

Fred felt tired, old. He thought of what Andy had said. *The world did not begin with war, and might not end with war. But there will be no peace in the time between.* This, too, was war, an assault on the land, on the animals who depended on the land.

"What are you going to do?" he asked again. "Let more animals die?"

"Death," Wittenberg said.

As Fred watched, he stuck his hand down the side of the cushion, came up with a gun.

"You tell them," he said as he raised the weapon to his head.

"Nooo!" As Fred got up he heard a loud bang. It felt like he had been hit in the chest with a sledgehammer. He smelled blood and was surprised. There was no pain.

15

Mars lights were flashing from three squad cars when Marti arrived at Wittenberg's house. She circled the block, didn't see Vik's car, and parked in the closest space available. An ambulance was parked out front, engine off, lights out. Not a good sign. According to dispatch, Wittenberg had shot an intruder. And, according to dispatch, there had been a disturbance earlier on Hemlock Street. Marti went to the evidence techs first. They were standing outside. One was smoking.

"Are you finished with Wittenberg?"

"Yes, ma'am."

"Got anything for me?"

"He fired the weapon. You'll have to wait for the reports for anything else."

The uniform standing at the front door pointed down the same short, narrow hall Marti and Vik had traversed the last time they were here. More uniforms were standing outside the door to the den. When she looked into the room, Ben and his partner, Allan, were there. They weren't saying anything, another bad sign. Marti couldn't see who they were working on. She could see that they had an IV going, and were giving oxygen from a portable unit. A defilibrator was on the floor. Ben was filling a syringe. After he injected the medication, he checked the victim's vitals again, said, "This is the best we can do," and asked for a stretcher. When that was wheeled in, Ben stood, and Marti saw who it was.

"Fred!"

Ben turned. "You know him?"

"The Gulf War vet," she said.

They lifted Fred onto the stretcher. She moved out of the way as they wheeled him out.

"How bad?" she asked, as Ben and Allan rushed past her.

"Real bad," Ben called without looking back. "Chest wound."

Wittenberg was in the kitchen sitting at a round table. It was a big room with bright ceiling lights. A uniform was sitting across from Wittenberg.

"Read that last part again, officer," Wittenberg said, then drank from a mug.

The uniform wrote something in his notebook, then said, "He came toward me. I pulled the gun from under the cushion. I always kept it there. He laughed and said, 'That won't stop me, you old fool,' and I shot him. He fell on me."

"How far away was he when you shot him?"

"He wasn't. He was right there."

Wittenberg saw Marti. "Detective MacAlister. Good to see you again."

Marti's first thought was that he neither looked nor sounded like someone who had just shot a man. She looked at him as she walked toward the table. He appeared sober, calm, and . . . smug. She wasn't sure what gave her that last impression, but he didn't seem the least concerned.

"Where's your partner?" Wittenberg asked.

If he didn't sound so lucid, she might have thought he was in shock.

"He's on his way." Dispatch had reached Vik at Lincoln Prairie General. When Marti called and suggested that she and Lupe handle this, he insisted on being here. "Mildred's okay. She's just here for observation. And Wittenberg's getting mugged one day and shooting someone the next—they can't be isolated incidents."

As Marti approached the table, the uniform held out his note-book, but she ignored it.

"So. Alderman Wittenberg. How awful. Tell me what happened. Mind?" She pulled out a chair and sat down.

"I don't know," Wittenberg said. "I just don't know. I was in the den, having a little brandy. Must have forgot to lock the door. I looked up and there he was. Scared the hell out of me. If I hadn't had a few drinks I might have reacted differently, but I'm not sorry I shot him. Man threatened me. I had a right. Gun's licensed."

Marti was surprised to hear he had been drinking. He sure seemed sober now.

"What did he say when he threatened you?"

"It was more like he was surprised that I was there. Like he thought the house would be empty. But when he came toward me, there was no mistake. He meant to do something. Strangle me maybe, the way those two in the Atkins place were strangled."

Marti wondered how he had found out about that. So far they weren't giving out any specifics. If anybody within the department was talking, and she found out who he was, she would have his ass.

"How do you know he was in the Atkins house?"

"I don't, but nothing like that has ever happened here. And nothing like this either. Sometimes when you add one plus one, it comes out two."

"Do you have any idea why he would come here?"

"No." The alderman emptied the cup. "Oh, you mean is he the one who mugged me and took my wallet? Could be, I suppose. I didn't see that guy. I didn't even think of him until you mentioned it."

"You seem to be handling this well. Did the paramedics check you out?"

"No. The officers asked if I was okay. I told them I was fine. It isn't every day that you have the opportunity to get someone who is trying to burglarize your home. They said it didn't look good for him. With any luck, we'll have one less criminal on the street. Can't say I feel bad about that."

Marti wondered what tomorrow's newspaper headlines would read. Wittenberg was obviously expecting some kind of medal.

"Had you ever seen the man you shot before?"

"There was something familiar about him." There was a scratchy sound as Wittenberg rubbed a shadow of beard. "Can't quite place him though. He's not someone I ever spoke to, that I remember, or who spoke to me. I just get this vague feeling. This was random, wasn't it? You don't think I was some kind of target?"

Marti didn't say anything.

Wittenberg ran his fingers through his hair. "Funny, isn't it? So close to that other . . . at the Atkins house. I go by there maybe twice a week, walk some part of my ward every day." He touched the bandage on the side of his head. "You don't suppose he saw me? Knew who I was? Someone has my I.D. Do *you* think he might be the guy who mugged me?"

Marti didn't answer. She remembered what Vik said about Wittenberg getting what he wanted for his constituents and didn't have any difficulty figuring out how he did it. He was probably a good used car salesman, too. She wished Vik were here and no sooner thought it than he walked in.

"Officer Jessenovik. Good to see you again." Wittenberg stood up, extending his hand. "Good man, just like your dad and your uncle. I knew them both well. Shouldn't take much to close this one. Cut and dry. Home invasion. Self-defense."

"If you'll excuse us for a few minutes," Marti said, before Wittenberg could say anything else. She followed Vik into the hall. The evidence techs were still working the den. She motioned toward the front door.

"A master manipulator," she told him, and repeated everything Wittenberg had said.

"So," Vik said. "We have no sign of a struggle. Fred just walks in for reasons unknown. Wittenberg shoots Fred. Man just comes toward him. Wittenberg pulls out the gun. The only thing Fred says is 'That won't stop me, you old fool.'" He shook his head.

"It doesn't make sense," Marti agreed.

"The only reason I would even consider Fred's being the mugger is because the guy who got Wittenberg did not intend to hurt him or he would have. And I think Fred would have left him where he could be found. But then the question is, Why? Why Wittenberg?"

"And whether he did it or not, why would Fred come here?"

"It takes a politician," Vik said. "We're going to have to take a closer look at our local friendly alderman. How is Fred?"

"Ben said it didn't look good."

"Let's get to the hospital then, MacAlister. This can wait."

They left without telling Wittenberg they were leaving.

Fred was in surgery. "Looks bad," the emergency room doctor told them.

While Vik went upstairs to see how Mildred was, Marti checked out Fred's X rays. The bullet had damaged two ribs and his shoulder blade. If the trajectory was a little lower, or the angle a little straighter, the bullet would have gone right through his heart. She called Ben.

"The entrance wound was lower than the exit wound," he said. "If Wittenberg was sitting, Reskov was standing, and Reskov is either taller or the gun was pointing up. The bullet went through the left lung. Major damage. I don't know how much they can do for him. He's in big trouble."

"Did you see any powder burns?"

"Too much blood."

She would have to wait for forensics.

"Anything else?"

"Sorry, there wasn't time. Reskov was damned near dead."

When Marti returned to the waiting room, Vik was there.

"How's Mildred doing? She's okay? What happened?"

"She fell. Nobody was home. It took her half an hour to crawl to a phone. I can't leave her alone anymore. She'll hate that. But if she falls, and it's worse than this . . . anything could happen to her in less time than that."

It hurt to hear the pain in his voice.

"What if she hit her head? What if she couldn't move? What in hell should I do? She doesn't mind having her sister with her. Mildred and Helen were always close. But, never to be alone . . . from now on if she's in the bathroom for more than five minutes, Helen will be at the door."

For whatever the reason, Marti thought of something she had seen at TOPS Dog Training Center when Trouble was being trained there: a dog being taught to walk alongside a wheelchair. She didn't say anything. Vik didn't dislike dogs, but he didn't seem to have any great fondness for them either. And she didn't know if a dog could be trained to do something in this situation.

Fred was in surgery for four hours. When the surgeon came in, he flopped in a chair and said, "He's alive, but barely. It doesn't look good. He's on a respirator and in intensive care. We had to remove half of his lung. Now we just wait. Has anyone notified his family?"

"I'll take care of that," Marti told him.

What really happened? she wondered as the doctor walked away.

A few minutes later the nurse let them see Fred. The room was little more than a cubicle filled with machines and computer screens. The nurse could observe him through a window. Fred was very still. The respirator controlled his breathing.

"Fred," Marti said. She believed he could hear her. "We need to know what happened. And Geronimo needs his owner. Don't check out on us now."

When they returned to the waiting room, Cowboy was there.

"I'll stay," he said. Marti heard a weariness, a helplessness in his voice and remembered that brief, almost silent vigil for

Johnny, the officers who came and who stayed even when they knew there was no hope.

Marti walked with Vik to the elevator, then waited until he got on. "Tell Mildred hi," she told him. "We'll all be praying. And don't forget, we've got a task force meeting at ten."

Vik put his hands to his head as if he didn't want to be reminded.

It was still dark when Marti walked outside. "Why?" she asked.

As Karl Wittenberg watched from the window, the last police car pulled away. It was over. He couldn't believe it when he saw that man standing at the door. He thought Reskov had come to kill him. Even now he wasn't sure why he *had* come. He seemed to be concerned about the land, but why? What was it to him? Pulling out the gun was just . . . did he mean it? Had he really intended to kill himself? No, of course not. That was why he took all of the bullets out but one. No, what had happened was what was supposed to happen. God had decided what was to be done. God decided that the bullet would be in the chamber when he pulled the trigger that time, and Reskov would die, not him. And, with Reskov dead, the secrets of Deer Woods would die with him.

People were not supposed to know. If they were, things would have happened differently. He wasn't a religious man, hadn't even had a church service for Hedda, but it was good of God to look beyond his personal lack of faith, and show him what was to be done. As soon as that cop asked the first question, it had come to him. Stay close to the truth. And he had. With minimal deviations, everything he told them had been true. For the first time since Hedda died, he no longer wanted to look back on his life. He was ready to look ahead. He was going to resign as alderman tomorrow, put the house on the market. By this time next week, he'd be living in Arizona. To hell with Deer Woods. It wouldn't be his problem anymore.

*   *   *

Cowboy went into Fred's room. He had asked the nurse for a chair and she agreed to let him stay there. Fred wasn't breathing on his own and he was unconscious, but the nurse said there were changes in his vital signs when Cowboy was with him that indicated he was calmer.

"Just hang in there," Cowboy said. "Geronimo needs you. Some of this war shit will never sort itself out. You get used to it being there after a while. Sometimes when I'm on the street and things get crazy and I know I could go down, I remember that desert and the heat and the sand . . . and now we're there again. I've got a nephew over there. It makes me wonder why I was one of the ones who came home. Crazy, isn't it? It's not like you draw lots. You're the one who spends the rest of your life wondering why. Surviving can be almost as bad as dying."

The machines kept clicking, beeping. Fred's eyes remained half open. The nurse came in and checked the IVs.

"He likes having you here," she said.

Cowboy didn't answer. He touched Fred's hand. Live, he thought. Dammit, you have to live. For a moment he felt as if his life depended on Fred's survival. No, he thought. This isn't war, and then, Maybe it is.

16

When Iris returned to Juneway Terrace Wednesday morning, she wore a coat Miss Lottie gave her and kept the red hat in her pocket. She checked the photos and walked the streets until she found the park, and then the place where the little girl's picture had been taken. As she watched, children who should have been in school went down the metal slide and swung on chains where swings had been and stood on top of a humpbacked jungle gym and yelled taunts filled with curse words. Iris walked past the children, past the men crowded around a barrel where a fire blazed, avoided a group of teenagers who sized her up as a possible mark, then laughed and pointed at her.

She did not expect to see the man who called himself Darrell Loomis here. She didn't not expect to see the girl in the picture either. And having found the place where the picture had been taken, she was no closer to finding them than she had been when she woke up this morning. But she knew she had to come back, keep looking, even though this might not be her child. The D.C.F.S. had lost Lynn Ella. The police would not find her. Not here in Juneway Terrace, not in a city as big as Chicago. Who would bother about a poor black girl anyway? Who would bother, but her?

She had bought both Chicago newspapers this morning and searched through them while riding the bus. There was no picture of Lynn Ella. No story about her being missing. Hell, they had no picture of Lynn Ella. They didn't know who was in the picture she got from Loomis. And if the picture was nailed to every light pole and telephone pole in the city, hung in the window of every neighborhood store, who would care, or even notice. It would get Loomis's attention, if he saw it, but if he knew someone was looking for the little girl, he would go someplace else.

She walked the streets from the six story V-shaped apartment buildings to the lake where the wind whipped the water into choppy, foaming waves that crashed against the slabs of rocks piled along the shoreline; crossed the street to the cemetery with fancy tombstones and tall crosses and graves decorated with angels. There were so many trees she thought it must look like a park in the summertime. A nice place to sleep forever. Peaceful. She passed old women with faces as dark and round and smooth as pecans who carried string bags filled with produce, and walked in pairs, and spoke with Island accents, most of it Pidgin English, and sometimes French or Spanish. Young men stood on corners and laughed at each other's lies and old men huddled in doorways drinking from bottles in brown paper bags. She walked to the edge of the park and stood looking at the place where the child had been, then turned away. The sky was gray. People glanced at her and looked away. Their faces were not friendly. She walked until her toes were cold and gloves were not enough and she had to put her hands in her pockets to keep them warm, and then she saw it. Po' Boys.

Marti got in a three-hour nap and still felt exhausted when she arrived at work. Lupe and Holmberg looked busy. She didn't ask what they were doing. Instead she said, "This could be your lucky day. If anything comes up, you get to decide who's duty driver. I feel like the walking dead." She gave them a summary of what had happened last night.

"You two went home early last night, didn't you? Got a good night's sleep, didn't you? I'm going to have to do something about that."

She put in a call to dispatch, told them Lupe and Holmberg

were to be copied on any calls that she and Vik received. Both officers were smiling when she hung up.

"You're used to having *a* partner," she said. "So are we. We'll figure out something."

Next, she checked her voice mail. There was no word from Denise. It was Wednesday and there was still no word from the FBI agent, Mark Dobrzycki. Ben had been home on break when Sharon called yesterday and said DeVonte was outside her apartment building. Marti was as skeptical as ever about the whole story, but, just in case, she had put in a call to Dobrzycki. The agent who answered advised her that Dobrzycki was either in Maryland, D.C., or Virginia, which probably meant he was somewhere on the West Coast.

"DeVonte Lutrell," the agent said. "Someone was just asking about him a couple days ago . . ." He paused, then added, "A Lieutenant Nicholson. I told her the same thing I'm telling you. I'll relay your messages to Agent Dobrzycki as soon as possible."

Marti interpreted that as "in my lifetime." If Nicholson hadn't been able to get any immediate action, it wasn't likely that she would either. Nicholson's butting in like that angered her, but it wasn't a surprise. Marti shrugged it off and called a friend who was an FBI agent in the Chicago office who promised to see what she could do.

Vik came in while she was on the phone. He got a cup of coffee and refilled hers.

"Get any sleep?" she asked.

He shrugged. "Those chairs ain't meant for sleeping." He turned on his computer. After a few minutes he said, "Listen to this one from Nicholson: 'Officer Jessenovik'—does that mean I've been demoted?—'Please note that you were not at roll call this morning. Please plan to attend even though your wife is hospitalized.'"

Marti brought up her e-mail. "Check this out: 'Absence from roll call is an infraction that could result in disciplinary action.' She didn't even refer to me as officer, but it does sound like I'm still on the force."

Neither she nor Vik replied, although Marti was tempted to e-mail Nicholson a question, any question, like, Is the sun shining today? She decided that given her present attitude, no response was a good choice and put in a call to Fred's ex-wife instead.

"Oh, my God," the woman said. She said that several more times.

Marti interrupted. "Who should we call?"

"His father will have to know. They haven't seen each other since Andy's funeral. Don't call him. It could be too much for his heart. I'll go over right now and tell him myself. He's going to want to be there with Fred." The woman took a deep breath. "I'll see to Fred's daddy," she said and hung up.

It was eight forty A.M. when Vik took a call from the sergeant. "Woman found in a vacant house on Burr Ridge Road."

"Dead or alive?"

"Guess."

"Not far from a forest preserve?" Vik said.

"Closer to a middle school," Marti said. She was familiar with the street because her boys had attended that school last year.

"Okay, you two, let's roll," she told Lupe and Holmberg. "You're going to have to do some legwork on this one." She was glad to have some real work for them to do.

Dr. Mehta was leaving when they got there. "Manual strangulation," he said. "No signs of rape. One stab wound while unconscious. Multiple stab wounds when dead."

"Why does that sound familiar?" Vik said.

"The violence to the body is escalating, but no damage to the face. One hammer blow to the skull."

"How long had she been here?" Marti asked. The answers to questions like this were imprecise at best, but Dr. Mehta didn't seem to mind answering. Nor was he reluctant to give them preliminary information before the autopsy. She liked that about him.

"Rigor's decreasing. My best guess based on the temperature in the house is ten to fifteen hours."

"Thanks." This would give her and Vik something to work with while they were waiting for formal examinations and reports.

"Realtor found her," the uniform told them as they went inside. "Came over to show the place to a customer. That's her in the squad. She's still pretty upset. Evidence tech walked her through what she did when she got here. We've got a statement."

Marti let Vik do the talking. She was an older woman and cried as she answered his questions.

"This is Lincoln Prairie," she said, "not Chicago. I've lived here all of my life."

Vik's expression was grim. Marti could remember when he said the same thing.

"Nothing like this has ever happened to me before, and I've been selling real estate for thirty-two years."

The evidence techs were finishing up when they went inside. Lupe was used to Marti and Vik's routines and wandered down the hall. Holmberg stayed close and said nothing. Silent and attentive—Marti liked that in a rookie. She had no patience with the know-it-alls, and the opinionated idiots were usually so far off the mark they made her crazy.

"So far, we haven't found much," the female tech told them. "Place is really clean, like the other one. At least we only found one victim this time. He won't be able to use this place again, now that we've found a body here."

Fifteen minutes later, Marti squatted beside the body. The woman had been dead long enough to lose any semblance of ever having been alive. It was like looking at a mannequin. Her hair was dirty and the odors of death were unpleasant but not overwhelming. The pink jacket the woman was wearing had a Winnie the Pooh emblem near the shoulder and was several sizes too small. A floppy cotton hat was on the floor.

"Homeless," Vik said, "from the looks of her. Just like the others. If Fred is our guy, he could have had time to do this before stopping Wittenberg's bullet."

"Do you think he is our guy?" Marti asked.

"I don't want to think that," Vik admitted. "But not because of the dog."

"Because he's a vet?"

"Maybe. The older I get the less war seems like some kind of a game that's played on someone else's field. The older I get the harder it is to see us as the superheroes saving the world for democracy. Maybe we should mind our own damned business, at least some of the time. I don't know."

"That sounds unpatriotic coming from you, Jessenovik. Especially after nine-eleven."

"Nine-eleven was a first for us. It's been happening in the rest of the world for a long time now. And no, I don't want terrorism to become a way of life here, too, but I'm damned if I know what to do about it."

He took a few steps back and walked around the victim. "We're getting a body count. How did this woman come to be here?" From the syntax, Marti knew he meant what had happened in her life, not just last night. "How did she become homeless?" he asked, and went on without expecting an answer. "How did the others? This is America, damn it. Why can't we take care of our own?"

Marti wondered if Mildred's illness wasn't the real root of Vik's discontent. They all knew Mildred would not get well, that M.S. was chronic and the remissions and relapses could go on for years.

"What time are they releasing Mildred?" she asked.

"They're not. The doctor wants to run more tests. He's thinking about changing or adjusting her medication. They're going to increase the physical therapy, too. It'll get her out of the house more often. She doesn't even want to go shopping anymore."

Marti stood, looked down at the pink jacket, at the appliqué of Winnie the Pooh with his hand in the honey jar, looked at the bruises on the woman's neck, and wondered for a moment how she had come to be here and who would mourn her. Then she got out her camera, adjusted the lens, and focused.

"So," she said. "Looks like he's done it again." Did this mean that he stayed in one place for a while, killing multiple times before he moved on? Were there other victims in Chicago? If he had some kind of quota system, and they found out what it was, they could estimate how many more people he would kill here before he moved on.

"That was a hell of a thought," she said aloud, and repeated it to Vik.

He just ran his fingers through his hair, but the way his wiry salt-and-pepper eyebrows almost met across the bridge of his nose suggested that it didn't sound that unlikely.

Marti turned to Holmberg. "Get the Polaroid out of the trunk. We need some shots for canvassing." It had been so long since she had used that camera she wasn't sure if the film was still good.

While Holmberg was gone, she ordered another unmarked vehicle. "You and Lupe are going to get going on this now. Go anyplace where the homeless hang out during the day. We'll take the most likely places—the shelters and the library. You've got any other place where someone will let them come inside. Check doorways, empty buildings, anyplace where they can get out of the cold. Show everyone in those areas those Polaroid shots. Talk up the jacket. It's distinctive. If we move fast, someone might remember her."

The Presbyterian Church opened their basement as a shelter when the temperatures went below forty. About two dozen men and women sat in folding chairs placed at long tables. An elderly woman was putting out packaged cups of instant soup. Marti showed her the morgue shot. The woman looked at it for a moment, wiped her eyes, then looked at Marti.

"She's dead, isn't she." It was a statement, not a question.

Marti nodded.

"She didn't freeze to death, did she?"

"No, ma'am."

"Good," the woman said, as if that were somehow consoling. "Her name was Jelena. She came here from Serbia. Ran out of luck a couple years ago."

"Do you know what her last name is?"

"Sorry. They don't tell us much. Sometimes they give us their street name, if they have one, but Jelena said she was named for her aunt and I believed her. She . . . my parents were immigrants, too." The woman turned away and began rearranging the cups. "You do what you can," she said. "It never seems to be enough. What happens now? Will you be able to find out who she is? Where her family is? If you don't, does she get a funeral?"

Marti was taken aback by the woman's distress. "Are you new at this?"

The woman turned to her, wiping her eyes again. "No," she said. "I've been doing this for years. Nothing ever seems to change."

"I'll let you know what happens." Marti patted the woman on the shoulder. There was little else she could do.

Their next stop was the library. It was easy to tell the homeless from the patrons, and not just because of the way they were dressed or unshaven. They weren't reading, for one thing, although they all had a newspaper or a periodical on the table where they sat. And they didn't sit near each other. Marti counted seven, and at least two chairs separated one from the other. The patrons stayed even father away and ignored them.

The security guard nodded as soon as he saw the picture.

"One of the regulars," he said. "Comes in just about every day. Maybe one, two o'clock. Can't tell you her name. They're not required to have library cards. It's cold out there this time of year. As long as they're quiet, I look the other way."

Vik caught her eye and raised his eyebrows. Marti nodded. They did have a talker on their hands, not necessarily a bad thing. It was escaping, once you had all the useful information you were going to get, that could be difficult.

"Do you remember anything different about yesterday?" Vik asked.

"Just the dude that stopped to talk to her. You'd think that with them all being homeless they'd be friendly toward one another, but they're not."

"Can you describe the man?"

Marti almost winced as the man described someone who could be Fred.

"We're late for that task force meeting," Vik said when they returned to their car. He made a quick call on his cell phone. "Winans's waiting for us. Are you alert enough to drive?"

"Probably not."

"Sounds good. Me neither. Let's go. There's always flashing lights and a siren if you need something to keep you awake."

Winans was waiting for them in the same small office. This time an older man was with him. Marti's antenna went up. The other man had cop all but written on his forehead, but for some reason she thought he might be a judge. Maybe he was just a lawyer. Some cops did get law degrees.

"This is an old friend of mine, Jed Daniels," Winans said without clarifying the man's occupation.

"Don't tell me you two are late because the body count has gone up," Winans began. He turned to Daniels. "MacAlister and Jessenovik seem to have what we commonly call a serial killer on their hands." He looked at them. "How do you two see it?"

"Most of the time we think of them as repeat offenders," Vik said.

"How do you define a serial killer?" Daniels asked.

"We don't," Marti answered.

"Why not?"

"Labels and profiles can get in the way. We can't afford to lose focus."

"What is your focus?"

"Stopping them."

Winans said, "So, you've got . . . what? Three, four bodies now?"

"Three here, two in Chicago."

"Is Chicago cooperating?"

"We've worked with them before."

"What's it like, when it's a smaller department?" Winans asked.

"Depends on how much ego is involved," Vik said.

"And how much information they're willing to give up," Marti added.

There was a knock on the door and a woman looked in on them. "Coffee, soda?" she asked. "Cookies?" They agreed on coffee and cookies.

"How *do* you handle a case like this?" Daniels asked.

"We don't make any assumptions," Marti told him. "We let the victims and the killer talk to us."

"Talk?" Daniels seemed puzzled. "How?"

"Method, scene of the crime, type of victim, weapon. Whatever stays the same, and if we get lucky, something unique."

"Then you do have a profile," Daniels said.

"We know how this guy kills," Marti said. "We know we don't have any copycat killings yet. Profiling, if you want to call it that, comes more into play as the case progresses, and then it's more a matter of the killer's habits, preferences, idiosyncrasies—the changes in his behavior and what that tells us."

The woman returned, making several trips as she brought in mugs of coffee, packets of sugar and creamer, and a plate of cookies.

"We are dealing with a nutcase here," Vik said when she closed the door. "A psychopath, if you prefer. Based on what we know about the victim found this morning, our subject is getting angrier. That could mean a number of things. The most important thing to us right now is not why he's becoming more violent, but how long it will be before his anger causes him to get careless, to make a mistake. That's what we're looking for at the crime scene now. We've also got more men out canvassing. There are a lot of ways to make a mistake, being seen or noticed is one of them."

"Is this his way of asking to be stopped?" Daniels asked.

"That cry-for-help crap doesn't carry much weight for me," Vik admitted. "Not until they turn themselves in or commit suicide."

"You don't think he wants to be stopped?"

"Sir," Vik said. Marti could tell he was getting annoyed. "This isn't a social service operation and we're not psychiatrists."

"As far as we're concerned," Marti said, "he's losing control and/or he has to behave more violently in order to get the same satisfaction."

"What's going on in his head," Vik added, "is important to us in terms of how it affects what he does and how that helps us catch him."

"So, you have a profile," Daniels said, "and you're using it to try and catch a serial killer."

"Yes and no," Marti said. She was becoming annoyed by the man's persistence. "We have five victims. We know there are certain consistencies in the way they lived and the way they died."

Vik was scowling. "We focus on those consistencies—not some abstract idea of who our killer is."

"We know who his target victim is," Marti explained, "and we know that could change. And if it does, his methods could change as well, but some of the consistencies should hold true. We know that there are other victims out there somewhere."

"How do you know that?"

Vik gave Daniels his "Duh" look. "Practice makes perfect," he quoted. "This guy is too good not to have practiced a few times."

"Then how are you going to catch him?" Winans asked.

"That might be tricky," Marti explained. "For instance, we have a few officers undercover at his pickup points of choice. But if he figures we're there, he'll change his locale or his victim population. I think he's at the point where he might begin making mistakes, that and a lot of plain old shoe-leather-hitting-the-pavement are probably what it will take."

"Or a lucky break," Daniels said.

"That does happen sometimes," Vik admitted. "But only a damned fool waits for it, or expects it."

Later, as they were leaving the building, Vik said, "Do you think they just wanted to pick our brains or was that a job interview? Either way, I don't think we told them what they expected to hear."

Job interview? Marti thought. What if it was? Was she going to need a job soon? Or just want out?

Po' Boys was a small but busy place, take-out only. Hand-printed signs advertised everything from breakfast sandwiches to burgers, hot dogs, and polish sausages for lunch, and even fish and chicken for dinner. Iris knew that if she went in there, asked if they recognized the photo or if they knew of anyone matching Loomis's description, they wouldn't tell her. Worse, someone might alert him. Right now she had the advantage. He didn't know she was here.

She circled the block a couple of times, then decided on a doorway near a bus stop where folks wouldn't pay much attention to her and she could keep out of the wind and watch who went in and out of Po' Boys. If nothing else, she'd find out if the little girl in the snapshot really did like hamburgers.

17

DeVonte lay in bed and looked up at the ceiling, wondering what he was going to do. His arms and legs ached. The pain in his gut wouldn't quit. And when he breathed, his ribs hurt. His chest felt like it did when his mother broke his ribs. If only he hadn't tripped over that branch he wouldn't be the one who was hurting. Then his knife fell just as he was about to stab that S.O.B. There was no time to pick it up. And then those men were running toward them. He had no choice but to get away from there, and fast. Next time it would be different. And there would be a next time. Nobody got the best of him now that his mother was gone. His knife. That knife was special. He had killed for the first time with it. He would have to get another knife. He would return to the woods, find that bastard, and take his time killing him.

Meanwhile, there was now. The child kept peeking in at him. Maybe he shouldn't have told her he had seen her mother. Maybe he shouldn't have said her mother would be here in a couple days. Maybe the child sensed that her mother was in danger and had conjured a spell. Maybe that was why so much went wrong last night. He would have to be careful. He would have to watch what he said to her. As for Iris, he didn't know where to look for her, but he would have to find her.

He braced himself for the pain in his chest and took another shallow breath. He was going to have to get up and get the child something to eat. Good thing Po' Boys was only half a block away.

Even though part of her expected to see Loomis, Iris was still surprised when she did see him walking across the street. She could tell right away that something was wrong. He was hunched over and holding one arm across his chest. Someone had got hold of him, and, from the looks of it, hadn't been in any hurry to let go.

She waited until he came out, and crossed to her side of the street, then she called to him.

"Mr. Loomis!" Hurrying, she caught up. "Lord, I didn't think I would ever find you. That woman tricked me. Took my hat and my coat while I used the bathroom, then told me the bus was delayed for ten minutes and she'd meet me by the pop machines. By the time I went looking for her, the bus was gone. I had to wait four hours for the next one. And you didn't give me any address, phone number, nothing."

"Then how'd you find me?"

"Po' Boys. You talked about getting burgers from there. I used to have a friend who lived on Juneway, not far from here. I've had a few of their burgers myself."

He didn't say anything else until they reached one of the apartment buildings. Then he stepped into the doorway and unlocked the front door. She followed.

"Car accident," he said.

"Is Lynn Ella okay?"

"She wasn't with us."

"Thank God!"

"My wife is in the hospital. I probably should be, too, but someone's got to be at home."

"How can I help? After all you've done for my baby . . ."

"Come up and meet her."

As he spoke, Iris wondered how he had got his hands on the child in the first place and what he wanted with her. If he was some damned pervert. She felt suddenly afraid, but shrugged it off. Hell, she had known a lot of perverts in her time, and drug addicts and crazy people as well.

She had to walk up three flights of stairs, but the hallways were clean and didn't stink. Loomis wasn't walking too fast and Iris was in no hurry to get wherever she was going. This man wasn't who he said he was. He hadn't come to meet her out of the goodness of his heart. He was up to something. She didn't know what and she didn't want to find out, but she had to know if he really did have a child with him, and, if he did, whose child she was and why he had her. She had been in enough jails, shelters, treatment programs, hospitals, and mental institutions to know that unless you were rich, famous, white, or knew Jesse Jackson, nobody was going to do anything for you. You had to do for yourself. And this child, whoever she was, couldn't.

Loomis stopped at the top of the stairs and leaned over, holding his chest.

"You okay? Can I help you? Where are we going?"

He handed her the bag from Po' Boys "Three-oh-two," he gasped. "Right there." He reached into his pocket and gave her the key.

Iris hesitated. What was she getting into? She turned the key in the lock.

Inside it was quiet, too quiet.

"Got to lie down for a while," Loomis said and went into the room across from the front door.

Iris walked down the hall, found the kitchen, put the bag on the table, and looked around. Clean. Just the basics. Nothing extra, but clean. No roaches either.

She returned to the hall, counted two doors besides the door to his room. The first was the bathroom. Clean. No odors. Two towels on the rack. Toilet paper. Soap.

She stopped when she got to the next door. It was closed. Was this where the little girl was? She could leave now. He couldn't stop her. If she was quiet, he wouldn't even know she was leaving. Even better, the little girl wouldn't know she had been here.

Iris went back to the kitchen, looked around. It came to her all at once. There was no woman here. He didn't have a wife, not here anyway. Whatever was going on, the child was here alone with him. This time—knowing this might not be her child, or, if it was, that the child might not want her—the closed door didn't stop her. She turned the knob, walked inside. Empty. Nobody was here. There was no child. What was he up to? Why had he lied? Was it some kind of trick to get her here? But why?

Then a little girl peeked out from the closet. A small brown face, short hair, uncombed—and dark eyes, slanted ovals just like Ma's, with thick eyelashes and naturally arched eyebrows like Ma's.

"Lynn Ella?" Iris whispered.

The child didn't move.

"Girl, you look just like your grandma."

Still the child didn't move. Iris went to her, saw the pillow, the blanket.

"Why are you sleeping in here?"

"It be there." She pointed to the bed.

"It . . . what?"

She went to the bed, pulled off the blanket. The sheet was clean. "I don't see anything." But there was fear in Lynn Ella's eyes. She was afraid of something that happened in the bed. If that man was abusing her baby, she'd kill him. "Is he hurting, you?"

The child shrank back. "Nooo. Nooo. I be here. I don't go. Nooo. I be here." She scooted into the closet, folded her arms, and said, "Don't want no mama. Don't want no mama, no more, never."

Lynn Ella sure talked funny, but maybe not. The D.C.F.S. had no record of her ever going to school.

"It's okay," Iris said. "I just want to be sure nobody's hurting you."

"Don't be hurtin' me here."

"Did they hurt you when you were someplace else?"

Lynn Ella looked at her with either anger or hatred, she wasn't sure which. "Don't be wantin' no mama. Don't be wantin' no mama, no, never again."

Then it must have been a mama who hurt her. The old

woman, maybe. And now here she was. A woman. Maybe another mama. Maybe someone else who would hurt her.

"What do you want, baby?"

"Want to be here. With DeVonte."

Iris was about to ask her who DeVonte was, but it had to be him, Mr. Darrell Loomis. But why did he want her baby? How did he get her? And now what did he want with her? None of this made any sense.

"DeVonte's not feeling so good today. He hurt himself, asked me to help out."

The child's look suggested that they didn't need her help.

"You comfortable in there?"

A nod.

"One pillow enough?"

Another nod.

"Are you hungry? There's food."

Lynn Ella shook her head. She was so thin. Iris wanted to cry just looking at her. She wanted to hold her, soothe her, love her, tell her she was safe, that she wouldn't be hurt anymore. But she hadn't been here to say any of that for so many years. She didn't think anyone else had told Lynn Ella that either. But now, for whatever the reason, this man had made her baby feel safe. He hadn't hurt her. He had gone out of here sick to bring her some food. Whatever the reason, he was taking care of her baby, better care of her than whomever the D.C.F.S. had placed her with.

Iris went to the kitchen and brought back the bag from Po' Boys.

"It be in there," Lynn Ella said again, but she scooted out of the closet.

"Food be in here," Iris told her. She took out one of the burgers and unwrapped it. Then she took the fries and spread them on a napkin.

"See," she said. "It's just food. It's okay to eat it."

Lynn Ella backed into the closet. Iris waited. After a few minutes Lynn Ella came out and began to eat. When the food was gone Iris went down the hall to DeVonte's room. She looked in to make sure he was dressed, then walked into the room.

"I don't know what's wrong with her," she said. "She's acting weird. But she is my daughter. She's got my mother's eyes."

"I have a hard time getting her to eat," he said. "And she doesn't want to play with the doll or go outside."

"You don't have a woman living here either," Iris told him. "And you're not feeling too good. My guess is you've been in a fight, not an accident."

"Car crash," he repeated.

Maybe, but she didn't think so. Mr. DeVonte lied a lot. "You want to tell me why you want both of us here?"

"I might if you can score something for the pain."

"No problem."

He reached into his pants pocket and gave her a hundred dollars. "Codeine would work. You need anything?"

"No. I'm not using."

"Prescriptions then?"

"I've got enough for a week."

"Good. You will come back?"

"What do you think?"

"You're an addict."

"And a mother." With a little girl who didn't want her, who had been hurt, and for some reason trusted this man. "I'll be back."

He gave her the money. She could see that he was in pain. It must be his ribs. He winced every time he took a breath. She could tape him so it wouldn't hurt as much, but that might be something she would need later—*if* she didn't just take Lynn Ella and get out of here while he was asleep.

Outside, Iris began walking. She needed to think. She could find a cop, take him up to the apartment, and give her little girl back to the state so they could lose her again. Or she could take Lynn

Ella to Miss Lottie's. Who would know? Or care? Lynn Ella wouldn't be any more lost with her than she was now as far as the D.C.F.S. was concerned.

Lynn Ella trusted this DeVonte, wanted to be with him. Wanted him to be her daddy. As far as she could tell, he wasn't mistreating her. But someone had, and if she just took the child away from him now and took her . . . where? . . . To what? She had no legal right to that child. The state owned her. But she had not been loved. Maybe not since they took Lynn Ella from her arms, except by this man. She didn't like him. She didn't trust him. But she could see the affection that had grown between him and her child.

She had never been a good mother. She was going to have to be now. She didn't just have to make amends to this child for what she had done, or neglected to do. She had to find a way to make sure nobody mistreated her baby again. She didn't know what the right thing was this minute, but she did have time to think about it. There wasn't much Mr. DeVonte could do right now, whatever his intentions were.

DeVonte smiled as he waited for Iris to return, in spite of the pain. Another woman. Another fool. This one would help him, just as the other women had. This one would do whatever he wanted her to. When he was feeling better she would die—along with that cop—along with Sharon. They would all die. Soon. He heard a small sound, looked toward the door, and saw the child peeking in.

"See," he told her. "I said I would bring your mother, your real mother, and I did."

The child remained in the hall. All he could see was her head. Her choppy haircut made him think of his own hair as a child. Shaggy, nappy, uncut.

"Come here, Lynn Ella."

She didn't move for almost a minute, then she came into the room, but stayed near the doorway.

"Did you eat?"

She nodded.

"You've been hungry before, haven't you?"

She looked down at the floor.

"When I was your age I had to go hungry sometimes, too. It was a poor place, the island where I was born, but beautiful."

Lynn Ella scuffed her gym shoe against the linoleum.

"Do you know how I got hurt?"

"No."

"Did you work root on me? Work a spell?"

"No. Don't never do."

"But you know how to."

She shrugged. "Big mama do. She dead. Don't want no mo' mamas."

Looking at her, he realized that he didn't want her to have a mama either. He couldn't do to her what he had done to the others. She was too small, too young. He had never hurt a child. This one was so small he could strangle her with one hand and break her neck doing it. But she wanted him to be her daddy. If he put his hands around her throat, the last thing she would know was fear; if he stabbed her, pain. Lynn Ella had known that for a long time now. He didn't want her to know that anymore. He didn't want her to go away. He *could* keep her with him. Women respected men who raised their children alone, trusted them, wanted to help them. Lynn Ella didn't need a mother. Iris was just another junkie, just like the woman who had sold Lynn Ella to him, just like his mother had been. The child didn't need Iris. Nobody needed Iris.

"Don't want no mo' mamas," she said again.

"Give me a few days," he told her. "And she'll go away."

Lynn Ella came closer. "Where I be when she go?"

"Right here. With me."

For the first time, the child smiled. DeVonte felt something he had never felt before. It was such a strange feeling he didn't know what it was.

* * *

"Things don't look good for Fred," Vik said as they left the County Building after their meeting with Winans. "We found that knife on him . . ."

"Two sets of prints," Marti reminded him. "Fred and someone else touched the handle. The prints on the blade aren't Fred's. They haven't found a match for the second set yet, and only that set was found on the blade."

"Then there's this story from Wittenberg about being attacked by Fred."

"Story," Marti repeated.

"Look," Vik said. "I don't like this any better than you do. Not because he's a vet or because he likes dogs. It just doesn't feel right in my gut. There are still some pieces missing, but if we don't find them . . ."

"Then I guess we'll have to," Marti told him.

"After we get something to eat?"

Reluctantly, Marti agreed to stop at the Barrister. She was more anxious to get back to work than to pay attention to the hunger noises her stomach was making.

When Marti got back to the precinct, there was a copy of the ballistics report on Fred's shooting in her in-basket. She had asked them to expedite things, but this had to be a record.

"That's odd, Vik. No bullets in the chamber. So there must have been just the one. Why do you keep a gun for protection and only have one bullet in it?"

"Sounds more like Russian roulette," Vik agreed.

Marti finished reading the report, then read it again. Next, she got out her copy of Wittenberg's statement.

"According to this report, the gun was fired from a distance of thirty-four inches. They found some scattered powder grains on Fred's shirt. According to Wittenberg, Fred was 'right there' when he shot him."

"No way," Vik said. "There were no soot patterns."

Marti visualized the room. "The doorway would have been at least nine feet from where Wittenberg sat when we were there.

The chairs where we were sitting were . . . what? Four feet from his?"

"That's about right, approximately forty-eight inches."

Marti read from Wittenberg's statement. "'I looked up and there he was . . . He came toward me. I pulled the gun from under the cushion. I always kept it there. He laughed and said, "That won't stop me, you old fool," and I shot him. He fell on me.'"

"Wittenberg's clothes were bloody," Vik said.

"At thirty-four inches—the distance according to ballistics— if Fred was sitting in the chair, he would have had to have taken at least one step forward. According to Wittenberg, Fred was right there. The blood on Wittenberg's clothing does indicate that Fred fell on him, but Wittenberg's story doesn't quite jibe with this report."

"He did say he'd been drinking."

"How drunk do you think he was when he gave this statement, Jessenovik?"

"Looked cold sober to me."

Marti returned to the report. "They're about the same height, and the entry wound is oval. The gun was fired at an angle. Upward trajectory. So, Fred was standing, Wittenberg sitting. That could indicate self-defense, but where's the threat? There's nothing in Wittenberg's statement to indicate Fred threatened him, only that he reacted when Wittenberg pulled the gun."

Vik drummed his fingers on his desk and said nothing. Marti waited until the finger tapping stopped. "Prosecution would say implied threat."

"But only if Wittenberg didn't let him in. We don't have any other reports yet, do we?"

"Nothing from the evidence techs yet."

"Well, let's just hope Fred comes through this and tells us his version. Maybe it will match up better with the facts. Meanwhile, we've got a statement with discrepancies from a man who says he had been drinking when the shooting occurred."

Marti made a call to the forensics lab. "Wittenberg's alcohol level was well below the legal limit," she said when she hung up. "The routine stuff is still being processed. Nothing yet on whose fingerprints were where."

Before either of them could say anything else, Lieutenant Nicholson sent for them.

This time there was no waiting to see the lieutenant. Not only was her door open, but she was pacing.

"Close that door," she said as soon as they walked in. There was no invitation to sit.

"Why haven't you charged Sergeant Reskov with this assault on Alderman Wittenberg?"

Marti looked at Vik. He raised one eyebrow. She blinked in agreement. This from the woman who did not want Reskov charged with homicide.

"Why would we, without sufficient evidence?" Marti asked

"We have Alderman Wittenberg's statement."

"Oh, so we charge Reskov because Wittenberg says to. Does that mean that, unlike our homeless victims, Wittenberg is important?"

"You listen to me." Nicholson jabbed her finger inches from Marti's face. "You have no common sense whatsoever. Wittenberg represents the people of this city. The people want police protection. They do not want muggings and home invasions happening in their neighborhood. You're damned right we'll prosecute Reskov."

"For this," Marti said. "And what about the homicide victims? Murder in one's neighborhood is okay as long as the victims aren't important?"

A vein bulged at Nicholson's temple. "How dare you—"

"How do we justify requesting charges for one crime and not the others?" Marti demanded.

Nicholson took half a minute to answer. "Because we don't have sufficient evidence." She sounded calmer.

"Have you read Wittenberg's statement and the ballistics report?" Marti asked. "There are discrepancies."

"Alderman Wittenberg was under a considerable amount of stress."

Smug, Marti thought. He had looked smug. Had he already known he had the lieutenant in his pocket?

"Stress?" she said. "You should have seen him."

If Nicholson caught the sarcasm, she didn't react.

"Have you spoken with the state's attorney about any of this, lieutenant?"

The lieutenant took a step back. Her hand fell to her side. "No," she said, "but I do expect you to."

"I can't do that," Marti said. "Not at this time. There are too many questions."

"Assuming there any inconsistencies in Alderman Wittenberg's statement, not only was he threatened by an intruder, but he was mugged the night before, perhaps by the same suspect," Nicholson said. "You will speak with the state's attorney."

"What's the rush?" Marti asked. "We don't even know if Fred Reskov will live."

The lieutenant seemed to consider that, then said, "Meanwhile, he's under guard. See to it that you have a case against him if he does wake up."

"Damn, MacAlister," Vik said as they walked back to their office. "I thought she was going to fire you on the spot. I was going to walk right out the door with you." He thought about that for a moment. "Too bad she didn't. Nothing like having a major life decision made for you."

"She still needs us," Marti said. "The other shoe will drop as soon as she doesn't." Right now, that couldn't happened soon enough. "Damned if anyone will own me. I didn't become a cop to become someone's flunky." Change be damned. Now she did want out.

*　*　*

Gail Nicholson clutched the clock on her desk and wished she could throw it. But she was not going to give anyone the satisfaction of knowing just how angry she was. Instead, she picked up a legal pad and ripped all the pages to shreds. That calmed her. She swung her chair toward the narrow window with its minute glimpse of the lake. She had finally gotten to MacAlister.

After all the years on the force, ten years working the streets of Chicago, the woman still believed in that stupid motto, To Serve and Protect. What a laugh. Marti MacAlister, champion of the underdog, the victim, the forgotten, the unwanted and unwashed. What a joke, comparable to the idea of martyrdom. And how stupid. All they would ever be to the underclass were pigs. This was a job, not a vocation.

And it was a job that would be done her way by everyone on her watch. She was in charge here, not Marti MacAlister.

Cowboy went to I.C.U. as soon as roll call was over. The uniform sitting in the waiting area nodded to him.

"Any change?" he asked.

The uniform shook his head.

Cowboy wondered why in hell the lieutenant would bother to waste manpower on a man not only unconscious but hooked to so much equipment that he was anchored to a hospital bed. Strange one, that Lieutenant Nicholson. Marti seemed to understand her, and Jessenovik had probably seen too many bosses come and go to give a damn, but he was fed up. He didn't need to deal with shit on the street and put up with it on the job, too. A little more of Nicholson's interference and he'd be out of here.

The nurse was putting medication in Fred's eyes when Cowboy went in. Fred looked the same as he did a couple of hours ago.

He mouthed the words, "No change?"

The nurse shook her head.

He wished he could bring Geronimo here. The dog might be all Fred needed to come out of this. When the nurse left, he went over to the bed, covered Fred's hand with his.

"Hey, man," he said, "I'm back. I'm here with you, okay? I'm right here. And I didn't just take Geronimo to the vet, I called a cop vet, a forensic veterinarian. I took him into our lab, got a local vet to draw the blood, and we're running the tests here and having the same tests run by an independent lab. We'll have two sets of results. Anything doesn't match up and we'll run that test again. And the vet checked him over, said she couldn't see any sign of poisoning."

He pulled the chair closer, so that he could keep his hand on Fred's. "Wake up, man. Tell me why you want Geronimo tested. I don't know what's going on here. I don't know how else I can help you."

The nurse came to the door and gave him a thumbs up. "Keep talking," she said.

Cowboy didn't know how she knew there were changes with Fred while he was there. He just hoped she was right, hoped that even if Fred didn't make it, he at least knew he wasn't alone.

"Look, man, you can beat this, you've been through a hell of a lot worse. It's been years since we fought in Desert Storm, and we're both still here. We've survived, Fred. We've survived. I see this real good counselor sometimes. He was a jarhead in 'Nam. He knows, man, he really knows. He's helped me a lot. There's none of this 'I know how you must feel' crap. He's been there, he's felt it. He knows. There's a lot of things in life that nobody can fix. But you've made it through one hell of a lot and you're still here. You'd be surprised at the stuff you can't fix that you can learn to live with. Jesus, man.

"Fred, I really don't want you to die. I owe you. You've given me something and not just by going in first in Iraq. When you come for Geronimo, I'm heading for the shelter to find a dog. This is the first time I can remember not wanting to be alone. Even with females, it's one-night stands. Well, maybe a week or two when the sex is good. But no commitments. I don't ever want to commit to another human being. I've got my sister, and I've still got my old man. That's enough. But I am going to find me a dog."

Cowboy felt Fred's hand move beneath his. When he took his hand away, Fred's hand was still. Maybe it was just a reflex, a spasm or something. But as he watched, Fred's fingers moved again. Cowboy reached for the call button.

There was a voice mail from Mark Dobrzycki. Marti listened to the message: "MacAlister? I got a call from your friend at the Chicago office. I'm sending her everything we've got on Lutrell. He has been making phone calls. Real friendly on the surface, no threats. Our guys didn't think they were that important. We've got transcripts. That and a copy of our file on Lutrell will be delivered to you by this afternoon. I know I don't have to tell you this, but it's my confidential file. You cannot use anything in it without the expressed consent of the department. If you need anything else, the quickest way to get in touch is to call your girlfriend again. She doesn't need clearance to contact me."

There was also a message from her friend in Chicago. "Call me." Marti did.

"Are you going to be in your office for a couple of hours?"

"I can be," Marti told her. "Why?"

"I can dispatch an agent with these files right now, but he won't be able to give them to anyone but you. And don't get your hopes up. Dobrzycki's not doing this out of the goodness of his heart. If he found anything he could use, you wouldn't be getting it." She repeated Dobrzycki's admonition about confidentiality, then added, "I can contact him as soon as possible if you need anything else."

When Marti told Vik they were getting an FBI file, he leaned back, looked at her for a moment, then said, "This is one of the reasons why Lieutenant Dirkowitz always gave us a heads-up, isn't it?"

"Maybe," Marti said. This wasn't the first time she had used contacts and old friends during a case.

"What do you think the odds are that Dirkowitz or Nicholson could do this without going through channels?"

Marti grinned. "Thanks, partner." This was the first time since

Nicholson had come on board that she felt good about being a cop. Nicholson would probably be furious at not being told, but when she had called her Sunday morning, Nicholson had said to let the FBI handle it. As far as Marti was concerned, she was. She thought about that for a moment and realized she no longer cared about Nicholson one way or the other.

18

Cowboy was sitting near the bed watching Fred's hand when the nurse came to the door.

"His father is here," she whispered.

As Cowboy followed her to the waiting room, he asked, "Is this going to upset Fred? His hand moved. It wasn't just a reflex. Maybe he's coming out of it. I don't want—"

The nurse patted his arm. "We know. Why don't you talk to his dad for a few minutes. He seems like an awfully nice man. He's seventy-eight years old and he looks like he has a few health problems. He's very concerned about Fred."

The man sitting in the chair when Cowboy walked into the room bore no resemblance to his son. He had thick, wavy white hair, and sideburns. He breathed with a wheeze. The jacket he was wearing wasn't warm enough for this late fall, northern Illinois weather.

"Mr. Reskov," Cowboy said. Mr. Reskov stood. He was at least six feet two. The hand he extended had veins as thick as cord. As they shook, Cowboy could feel the tremors.

"Why is he here?" Mr. Reskov asked, nodding toward the uniform. "What's my boy done? How is he? The nurse said she's sent for the doctor to come talk to me. That doesn't sound too good."

Cowboy guided the man to a chair and sat beside him. He filled him in on what he knew about what had happened.

"You're a cop, aren't you?"

Cowboy nodded. "Fred has a dog, a red-nosed pit bull. I'm taking care of him. We both served in Desert Storm. I owe him."

Mr. Reskov seemed to relax when he said that. "War," he said. "One way or another it's taken all of us, not just Andy. I kept trying to tell Fred, you've got to learn to live with what you saw there, what you did, even if you can't make peace with it. If you don't figure out how to live with it, it'll eat you alive. I never could help him, though, even though I'd been through a worse war myself."

Reskov rubbed the back of one hand with the palm of the other. "Intensive care, half his lung gone. It doesn't look good, does it? Even if he makes it, he's got that." He glanced at the uniform.

"Don't worry about that now. Nobody here is out to get Fred. All of us just want to help him, same as you."

"When can I see him? Or would it be better if I didn't?"

"Do you want to see him?"

Reskov's eyes filled with tears. "Fred's the last button on the old man's overcoat. My wife called him our bonus baby. The last time I saw him was at Andy's funeral. He was so . . ." He wiped at his eyes. "Hard thing, burying your only son, worse than my burying my youngest—and favorite—grandson. I didn't have any words for him then. He didn't have any for me."

"But you're here," Cowboy said.

"We used to . . ." His voice broke. "The war. A long time ago, when Fred was a kid . . ." His voice broke again. He cleared his throat and went on. "We'd go to the cabin. The fishing was good there, but we didn't hunt. I never could bring myself to raise a gun to an animal. I never could teach Fred to shoot like my daddy taught me. We were mountain people, born and raised in the hills of Kentucky. But we never did shoot or trap anything, me and Fred. Not even a rabbit. We never could."

"If that's what you remember," Cowboy said, "maybe that's what Fred remembers, too. He mentioned heading for a cabin in Montana for the winter."

Reskov smiled. "And he had a dog."

"A good dog. Trained."

"Fred always had a way with animals."

"I keep reminding him that Geronimo needs him."

"Geronimo. We had a dog by that name when Fred was growing up. That old boy lived to be seventeen. It broke both our hearts when we woke up one morning and found him dead right there at the foot of Fred's bed. Fred went off and joined the Marines not long after that."

The nurse came to the door. "Would you like to see your son now, Mr. Reskov?"

The old man muttered "arthritis" as he pushed himself up from the chair. His shoulders were stooped and he walked as if his joints were stiff.

A few minutes later, the nurse returned. "I'm sure Fred knows his dad is there, and there's no adverse reaction."

"Thanks," Cowboy said. "I won't be gone long." Geronimo was waiting for him at the forensics lab.

"Too many bodies in too short a time," Marti said as she and Vik left the coroner's facility. Looking at Jelena had been almost painful. She was tiny with small bones, small breasts, and thin. She was much too thin. "Undernourished," Dr. Mehta said. She died the same way as the others. There were more stab wounds, too many more. "It looks like he's losing control."

"He sure is angry," Vik said.

"Do you think the Serbian fraternal organization will be able to find any relatives?" Marti asked, changing the subject.

"Maybe. They found out her last name. And fast, too."

"Nice people," Marti said. "They're taking care of the burial, and if they can find any relatives in the next week, they'll bring them here for the funeral. At least, according to the autopsy, she never had children." She wasn't sure why that made any difference, but for some reason it always seemed to.

* * *

Vik had to go to the hospital to meet with Mildred and her doctor. There wasn't enough time to have breakfast. They settled for jelly- and custard-filled doughnuts instead.

"Geronimo!" Marti said when Cowboy came in with the dog. Then, "Fred's okay, isn't he?"

"His dad is with him," Cowboy explained. "Geronimo, here, had to go in for some tests, didn't you, boy? Fred called me yesterday, worried about his having some kind of poison in his system. Lead, mercury, maybe."

"Did he say how he thought he got it?"

Cowboy took off the dog's long leash and snapped on a short lead. "No. Be back in a minute."

Geronimo trotted over and sat near her. Marti massaged him behind his ears like she did her dogs. His neck was solid muscle.

When Cowboy returned he had two cups of water. Geronimo drank both.

"What else did Fred say?" Marti asked. "Why did he want Geronimo tested?"

"Here, it's still on my voice mail."

Marti listened: "Get Geronimo to a vet, please, right away. Have him checked for lead and mercury poisoning. I just found out he's been exposed. Make them check for any kind of environmental water or ground poisoning they can come up with. Please, right away. Don't let anything happen to him."

"Well," Marti said. "There's no question he was upset. What that has to do with anything beats me. Maybe it'll make sense to Vik. He should be back from the hospital soon."

"How's Mildred?" Cowboy asked.

"That's what they're finding out."

Marti wondered if seeing her without Vik seemed as strange to Cowboy as seeing him without Slim seemed to her. Slim was giving Holmberg a view of life on the street and Lupe had tagged along. Cowboy had gone right to the chief to request personal time to be with Fred. The most interesting think about that was that the chief didn't even mention going through channels, namely Nicholson. Even though they didn't discuss it, Marti thought they all recognized not just Fred's need to have Cowboy around, but Cowboy's need to be there.

Cowboy put on another pot of coffee.

"We should get you a coffee maker like the one you've got at home," Marti said.

"And the coffee beans." He sat down and began going through his in-basket. Geronimo collapsed with a sigh by his chair.

"Do you know much about dogs?" Marti asked.

"They eat, sleep, and shit," Cowboy said. "And they need exercise." He looked down at Geronimo. "No offense, man. They also appreciate kindness and offer unconditional love. In fact, when Geronimo goes back to his master, I'm heading to the shelter to look for a replacement."

Marti just looked at him for a moment or two. This Cowboy, the man she didn't know, was full of surprises. She told him she had been thinking about a companion dog for Mildred, but hadn't mentioned it to Vik.

"Why not?" Cowboy asked. "The man's desperate. Maybe they can train the dog to do something. If nothing else, they're good company."

He picked up the phone. "Forgot to check my voice mail this morning." He listened for about a minute, grabbed a pencil and began writing. He pushed a piece of paper over to her, kept listening.

She read a license plate number, then "Hemlock Street," then "from Fred."

When Cowboy hung up, he said, "Mean anything?"

"It must, but I'm not sure what." She ran the plate number, came up with a James Morgenstein and an address in unincorporated Lake County. She ran a check on Morgenstein. "Well, I don't think he's our killer. Eighty-three, visually impaired, no longer has a valid license." She ran another check. "Great. Car was reported stolen almost a year ago. 'Eighty-eight Chevrolet Cavalier, brown.'

Could be the car our only witness saw. She did say the car she saw could have been brown, but she also said it was small."

Marti made a few calls. Associating the car with a double homicide significantly increased the odds that, statewide, law enforcement agencies would be on the lookout for it. Then, on a hunch, she put in a call to the Lake County Sheriff's Department because the unincorporated area was under their jurisdiction. She asked to be put through to homicide. The detective she spoke with sounded interested. He agreed to check his records for homicides with similarities to the Hemlock Street cases.

When Vik came in twenty minutes later, Marti could tell by the expression on his face that the news was not good. Neither she nor Cowboy said anything as he poured a cup of coffee and helped himself to a doughnut. As soon as he sat down, Geronimo went over to him.

"Hi, boy," Vik said. "You pick up any bad habits from your new roommate yet? What? No womanizing? No boozing it up? Gotta watch out for these vice cops. Crazy, all of them."

Marti looked at Cowboy. He tipped his five gallon hat in her direction and winked.

"How's Mildred?" she asked.

"She might be coming home tomorrow," he said. He gave Geronimo a piece of his doughnut. "They're trying a different medication and want to monitor it for a day or two. They are also taking her to physical therapy twice a day. She hates it. We had to talk her into going to a physical therapist when she's released. She wanted one to come to the house, but getting out will be good for her."

"Is Helen okay? Denise Stevens has help coming into care for her mother, and she belongs to a caregiver's support group."

"Helen will be a nervous wreck now that this has happened. Maybe Denise can talk to her about this group, take her to a meeting. My son will be staying at the house at least until we get these cases closed. By then I may have come up with something."

"Like what?" Marti asked.

"I don't know. Right now, this seems more like taking her to jail than taking her home. She'll have privacy, but she'll never be alone. I am having a contractor come in to see if we can make any changes to the house that will make it easier for her to get around. We've lived there since we were married. I hate to take that away from her, too." Vik began petting the dog.

"Geronimo sure seems to like you," Cowboy said. "You and Marti are the only ones he's gone to since he's been here. Though at least he hasn't bit anyone yet."

"Take him in to meet Nicholson," Vik suggested. "What's he doing here, anyway? Are we deputizing him?"

Cowboy explained about the lab work. Vik didn't say anything, but he looked thoughtful until Cowboy asked, "Have you ever thought about getting a dog?"

"A dog?" Vik said. "We used to have a dalmatian when I was a kid. Firehouse dog. My uncle the fireman decided to give us kids a puppy one Christmas. He wanted us to call him Sparky, but we named him Kringle instead."

"When I was at TOPS training Trouble . . . ," Marti began. She told him about the dog learning to walk alongside a wheelchair. "Maybe Mildred could get a companion dog. I'm sure that, if nothing else, they could teach him to let someone in the house if she needed help. They might even be able to train the dog to do something if nobody else was at home, like if she were to fall."

Vik didn't say anything. Marti thought that was a good sign. He did keep petting Geronimo. Then, he looked down at the dog and said, "What do you think, boy?"

Geronimo wagged his tail.

"I must be desperate," Vik admitted. "How do we go about doing this?"

There was knock on the door before Marti or Cowboy could answer. The FBI agent was there. He had a buzz cut and stern expression. He looked young enough to be a new recruit and the office errand boy.

* * *

"What's this?" Vik asked. When Marti told him they all but fought over who got what. He took the most recent documents, including the transcripts of the phone calls from DeVonte. Marti was more interested in the family history.

The oldest reports were police calls to the house for domestic violence. In the early calls, the father was the abuser. Over time, he began complaining that his wife was the one beating him. Both were battered and bloody. Neither was willing to file a complaint. The calls became less frequent as time went on, but the severity of the injuries increased. Hospital reports became interspersed with the police reports. She had a broken arm. He was hospitalized several times with concussions. His last hospitalization occurred four and a half months before he died. A knife wound to the abdomen. The wife pleaded self-defense and was released. Her last trip to the hospital was two weeks before his death. Bruises and contusions about the face, shoulders, and back.

Marti read through the police reports again. There were only two mentions of a minor. In both instances one parent went to the hospital, the other to jail, and an unnamed male child was taken in by a neighbor. Hemp plants growing in the yard were also mentioned several times, but no charges were brought against the parents for possession.

Marti paper-clipped those reports and looked at those surrounding the father's death. According to the autopsy report, he died of a stab wound in the back that pierced his heart. There were numerous postmortem stab wounds. And—she caught her breath—one blow to the top of the skull with a hammer.

"Bingo."

"What have you got?" Vik asked.

Marti shook her head, kept reading. The mother was acquitted. Self-defense. The domestic violence reports didn't begin again for five years. By then DeVonte would have been about fifteen. The calls were frequent at first, mother blaming son, son accusing mother, no action taken. Then, once again the neighbors seemed to become accustomed to the violence and only called when the situation seemed serious. At sixteen, DeVonte was hospitalized with broken ribs, but said he fell down. Four months later he was found in an alley a block from his home, beaten severely with bruises on his neck, as if he'd been choked. This time he said he didn't recognize his attackers.

DeVonte was seventeen when his mother died, assailant or assailants unknown. As Marti read her autopsy report she wondered why nobody else had seen what she saw now. Or if perhaps someone had decided that justice was served with the mother's death. One stab wound through the back to the heart. Multiple postmortem stab wounds. Hammer blow to the head. And choked until unconscious.

Without speaking, she handed both autopsy reports to Vik.

After he read them he said, "DeVonte killed both of them."

"No," Marti said. "The mother killed the father. DeVonte killed his mother the same way."

"DeVonte is still killing her," Vik said.

Marti glanced at Cowboy. He was sitting there with his mouth open, listening, saying nothing. Geronimo, still by Vik's desk, was sound asleep.

Marti bypassed Nicholson, called the state's attorney's office and requested a warrant for DeVonte's arrest. Cowboy agreed to pick up Sharon and bring her in. The desk sergeant ordered additional patrols at Marti's house. Ben agreed to have someone take his watch for the next few days so he could stay home. Momma told her not to worry about anything, that "God still sits on the throne."

"Now what?" Vik said.

"God still sits on the throne," she repeated.

Vik hesitated, then said, "That's one of those southern Baptist quotes, isn't it?"

"Most likely," Marti agreed.

"I wish our priest could come up with a few sayings like that instead of giving a homily. Mass would be over much faster if he did. And, you'd still get the gist of things."

Marti had no comeback for that. Church was an obligation to Vik. It was a social event for her.

"Read through what I've got, Jessenovik, and let me see the transcripts of those phone calls." As she read through DeVonte and Sharon's brief conversations, Marti felt relieved Sharon was telling the truth, but angry because she had brought DeVonte Lutrell, the worst possible Mr. Wonderful, into their lives.

"There is nothing here that indicates where he is," she concluded. "The cell phones he used were stolen from people living in the Chicago area. One of the calls places him here the night Jelena was killed. Maybe Sharon can tell us something we don't know."

While she was waiting for Sharon, Marti put in a call to Denise Stevens. She shook her head when she hung up. "Nothing on the child."

The first thing Sharon said when she came into the office was, "I have to stay home in case he calls."

"Don't worry. He'll call back."

"He'll think I'm up so something."

"Up to what? Getting the pension fund money you're giving him tomorrow?"

Sharon stood there with her mouth open, as if she was about to say something, but didn't.

"Take off your coat," Marti said. "And sit down."

"What do you mean? What is this? Why the cop routine?"

Marti looked at Vik, nodded to indicate that she would handle this. Then she said to Sharon, "Sit. Now."

Sharon took the chair by Vik's desk.

The back of Cowboy's chair hit the wall as he stood up. "Gotta get back to the hospital," he said. He put on Geronimo's leash, and tipped his five gallon hat toward Sharon. "Be seeing you, little lady."

"Now," Marti said, as the door closed, "I've got transcripts of all the conversations since Sunday."

"So, now you believe me, now that the FBI—"

"What exactly did DeVonte say to you Friday and Saturday?"

"You expect me to remember?"

"Do I . . . ? Sharon, this isn't game. We're not playing De-Vonte, DeVonte, where is DeVonte. He's here and he might have a woman and/or a child with him."

"Oh, dear Lord," Sharon said. "Why did I ever involve you in this? I should have just handled it myself." She looked about the room as if she wanted to leave. "Do you know what this is doing to me? Do you know the last time I ate?"

"I don't have time for the drama, Sharon. What did he say?"

"You're mad at me, aren't you?"

"Sharon! What did he say? What did the woman say? What did the girl say? All of it. Now."

"You never—"

"Now."

"I-I-he put Iris on the phone . . ."

"Their words, not yours."

"Okay. Okay." She thought for a moment. "She said, 'It's me, Iris, Johnny's sister.' Then he said, 'Hi, hon, it's me. I'm just giving Iris a ride home.' I told him he was lying. That Iris was dead. He just said 'Is she?' I asked him not to hurt her. He just laughed and hung up the phone."

"That's everything?"

"Yes."

"You're sure?"

"I said I was, didn't I?"

"Think hard. The life you save might be someone else's."

Sharon gave a deep sigh. "That's it. I'm sure of it."

"And the next call?"

"He said someone wanted to talk to me. I asked him who and he said Iris's daughter. Then the little girl said, 'Hi.' I asked her what her name was. She said 'Lynn Ella.' "

"That's all, no last name?"

"No. He took the phone away from her."

"Damn."

"What?"

"Nothing. What about the next call."

"Saturday night," Sharon said. She began rubbing her arms as if she were cold and trying to warm them. "He said he wanted money. I . . . I didn't know how to get it. He told me to find out and he'd call back on Monday."

"And that's it?"

Sharon nodded.

Marti leaned back. If she asked Sharon to repeat everything now, she'd just parrot back what she had just said. If she waited, Sharon might remember something else. She looked at Vik and raised her eyebrows. He got up, took his cup and hers, and re-filled them.

"Coffee?" he asked Sharon.

"Please."

"Cream? Sugar?"

"Two sugars, no cream." She picked at her slacks, rubbed her arms again. "Cold in here. I should have worn a sweater."

"You're nervous," Marti told her. "What is it?"

Sharon bit her lower lip, then said, "I'm scared to death of him."

"You should be," Marti told her.

"I brought him here. I brought him into our lives . . ."

"Don't even go there, Sharon. You've been bringing your Mr. Wonderfuls into our lives, into Lisa's life, for years now. This one just happens to be a psychopath. And just so you know, Lisa will be living with me from now on. You both need some kind of counseling. And if you're still not smart enough to get help, I'm going to make sure that she does."

As Marti expected, Sharon put her head down and began to cry. "This is my fault. Everything is my fault. If he hurts them . . ." She sniffled noisily. Marti waited until Sharon looked up at her. Sharon's face was streaked with tears.

Marti handed her a box of Kleenex. "Sorry, Sharon, a thousand tears and a hundred apologies will get you nowhere. Not because I'm angry with you—and I am, but I'll get over that—but because I just don't have time for this right now."

Sharon dabbed at her face, dried her eyes, blew her nose, and said nothing.

Marti put in a call to her FBI friend in Chicago and asked to have the transcripts of all future calls from DeVonte faxed to her as soon as possible. Then she put in a call to Lupe and Holmberg and told them to return to the office.

"We're going to have to bring them current information on what's going on, Jessenovik, and make sure we aren't overlooking anything."

When Lupe and Holmberg arrived, she introduced Sharon, then told her, "We cops are going to have a little meeting and you're going to keep the desk sergeant company while we talk."

Good judgment and common sense had not been among Sharon's strong suits lately. She had no intention of telling her anything.

The phone rang. Vik took the call. When he hung up, he waited until Holmberg returned from escorting Sharon to the sergeant's safekeeping, then said, "They've identified our he-she victim from Milwaukee. I told them Marti and I would drive up there later tonight. They've got a couple of people who are willing to talk to us, but they weren't able to find out much when they interviewed them."

"I need a really big favor," Marti told Lupe when the meeting was over.

"Sharon," Lupe guessed. "We don't want DeVonte to know she's talked to us. She needs to stay at her place and take his calls, or be there if he shows up, but she can't stay there alone. I volunteer. How much does she know?"

"Assume she knows nothing and don't tell her anything. I can't predict what she might do." As much as she hated saying that, she had to admit that Sharon had become a person she frequently didn't understand and occasionally didn't know.

19

When Iris looked in on DeVonte, he was sleeping. She had some questions for him about Lynn Ella when he woke up. The child worried her. She did not come out of the closet and seemed scared to death of a little baby doll that looked brand new.

"It be in there," she repeated again and again. "It" was in the food, the bed, the doll. Sometimes Iris was sure Lynn Ella was scared; other times "it" seemed like a safe way to say no.

Iris continued down the hall and went into the bedroom she was sharing with Lynn Ella. She had left the room a few times, made sure Lynn Ella heard her walking to the kitchen, then tiptoed back to see if she came out of the closet when nobody was there. She didn't. She only came out to eat.

There was no radio, no television. There were no books and no toys except for the doll. She asked Lynn Ella if she wanted a television just to see what she would say. "It be in there." And again, she would not or could not explain what "it" was. It wasn't natural, a child sitting in a closet all the time. Iris had never seen a child who didn't play, who didn't even seem to want to play. What had they done to her baby? Could it ever be fixed? She sat on the floor near the open closet door.

"Hi, Lynn Ella. How are you?"

There was no answer.

"I thought I would fix us some supper. What do you like to eat?"

Nothing.

She had paid seventy-five dollars for the codeine, then spent six dollars at a secondhand store for a couple of pots, a frying pan, a few dishes, and some knives and forks.

"There must be something I can cook for you."

Lynn Ella looked at her. Mama's eyes, Iris thought. Her baby had Mama's eyes. She remembered Mama's voice. "Be still, child!" "Stop that jumping around!" "Stop talking so much!" She never could. Poor Mama. She would have liked having this child around.

"How about some fried chicken?" she asked.

The child's expression didn't change.

"Neck bones and cabbage."

Nothing.

"Spaghetti."

Lynn Ella's eyes widened.

"Good. I've just got to go to the store. DeVonte is sleeping."

"Nooo." Lynn Ella went from indifference to alarm.

"He's okay, baby. I promise. He's okay." How had this child, who didn't want to have anything to do with her, become so attached to this man? "I got him some medicine that will make him feel better."

Iris reached out to touch her and the child moved as far into the closet as she could. Dispirited, Iris got up and put on her coat.

As soon as she heard the front door close, Lynn Ella ran down the hall to DeVonte's room. She tugged at his sleeve until he opened his eyes. "Dead?" she said. "No be dead."

"No. Just sleeping," he said. "Feeling better. Be good." He closed his eyes again.

Lynn Ella could hear him breathing. She got on the bed, sat beside him, listening. Not dead, she thought. Not dead. Then, Daddy. She patted his arm and he smiled.

Vik was quiet as Marti headed for Route 41. She didn't feel much like talking either. She thought of Sharon, the way she was at seventeen, going off to college in Atlanta, demonstrating for civil rights, human rights, animal rights, women's liberation. Marti knew when the changes began—when Sharon met her first husband, Frank. But she couldn't figure out why. Nothing had ever been the same after that. After the divorce, it was one Mr. Wonderful after another. And with each, things just got worse. Now here Sharon was, with no job, no pension, no causes to fight for, not even her own. Worse, Sharon seemed to get some perverse satisfaction from making a mess of her life.

Route 41 merged with Interstate 94. Traffic was light. It wouldn't take her much more than half an hour to get to Milwaukee. Beside her, Vik muttered, "Wittenberg."

"What about him?"

"The car dealership."

"Uh-huh."

"It was right up the street from Deer Woods."

Marti moved into the passing lane, passed two trucks, and switched lanes again.

"Remember that old battery case I tripped over?" Vik said. "What if there are a lot of them?"

Marti thought about that. "Lead," she said.

"Right."

"And Fred asked to have Geronimo tested for lead."

"Mercury too. What would have mercury?"

"Beats me, Jessenovik. But I do know that lead doesn't go away."

Vik lowered the heat. "We'd better get someone from the EPA out there. The City Council has decided to award some company a contract to develop the place."

They drove in silence for a few minutes, then Vik said, "I guess that gives Fred a motive, with Wittenberg at least."

"Or vice versa."

"Fred's really attached to that dog. I can see him getting angry over the possibility that Geronimo could be sick. I can also see Wittenberg getting really upset about a family secret getting out.

210

It would be bad for business. He and his brother still own that dealership. And it would be death for a politician. I wonder if they can impeach aldermen."

"My bet's on Wittenberg," Marti said. She accelerated until the car was moving fast enough to pass a trucker doing eighty.

The Milwaukee cops they had spoken with before met them at what would be called "the projects" in Chicago. Here it meant several blocks of three-story buildings for people with low income. There was no loitering and almost no litter.

"Your victim used to live here," the older cop said.

"Gina Kam," Marti said.

"Eugene Kamren to his family," the young cop explained. "His mother, his sister, and a friend all have apartments here. We're going to the sister's place. The mother says she has no son named Eugene, refused to talk with us at all. We're going to take the sister to Lincoln Prairie tomorrow to make a formal I.D."

Kamren's sister was an older woman with skin the color of walnuts. There was a cluster of tiny black moles just below the corner of her left eye. Marti didn't see much of a family resemblance. They stepped into a crowded living area. Two sofas, a love seat, a recliner, and two overstuffed chairs were crowded into a room big enough to hold half that much furniture. There were also three tables, all with lamps that were lit. Graduation pictures were lined up along one wall. Marti recognized Kamren in a maroon cap and gown. When the woman invited them to be seated, Marti had to walk sideways to get to a sofa. Then she slipped off her coat. Even with a window open, the heat was stifling.

The sister sat beside her. "Eugene never caused any trouble," she began. "He just was who he was. I've got three other brothers, none like him. They're big men. Eugene, he was always small like me. Maybe he was supposed to be a woman like me, too, but something didn't go right.

She reached under the coffee table and got a photo album. Opening it, she said, "See? That's Eugene when he was twelve."

A boy in shorts with knobby knees stood by a chain-link fence. He wasn't smiling. "He never got taller than that," his sister said.

She closed the album and sat with her hands on it. "Granny died a month ago," she said. "The last time I saw Eugene he was sitting in the waiting room at the hospital, my mother was sitting across from him. Someone she knew from church came in and they talked for a while, said they'd pray for each other, all of that. Mother told her who I was, but she never introduced Eugene. He was wearing women's slacks that day and a pair of women's shoes, but he wasn't wearing a wig. You could tell he wasn't a girl. After that woman left, Eugene did, too. I haven't seen him since. He didn't even come to the funeral, and Granny loved him so. I've gone looking for him a couple of times. And a few of the neighbors said they saw him around here, but I haven't seen him since he left the hospital that day."

They went to one other apartment. "This guy had seen him in the past couple weeks," the older cop said.

This guy was in his mid-thirties, light skinned, and slender. He wore a loose-fitting cowl-neck sweater and slacks. He was barefoot and several pairs of shoes were lined up near the door. The living room walls were painted a pastel salmon pink and the couch and chair upholstered in a peach, jade, and maroon pattern.

"I tried to tell Gina just to be who she was. And she did try. But that family of hers . . . You've got to give them up, I told her, just like I did. You've got to cut family loose. They just get embarrassed when you're around. But Gina couldn't stay away. The only ones in her family who would have anything to do with her were her sister and her grandmother."

"When's the last time you saw him, er, her?" Vik asked.

"Wednesday. I went looking for her at this little place where we go, sometimes, to socialize. I should have known when she asked me for money that she was going to take off. I don't know why she took to the street though. There wasn't any need for that. She could have come here, stayed with me. And I can't even guess why she went to Lincoln Prairie. It's a shame her grandmother died. That old woman was all she had."

Marti watched his Adam's apple bob as he cleared his throat.

"Like I told her, 'Self-acceptance, Gina. You got to accept yourself, and to hell with those who don't.' But Gina, she had a lot of faith in people, a lot of hope for them." He paused again, arms folded. "We—meaning Gina's real family, her real friends—are taking up a collection. We are going to see that Gina gets laid to rest real proper. I already picked out her dress."

Marti went away with a lot more respect for "that guy" than she had going in.

It was a little after ten when Marti got home, well past the boys' bedtime. She was hoping the girls were still awake. Ben was in the kitchen. She went to him, and he put his arms around her.

"I need you," she said.

He held her tighter.

"I really, really need you."

He kissed her, then said, "Rough day?"

"We've got to talk to the kids, at least to the girls, right away."

"It might be a good time to let Lisa have some say in what's going on."

"Maybe you're right. I don't like the idea of her feeling help-less, the way Sharon does."

"And we can always overrule her," Ben added.

Marti smiled. "Momma needs to be here, too. Is she still up?"

"In the den, watching the news."

When Momma came upstairs, she put the kettle on, and got cups, tea bags, cider drink mix, and cocoa. When she brought the cookie jar to the table, she said, "You okay, baby?"

"No," Marti admitted. "I'm mad at Sharon. Worse, I'm worried about her. Why is she always such a damned fool when it comes to men?"

"Hard to say."

Marti looked at her. It wasn't like Momma to make comments like that.

"Time was," Momma went on, "when I'd say it was because of her mother, but the day comes when you'd better outgrow that. It looks like, with Sharon, that day has come and gone."

"I told her I was keeping Lisa."

"Good," Momma said. "Lord knows we don't need two of them. I just hope it's not too late."

Marti waited until everyone was assembled around the table except for Theo and Mike. When they each had their beverage and cookies of choice, she said, "Sharon wasn't lying about DeVonte."

Lisa's hand went to her throat. "He's here?" Her voice was just above a whisper.

"We don't know exactly where he is."

"But he's here. Out there. Somewhere. Close." She put her hands to the sides of her head. "He's . . . he's . . ." As Marti watched, she could see the fear come into Lisa's eyes. "Why did she do this to me? Why? Whyyy?" The last why came out like a moan.

Joanna was sitting beside Lisa. She took Lisa's hands, pulled them away from her head, and held them. "Deep breaths," she said. "Come on."

Lisa closed her eyes, breathed in, held it, then slowly exhaled.

"Good. Again," Joanna coached.

In a few minutes Lisa was calm, the fear had lessened, and she was looking at Marti. "What now?" she asked.

"That's what I'm asking you," Marti told her.

"Well, if you had bothered to ask me Tuesday, I wouldn't have had to miss the season's end rally for the football team!"

Marti saw in Lisa a glimpse of the old Sharon, feisty and determined. She felt sad and tried not to compare this Lisa to the Sharon she knew years ago. "What do you think we should do?" she asked.

"I don't want to miss school again. And it's not because of some cute boy either. I didn't pass anything the first half of the quarter. I got some of my teachers to agree to let me do make-up work. That, and a lot of studying, and I'll pass. But if I start missing class . . ."

"We've been working on self-defense techniques," Joanna said, "and we each have a perfectly legal can of hair spray in our purses."

"Lisa," Marti said, "you know DeVonte. You know that's not enough."

"I got away from him when he tricked me into going to meet him and Sharon in the Bahamas. He won't fool me again," Lisa reminded her. "Besides, the school is on Code Yellow."

"Which means . . . ?" Ben asked.

"Tighter security, random searches, a few more cops walking around," Lisa explained.

"Why?"

"Rumor is that there might be a gang fight," Joanna said.

Marti exchanged looks with Ben. That was part of the reason why they had taken the boys out of a public middle school and put them in a small private school.

"Do you feel safe there?" Ben asked.

"We're in the college prep program," Lisa said. "We have our own section of the building and the kids we're around are all preppies. Of course Joanna does have to mingle with the peons because she's a jock."

Marti felt uneasy. She was going to have to talk with the coppers assigned to the high school. Both girls were juniors. Both wanted to stay there. "All right," she agreed. "Everyone goes to school tomorrow. And everyone comes right home. But you both will have an off-duty officer shadowing you. Deal?"

Both girls agreed.

Marti and Ben sat at the table drinking cocoa while everyone else went to bed. When the house was quiet, they went into the living room, hand in hand, and sat in the darkness. Trouble came in, trotted over to be petted, then, as Marti listened to her paws tap against the hardwood floor, went from window to window and looked out.

"A guard dog," Marti said. "An alarm system."

"A Beretta *and* a service revolver."

"A cop and a fireman."

"Security," Ben said. "An illusion." Then, "Sounds like Joanna's been coaching Lisa."

"I hope she does a better job with her than I did with Sharon. Why couldn't I help her?"

"This isn't your fault, Marti."

Marti turned to him, kissed him. "Tell me that again," she said. "And then let's go to bed."

"You must be tired," he teased. "Long day."

"Not that long." She rested her head against his chest and felt his arms around her. It was good to be with someone she didn't always have to be strong for. When Johnny was alive, he needed her to be strong for him, self-sufficient, so she was. It was different with Ben. She loved them both and always would. But unlike Sharon, she would never allow any man to use or mistreat her.

Sharon once said that you had to kiss a lot of frogs before you found the prince. She would do without before she would do that. But then, as far as she was concerned, there was no Mr. Wonderful. She wasn't always on the lookout for him. She just wanted someone who was secure, dependable, and, as the song said, ready for love.

"Let's go upstairs now," she whispered.

Cowboy felt as if time stopped in the I.C.U. Nobody dimmed the lights. There were no windows, no blinds or curtains to open and close. Activity increased just before a shift change, then everything was quiet again. He had a date with one of the night nurses whenever Fred got out of here.

He looked down at Fred. "I took your dad and Geronimo over to my sister's house. I didn't think your father should be alone, and those chairs are no place to spend the night. He'll be fine there. My sister took care of my dad until we had to put him in a nursing home."

He stared at Fred's hand, willing it to move. "You've got to

216

come out of this, man. Must be nice, not being here, not being there, not being anywhere, but you've got to come back. All of the test results on Geronimo are negative so far. We're waiting for the results on a couple more. He took to your dad right away. A little shy around my sister, but I think she's an undercover cat person. My dad is allergic to cat dander, so we never had one."

The doctor came in while he was talking, motioned for him to stay. He moved away from the bed, watching as the doctor listened to Fred's chest, then did something with one of the machines.

"What's up?" Cowboy asked when the doctor brought in a chair and sat down.

"He's trying to breathe on his own."

"You mean that!"

The doctor smiled. "If all goes well we'll have him off the ventilator by morning."

"Will he be able to talk?"

"Typical cop question. It'll take a while for the sedation to wear off, and he might have a sore throat, but from the looks of it, he might be able to say a few things. Now that's just step one," the doctor cautioned. "But getting him off life support is a big step."

Cowboy got up, went to the bed. "You hear that, man? You're doing good. You're coming out of it. You'll have that tube out of your throat by tomorrow. Know what? As soon as you can walk to the window I'm going to bring Geronimo here so you can see him."

He patted Fred's hand, said a silent thank God, and hoped that somebody heard him. It had been a long time since he'd said any prayers, but he'd come real close these past couple of days.

20

After roll call, Marti, Vik, and Slim walked to their office. Cowboy was at the hospital. They decided to go on mission round-the-station-house to see if they could beg or steal a decent cup of coffee. It was that or the over-brewed mud the hot-drink machine kicked out. Slim led the search. If he found anything drinkable, Marti promised herself she wouldn't complain about the odor of Obsession for Men for a whole day. Then she hoped either she or Slim would make that easier by being out of the office. When they stopped at the traffic department, nobody was there, but the aroma of coffee was in the air. They each grabbed a paper cup, filled it, and made their escape.

Three phone messages from the third-shift desk sergeant were on Marti's desk. She sat down, leaned back, and blew across the surface of the cup, trying to cool the coffee. Then she read the messages in order.

"Fred is coming out of his coma."

"Yes!" Slim said.

"Lonesome?" Vik asked. "Miss your sidekick?"

"Dealing with Nicholson is much easier when there are two of us. I take her criticism less personally with Cowboy there to share it."

"Well, well," Marti went on. "DeVonte did take time out for homicide while he was looking for a car to steal."

"The unincorporated area?" Vik asked.

"Right. February third." She checked her file. "Car wasn't reported stolen until March twenty-sixth."

She thumbed through the reports the state police had faxed. "The owner doesn't know when it was stolen. He kept it in a barn with the key under the floor mat, went out one day and saw that it was gone. According to the police reports, there was about a foot of snow on the ground when they got there and no tire marks."

"Did they I.D. the victim?"

"Waitress," Marti said. "Bartender says she left a little after two A.M. Boyfriend usually dropped her off and picked her up, but she drove herself to work that night. Lover's quarrel." She turned to the next page. "Her body wasn't found until May. It was in a duck blind. Her car was found in a field about three miles from the barn. Hard to say if he waited for her or if she was just a random victim, but the M.O. matches. How unlucky can you get?"

"What do you want to bet that we turn up a few more waitresses?" Vik said.

"He keeps moving down a little lower on the food chain," Slim said. "Matrons with money, waitresses and maybe other service workers, now the homeless. Johns and druggies do that, too. Maybe it's instinctive. On the other hand, each step down increases their invisibility. Who wants to look at a drugged-out hooker who turns five-dollar tricks? Who wants to notice street people?"

"And who gives a damn if some homeless nobody is murdered?" Vik said with bitterness.

Marti read the third message. "Which brings us to—ta-da—someone called Hyacinth, deceased female."

"A.k.a. Rosebud?" Vik asked.

"Let's show some respect for the dead," Slim suggested.

Marti knew she was sleep deprived even though last night with Ben it had been by choice. Vik sounded like he could use a long winter's nap, too. "The call came in from downstate. They must think she's one of DeVonte's victims."

"Downstate," Vik considered. "Maybe we'll get real lucky and Hyacinth will be one of his early victims, killed while he was still perfecting his techniques."

Marti dialed the number and spoke with the chief of police. "I've got to talk with the coroner, but it looks like we might have a live one."

"Who?" Slim asked. "The corpse?"

"Recently deceased," Vik explained.

"She died last Sunday," Marti added.

"And you two don't consider that a cold case?"

"The waitress that was found on February third is a cold case. This one is still warm." Marti looked into her cup. Empty. "No coffee and Lupe's with Sharon."

"Lupe's coffee is almost as bad as yours, MacAlister," Vik groused.

"True," Slim agreed.

"So, where's Holmberg? His is drinkable."

"He must still be at the county jail handling a couple of bookings," Slim explained. "Have you got any plans for him today, other than making coffee?"

"We'll see." Marti picked up the phone again.

"Looks like we're going for a ride," Marti said after she talked with the coroner. "Manual strangulation, stabbed through the heart, multiple postmortem stab wounds, dent in the top of her head. Town's got twenty-seven homeless people. All of them hard core, either alcoholic or mentally ill. They keep to one part of town where they can get food and clothes and a place to sleep. Even better, they all know one another. Hyacinth's body was found the same day she died because she didn't show up for supper."

"Who's driving?" Vik asked. "Holmberg?"

"Looks that way," Marti told him. "I hope he got a good night's sleep." She would have liked to have Lupe along, but she needed someone to be with Sharon who she could rely on when DeVonte called.

She called Sharon. "Hear anything yet?"

"Nothing."

"Put Lupe on."

"What's up?" Lupe asked.

Marti explained.

"Sounds like a fun trip."

"Got any favors you can call in?"

"Always."

"It will have to be a female officer. Sharon's good with men. And warn her that Sharon might think she can get away from her and go to him. But once that call comes in, they go to the bathroom together."

"Marti, this guy tried to kill her."

"I know," Marti admitted, "but she believes he is holding a woman and a child, and that it's her fault. I'm not sure what she will do. So, nobody takes any chances."

Her friend the Chicago FBI agent was in the field. She called Dobrzycki's number. He wasn't available either. She left a message so he would know what was going on. The agent who took the call said it was an interstate and local problem, and as such didn't come under their jurisdiction at this time.

Gail Nicholson smiled at she spoke into the telephone receiver. She had been surprised, but pleased, that Frank Winans called.

"So you would say that they think outside of the box," he said.

"Way outside the box," she agreed. "They don't even know there is a box."

"Anything else I should know?"

"Well, MacAlister doesn't know a computer terminal from a fax machine."

"What about their work ethics?"

"The overtime when they are working a case is astronomical. I'm following the case they're working on now very closely. There has to be a more cost effective way to get the job done. Problem is, they've still got that Baker Street Boys mentality. Too hands-on, too independent, resistant to authority. They need to become proficient at using all of the technological tools we have now that weren't available when they became cops. I've just about given up hope on either one of them ever joining the twenty-first century."

She was still smiling when she hung up. Too bad it was so early in the day. This called for a drink. She would remedy that when she went to lunch.

"Yes," she said aloud. "Yes!"

Not only would they not be offered a job on that task force, but once Winans spread the word, nobody would want them. Jessenovik might take early retirement if she pushed him hard enough. And as for MacAlister, she could comply with her directives and join the new world of policing or look for a new job.

Still smiling, she picked up the phone and pressed a couple of buttons. "Get Jessenovik and MacAlister in here."

Less than a minute later, her secretary called back. "Sorry, ma'am, they've already left the precinct."

Nicholson turned to her computer and pulled up their files. Even though she was certain the desk sergeant knew what was going on, she added "leaving without notifying senior" and "whereabouts unknown" to their list of offenses. The infractions were minor, but they were adding up.

DeVonte opened his eyes when Iris came into the room, then closed them. Now what did she want?

"How are you feeling?'

"Better than yesterday."

"Good, because we've got to talk. I haven't seen that child since she was three months old, but even I can tell that something's not right with her. How did you get her?"

DeVonte looked at her. "You're worried about her after all these years?"

"I always believed she would be better off without me. I thought she was in a home where she was wanted and loved. My other child is, but that didn't happen for Lynn Ella."

DeVonte didn't say anything. Iris believed what she was saying, but that didn't make it so. Words meant nothing. It was what Iris did as a mother, and that had been little to nothing. "Did *you* ever try to find out how she was?" he asked.

"They took her away from me permanently. Who would I ask? Who would tell me?"

"*I* knew somebody in the system, somebody with access to the D.C.F.S. files. *I* found out that some old lady had her. When *I* went there, the woman was dead. *I* talked to the neighbors. One of them told me where the woman's daughter lived. It was a whorehouse, a hangout for drug addicts. Lynn Ella was tied to a bed. I paid the woman two hundred dollars for her and brought her here." Talking so much made him feel tired. He rested for a few minutes, then said, "I have a hard time getting her to eat."

"Try canned spaghetti," Iris suggested. "Without the meatballs."

"It be in there," he said.

"I wish I knew what 'it' is."

"Me too," DeVonte agreed.

"Would you like some scrambled eggs?" Iris asked. "I've got some sausages, too. There was some money left after I scored the codeine."

"There's nothing to cook it in."

"I took care of that, too."

DeVonte considered that for a moment. She could have taken the money and kept going. "Why did you come back?"

"Lynn Ella. Why did you want me here?"

"To help with Lynn Ella." For a moment he regretted lying to her, but he couldn't tell her the truth. "The food sounds good. It would sound even better if you could get Lynn Ella to eat some of it, too."

"Get some rest. Eat. Then tell me the truth about why you came to get me."

Instead of taking a nap, DeVonte tried to figure out how he was going to get the money away from Sharon. His original plan was to go to Lincoln Prairie, sweet-talk his way into Sharon's apartment, have her get the cop over there, kill her while he was waiting for the cop, kill the cop, take the money, and leave. A simple plan. Foolproof. That was before the fight. Now he could still take care of Sharon, but would he be able to take out the cop?

Sharon hadn't told anyone anything. He was certain of that. He told her not to and Sharon was the kind of woman who would do as she was told, by a man at least. She was probably going crazy waiting for him to call. He would have to drive there. He would take the fake gun. Sharon wouldn't know it wasn't real. And he would kill them both.

Cowboy stood on one side of Fred's bed, Fred's father stood on the other side. Fred blinked a few times, swallowed, then frowned. He opened his eyes, looked at Cowboy, then at his dad, and closed his eyes.

"Geronimo's fine," Cowboy told him. "All the tests are back. There were traces of lead, that's all. They ran tests on you, too. Just traces."

Fred raised his hand, touched Cowboy's sleeve. "Car," he said, speaking just above a whisper. He voice sounded hoarse. "Man, woman, black . . . Hemlock."

"You saw who went into the house on Hemlock Street," Cowboy said.

Fred nodded, "Came back. Fought. Hurt him. License." His hand dropped to the bed. He opened his eyes for a moment and whispered, "His knife."

Cowboy stayed until he was sure Fred was sleeping, then he went back to the waiting room, put in a call to Marti's cell phone.

"Fred saw a black male and female going into the house on Hemlock. Guy must have seen him, too. Came back. They fought. Fred says the guy is hurt. He said 'license,' too. That has to mean he saw the car the guy was driving. And I think that knife he had on him might have belonged to the guy. The last thing he said was 'his knife.'"

"That's great!" Marti said. "Does he know Geronimo's okay?"

"That's the first thing I told him. He's still in and out, though. The sedation hasn't worn off. He doesn't remember going to Wittenberg's yet. He was surprised when I asked about it."

"We don't have a photo of DeVonte, but there is a drawing an artist did for me a couple of years ago in my file. I'll have Slim bring it over. See if you can get a description from Fred of whoever was driving the car, or going into the house, and if it matches up. Don't show him the drawing, though, not yet anyway. DeVonte has probably done something to change his appearance."

"Where are you?"

"Heading downstate. We've got a victim who matches the M.O. She was killed last Sunday."

"Ah," Cowboy said. "The trail might not be too cold."

The next time Fred woke up, Cowboy asked him what the man looked like.

"Black," he repeated.

"Think you'd recognize him if you saw him again?"

"Yeah," Fred said, then, "Geronimo?"

"He's fine, man. Soon as you can walk over to that window, I'll bring him over so you can look out and see him."

"Good dog," Fred said and went back to sleep.

According to the map Marti printed from the computer, getting downstate would take five hours. Holmberg was driving and he had a heavy foot. She was guessing it would be closer to three.

"I'm glad Fred's going to be okay," Vik said. He had been quiet since they left the precinct. He hadn't even suggested stopping for coffee or food.

"According to Cowboy, Fred said 'his knife,' meaning someone else's. So I called the forensic lab. According to them, its got an eight-inch blade, short handle, and it was sheathed. They've matched it to the stab wounds of the most recent victim. I don't know where that puts us. How could Fred have gotten the knife Tuesday night?"

"And why didn't he mention it when he called?" Vik added.

"Now that Fred's coming around we'll be able to get a few things sorted out."

Vik grunted. A few moments later, he said, "Wittenberg."

"Did you call the EPA?"

"Damned right."

"They'll check it out. That's not the only place in town that's polluted. We've got brown fields and industrial waste along the shoreline, pollution in the lake."

"And it's all about money," Vik said. "We used to go to Deer Woods to see the deer herds. Now there aren't any deer. The beach is closed more often than it's open. And I can teach my grandson to fish off the ComEd pier, but we can't eat what we catch. A man and his dog camp out for a couple of nights and get traces of lead poisoning."

He fell silent again.

"If they do find batteries there," Holmberg said, "this would have happened . . . What? Fifty or sixty years ago?"

"Maybe," Vik said. "Give or take."

"Then most of the people who caused the problem aren't even alive now. It doesn't look like we'll be able to make many arrests."

"Are you being sarcastic, Holmberg?"

"Something like that," he admitted.

When Iris came in with the eggs and sausages, she put the plate on the bureau, then propped up the pillow behind him before bringing him the food.

"Now, why are we here?" she asked as DeVonte ate.

He wasn't sure what to tell her. An easy smile, the Island accent, and sweet-talk weren't going to work with this one. Unlike most other women he had known, she wasn't the trusting kind and she might know even more about the street than he did.

He answered her question with one of his own. "Why do you think?"

"Because there's something in it for you. But that's the part I can't figure out. It's not like either of us has anything anyone would want."

"Let's just say my wife has something I want and I needed a little leverage to get it."

"So, you want me to believe that somebody knows we're here and that that's important enough for her to give you something. Maybe if you try telling me the truth I won't just take my baby and walk out of here. It's not like you could stop me."

"Ummm . . . ," he said as he speared a sausage with his fork. "This sure does taste good. Someone's got some money that belongs to me. I've got to make the pickup, but I need a little collateral."

She cocked her head to one side. "We can't be collateral unless this is someone we know."

"She doesn't know you, but she does know who you are. Johnny MacAlister's sister."

"Johnny's dead," she said. "He got shot."

"What else do you know about him?"

"I left home when I was seventeen. Went back once. A neighbor woman said Johnny and my mother were dead."

"This goes back before then. It's an old debt between me and him. I'm just calling it in."

"Then what happens?" As he expected, if Johnny had done anything wrong, Iris didn't want to know what it was.

"What do you want to happen?"

"I've been thinking about that. Nobody knows where Lynn Ella is. They haven't known where she is for a long time. They don't have to find out now. There must be some place to take her where people wouldn't ask too many questions." She then added, "You were smart enough to find us. You can figure out how to make that happen, too. I'm going to need a birth certificate. That should be enough."

"I'm going home to the Islands," he lied. "You could both come with me. Everything would be easier there: getting her into school, whatever." He ate the last sausage, the last mouthful of egg. The pain made him wince as he lay back against the pillow.

"How are you going to get what's owed to you while you're feeling like that?"

227

"I'll do it. I have to."

"I could go get some tape and get you fixed up good enough to drive," she said. "I've seen it done. I know how to do it right."

"And you'll come back? Again?"

"I've left this place twice already. And in case you haven't noticed, you do sleep occasionally."

He gave her twenty dollars. "Get Lynn Ella a chocolate milk shake from Wendy's. 'It' isn't in there. And buy a couple of cans of spaghetti, too—without the meatballs."

"I need another five dollars," Iris said. "To get what I need to fix her hair."

He gave her that, too.

21

Instead of being apprehensive about going eighty-five miles an hour, Marti wished Holmberg would drive faster. They had traveled so far south there was nothing but trees and occasionally another car on the road. When signs indicated an exit or a town, there was not one building tall enough to be seen above the trees.

"Boring," Holmberg said. "We'll be there in about twenty minutes."

There was break in the trees a few minutes later. An acre of grass surrounded a sprawling brick building with a tall chain-link fence topped with razor wire.

"There's no prison out here," she said.

"State mental hospital," Vik told her.

"And why are you more familiar with where it's located than I am?"

"When's the last time you drove to St. Louis?"

"When we do, we take I–Fifty-five, Jessenovik. It doesn't take as long. This is the scenic route minus the scenery."

"So now you know what you've been missing."

A picture of the town could have been used for a calendar or a greeting card. One main street with a church at the end that was painted white and had a belfry, then a hardware store, a market, and a drug store than wasn't owned by a chain. There was a sign in front of an old red brick building with parallel parking. Holmberg pulled in.

"See, Marti," Vik said. "Police Station, District Court, and City

Hall. One stop and you can report an accident, get married by a judge, pay your water bill, and get your car sticker. Things used to be like this in Lincoln Prairie."

"And you remember when."

"My dad told me."

"What happened when somebody died?"

"The coroner here probably works right out of the hospital or the funeral home."

"And you expect these people to have documents and a chain of evidence that will stand up in court?"

"One never knows."

Lupe snickered.

"Right," Holmberg agreed.

Based on the pictures lined up on one wall, Marti assumed that there were five uniforms and a police chief.

"Six cops," Vik said. "This place must be a hotbed of crime."

The chief would have looked Holmberg's age if it wasn't for the creases at the corners of his eyes and the gray that streaked his light brown hair. He was Vik's height and wore a tan-and-brown uniform. Everyone introduced himself.

"Well, well," the chief said as he called for more chairs. "Must be a big case. I wasn't expecting four of you."

The officer who had been at the desk brought in the chairs. He was followed by a woman in civilian clothes carrying a tray with an assortment of canned pop.

"Trust me," the chief said when she left. "You don't want any of her coffee. I've just about talked her out of making it." He went to his desk and sat down. "Now, like I told you on the phone, we've got twenty-seven indigent residents. Five of them belong here. The others have gotten out of the hospital down the road over time and don't have any place else to go. They're peaceful for the most part, and don't cause us much trouble. Occasionally someone has too much to drink and we lock him up overnight."

He pulled the tab on a can of pop. "We've got a storefront where they can eat, hang out, and find clothes. Got a center where they can sleep, have their mail sent, bathe, things like that. Keeps them in one part of town, and keeps them from needing to steal."

He took a long swallow of pop. "The drunks are the only ones who can be a nuisance. We can't blame the others for being a couple of pickles short of a Big Mac. Every so often some well-intentioned busybodies decide that they need rehabilitation, but they either shut up or go away. It's hard to get people riled up when they have what they need. This might seem odd to you, coming from the city and all, but it works for us."

He picked up a manila folder, held it out, and said, "This is what you came here to see. Go through it, ask questions, then I'll take you around to meet Hyacinth's friends and the people who look out for them."

Marti took the folder. There were half a dozen reports. She passed along each sheet of paper as she read it. Then she summarized aloud what the reports said. "Solid chain of evidence," she said. "The men's clothing with traces of blood takes care of a major missing link. Fax me a copy of the DNA results as soon as you get it."

"You sound like you know who did this," the chief said.

"We think we do," Marti told him.

"Important case, huh?"

"This is the seventh victim," Vik said. "So far."

The chief whistled. "A serial killer, and he was right here in our town. Man. You think he killed anyone else around here? Nobody else has been reported missing. We check on everyone who lives alone once a week; two or three times when the weather's bad."

"Is there any way to get here other than car or bus?" Vik asked.

"No way that makes sense."

"What's the bus schedule?"

"One bus a day going to St. Louis, one in the evening heading into Chicago. Got four buses on Sunday. Three going into Chicago, two during the day, one in the evening, and one coming out of Chicago in the morning."

Vik took out his notebook. "Why?"

"Sunday is visiting day at the hospital and the day they release whoever is getting out each week."

"We'll need to go the bus station," Vik said. "Talk with the people at each of those places you mentioned, and take a walk around town. Let's say a three-block radius around the place where she was found."

"An empty building," the chief said. "The mayor's been talking about tearing it down for two years. Maybe now he'll do something. We already talked with everyone at the centers. None of them remembers seeing Hyacinth with anyone they didn't know."

"We'll have to talk with them, too," Vik said. "Good thing you're coming along with us. It sounds like you know everyone in town."

The chief smiled and took a brown leather jacket off the coat rack. "Glad to help."

"Did you know her?" Marti asked him.

"Hyacinth? Half the town knew her. She dressed weird, talked strange, but she was an English professor at some state university before she took sick. Funny thing about some people we consider crazy—a lot of the time they make sense. She was always quoting one poet or another. Kept me wondering about just what she meant by it. Never did take the time to look any of it up though. I don't know why she called herself Hyacinth. As you saw in those reports, her given name is Margaret Mary Mulligan."

"Nobody's claimed the body?" Marti said.

"People are strange like that, aren't they? She does have family, but we had to send dental X rays to make an identification. I don't know if it's shame or what. They only live in Missouri, but not one of the six relatives I spoke with would come here. Though they did say they would pay to have her cremated."

* * *

Marti asked the chief for a map of the town and had him high-
light the place where the body had been found. She drew a
square around the surrounding three-block area, and divided it
in half. After they went into the vacant building to see where the
body had been found, Marti, Vik, and the chief took one section.
Lupe and Holmberg took the other.

"Talk with her friends and the people at the homeless facilities
as well," Marti told them. She didn't think they would find out
much—it was unlikely that DeVonte walked up and introduced
himself, but it would be a practical experience for Holmberg.

Marti, Vik, and the chief began at the outer perimeter of their
area. The houses were small with big yards. Some had American
flags hoisted on poles. A few had plastic yellow ribbons tied
around trees. None was empty. Marti and Vik watched the curtains. They knocked on the door when the curtains moved.
Nosy neighbors were the best kind. Nobody remembered seeing
Hyacinth. When they came to the diner they paused. It looked
like the dining car on a train, wheels and all.

"Real train car?" Vik asked.

"A long time ago," the chief answered.

The silver metal was battered in places, the windows bare.
The door didn't hang even but it did close. Inside, one waitress
was behind the Formica counter, talking on the phone.

She looked up. "Coffee? Here, or to go? Oh, hi, Chief." Without hanging up she reached for a thick, white mug.

"We need to talk with you, Darlene," the chief said. "Mind
hanging up?"

"Oh. Sure." She spoke into the phone. "Gotta go. Official police business. Tell you about it later."

"Were you working here last Sunday?" Vik asked.

"Work here every day. My folks own the place."

"Did you see any strangers?"

"Always see a stranger or two on Sunday. That's visiting day at
the nuthouse."

233

"How many strangers came in last Sunday?"

"Slow day. Only two. The lady was dressed like she was going to church. The man, well . . ." She shrugged. "Wanted coffee and a couple of doughnuts."

"What did he look like?"

"Black," she said, then she looked at Marti. "African-American."

"Ever see him before?"

She shook her head. "Wasn't from around here."

"Notice anything else?"

"Well, when he came in that morning he was wearing this blue jacket with the hood pulled up. When he walked by in the afternoon he had on a black overcoat."

The chief nudged Marti. She nodded. A sports bag with a blue jacket and a hammer inside had been found in a Dumpster near where Hyacinth was killed. The jacket had the blood stains. Now that they had the knife that had been found in Fred's pocket, and were reasonably certain that it was DeVonte's, they would compare it with the victim's stab wounds. They were finally getting the physical evidence they needed. Even better, they had two witnesses, this young lady and Fred.

The clerk in the bus station confirmed that a black male had got off the bus wearing a blue jacket and got on the bus wearing a black coat.

"Do you remember the time?" Marti asked.

"First bus in from Chicago, second bus out of St. Louis."

While Marti checked the bus schedule, the chief said, "That's the bus the people being released take if they're going to Chicago."

"Right," the clerk agreed. "If the bus is early or the van from the hospital's running late, we wait for 'em."

Outside, Marti said, "Do you know the number to the hospital?"

The chief nodded.

"Do they know you?"

"Real well."

"Can you call them and ask if anyone named Iris was released last Sunday."

"Last name?"

"I'm not sure."

He made the call, waited for a few minutes, then put his hand over the mouthpiece and said, "Iris O'Neill?"

Marti nodded. "Could be. When was she admitted?"

"Ten months ago."

"Do they have photographs?"

"Sure. We take one when they come in and another before they leave."

"Can you get copies for me?"

He spoke into the phone again. "It will take about an hour. That gives us time for lunch." He looked up. "Time flies. It's getting dark. Make that an early supper."

They met up with Lupe and Holmberg first. Neither had talked to anyone who remembered seeing a stranger, let alone one wearing a blue jacket or a black coat.

The diner was clean, Marti reasoned as they returned. She didn't see any rodent droppings or crawling insects as she slid into the booth. Even so, she played it safe, she hoped, and ordered a burger well done. Vik decided to live dangerously and have the daily special: meat loaf and mashed potatoes covered with gravy, and canned string beans. The chief ordered that, too. Lupe and Holmberg had club sandwiches.

The chief's cell phone rang while they were on their third cup of coffee. "They'll have those photographs waiting for you at the front desk." He wanted to pick up the tab but Vik insisted.

"Been a real pleasure," the chief said, as he walked them to their car. "Be glad to have you back anytime. I'm looking forward to coming to Lincoln Prairie to testify."

As they headed for the interstate, Holmberg said, "Admit it, everyone. We were all expecting a hick cop, a hick department, and a hick town."

Nobody said anything.

* * *

Inside the hospital, the clerk handed Marti an envelope. She didn't open it until she was back in the car. If this Iris O'Neill was Johnny's sister, Marti wasn't sure she would be able to recognize her after all of these years. The woman who stared at her from the before-photo looked haggard, unkempt. The woman who left the hospital last Sunday had gained weight, got her hair cut and styled. Marti knew who she was because of her eyes. From the nose up, it was like looking at Johnny's mother.

She put in a call to Denise Stevens and asked her to do a search as soon as possible for a Lynn Ella O'Neill. Next she called the office, got Slim, and asked him to do a search for anything he could find on Iris O'Neill.

"That's her?" Vik said. "You're sure?"

"She's got her mother's eyes."

"I wonder how in hell DeVonte Lutrell managed to find her."

"He's been in the area at least ten months that we know of. Had plenty of time." Time she hadn't had, time to search marriage records.

"Does Sharon just have a big mouth?" Lupe asked. "Or is Lutrell that good?"

"A little of both," Marti told her.

She called Sharon, spoke with the female officer. No incoming calls all day. They had picked up the check for the pension payout. The bank refused to give them the $90,000 until the check cleared in three to five days.

"You know the plan," Marti told her. "Listen in on the FBI line. He won't know you're there." And, Marti added silently, Sharon won't be able lie about what he tells her, or let him know we're in on it.

DeVonte woke up, checked the clock, saw that it was after six thirty, and called for Iris.

"I've got to get out of here."

"I'll get the tape."

He sat up with reluctance. He didn't like women to touch him and derived no pleasure from being with them. Physical contact was just a necessary part of his scam. The only thing that he enjoyed doing to women was killing them. Iris's death had to be postponed, but she too would die.

"You've got to take off your shirt," Iris told him when she returned. "And keep still. It'll hurt some at first, but you'll be feeling real comfortable by the time I'm through."

She wrapped gauze around him first. After the first layer of tape, she said, "Good thing I'm here."

"I would have managed without you."

"You would have," she agreed. "But it would have hurt like hell. Now, unless you cough, sneeze, or have to jump or run, you won't have much pain at all."

Lynn Ella came to the doorway. She was sipping her shake. Iris had combed her hair. Cornrows began at her temples and ended at her neck. She even had red and yellow barrettes. He smiled at her and winked. Iris was so intent on wrapping the tape around his chest she didn't notice.

Holmberg drove back. They made good time until they hit Chicago. Marti called twice to make sure there had been no word from DeVonte. "Nothing," Marti told the others. "He should have called by now." Then again, why should he be concerned? He had told Sharon to do something, therefore Sharon would do it. Marti realized she was clenching her teeth and tried to relax. At this rate, and with this traffic, when they did find out what DeVonte's plan was, they might not have enough time to react.

They were trying to get around an accident on the Dan Ryan when the desk sergeant called. The car had been found. "Have them tow it," Marti said. She wondered what effect that would have on DeVonte's plans. He'd either have to steal another car or take public transportation. "Where did they find it?"

"In Chicago. On . . . North Haskins Avenue."

The name of the street didn't mean anything right away. As they cleared the accident, it came to her. "The Juneway Jungle," she said.

"What about it?" Vik asked.

"Juneway Terrace. Where they found the stolen vehicle. North side of the city. A lot of people from the Islands live there." It reminded her of what Slim had said about moving down the food chain until you became invisible.

Slim was on his computer when they got back to the office.

"There's some cold pizza if you're hungry."

"Find anything?" Marti asked.

"Look on your desk."

There was a stack of printouts waiting for her. Before Marti could look at them, Denise Stevens came in.

"Bad news," she said. She was wearing a rust-colored, wide-brimmed felt hat that matched her coat and complimented her sable brown skin. She took off her coat, tossed it on Cowboy's desk, and sat in the chair nearest Marti.

"There is no Lynn Ella O'Neill?" Marti said. The possibility of having a niece she had never seen was such a new idea that she still felt detached.

"It's worse than that," Denise said. "There is a Lynn Ella O'Neill, but they've lost her."

"Lost her?" Then it hit her. "Oh, no, Denise. Don't tell me she's dead."

"No. She's lost. The D.C.F.S. terminated the mother's parental rights when the child was three months old, took custody of her, and lost her."

"They don't know where she is?"

"The foster parent taking care of her died six months ago. The mother, Iris O'Neill, was released from a hospital downstate on Sunday. According to the mother, a Darrell Loomis met her at the bus station and said he and his wife were her foster parents. He said they wanted the child to meet her birth mother on Monday. But no one at D.C.F.S. followed up. Bottom line, Lynn Ella is eight years old now and nobody knows where she is. There are no school records, nothing."

238

Iris, Johnny's sister, and Lynn Ella, his niece—her niece—were with DeVonte. But how? Why? Marti put her face in her hands. She suddenly felt overwhelmed. First DeVonte tried to kill Sharon and Lisa. Now he had Iris and her daughter. She cursed aloud, filled with a sudden rage, and banged her fist on her desk.

The theme from *Dragnet* interrupted her. She spoke into her cell phone. "MacAlister."

It was the chief calling from downstate. "I thought you might want to know this. I talked with this Iris's doctor. According to him she's bipolar with attention deficit hyperactive disorder."

Marti thanked him. Then, calmer, she sat back in her chair, contemplating the stack of computer printouts. She put them in piles and said, "Okay, let's take a look at this."

As she went through the orders of commitment for Iris, she remembered a little girl who could never sit still, who was disruptive in class, who was spanked by her Sunday school teacher. That little girl grew into a teenager who danced, sang, and talked nonstop, who changed her clothes, her hairstyle, and redid her makeup half a dozen times a day. Even when Momma talked about Iris, she said, "Being around that child for any length of time is enough to make you crazy."

Marti took out the photos. The Iris who left the hospital looked so different from the Iris who went in. Everyone, even Johnny, had assumed that Iris was on drugs, but although drugs were involved, the committals were for mental illnesses—paranoia, schizophrenia, suicidal depression, but not A.D.H.D. or manic depression. She took another look at the photos. Maybe they got it right this time. She turned to Denise.

"What do we do about Lynn Ella?"

"Find her, alive, hopefully. There are three to five hundred wards of the state that nobody can find. The numbers depend on who you talk to. This one has been identified so recently that it hasn't even been assigned to a caseworker yet. I made a few phone calls, got some visibility. The kids who aren't really lost, but look as if they are because of missing or erroneous paper-work, are found relatively fast, but in a case like this, they may never find her."

"We know who she's with," Marti said. "DeVonte Lutrell."

Denise's eyes widened. "Sharon's husband the psycho? My God."

Vik ran his fingers through his hair, then put his head in his hands. He muttered curses in Polish for a few moments, then be-gan looking at the paperwork again. Lupe didn't say anything. Finally Holmberg said, "This sounds impossible. Chicago is huge. How big is this Juneway Jungle . . . Terrace . . . whatever?"

"It's too heavily populated for a house-to-house search, and there's not enough time for the officers who work that area to try to find her."

"So, what do we do?" Holmberg asked.

"Wait for DeVonte to make his move," Marti told him.

"But that means he's in charge."

"You got it," Vik said.

22

DeVonte walked to the corner of North Haskins. He knew exactly where he had parked his car, but it was gone. A Buick was parked there now. Son of a . . . Someone had stolen his car. He left it there for two days and they took it. He had parked it on this street in this block for almost a year and nobody bothered it. Now, the one time he really needed it, it was gone. He stood there for a moment. Tonight. It had to be tonight. Sharon would have the money by now. She was waiting for him to call. He had planned just to drive there, surprise her. He knew how to get into that apartment building. Now what?

Ever since he went back to that house on Hemlock and that bum saw him, things had been going wrong. He should have killed him while he had the chance. He would have if he hadn't dropped his knife. Then he fell and broke his ribs. Now his car had been stolen, and he would have to change his plan again. The wind was blowing in his face. He coughed. It didn't hurt like it did before Iris taped him, but he didn't want to cough again.

He stepped into a doorway. Sharon would have to come here. He thought about that for a few minutes. She was at her best when she was scared, and she was afraid of almost everything. She could meet him by the lake. She was afraid of water. And it would remind her of what he had almost done to her in the Islands. She would be paralyzed with fear, just as she was then.

No. Too open. Too easy to attract attention. Too easy to get away. There was a cemetery. Yes! Isolated, dark, tombstones, crypts, graves, dead people. Yes! Sharon would be terrified. He had never been in there, but he had walked past. There was a gate facing the lake and a road there that went into the cemetery. If he told Sharon to be there at . . . eleven o'clock . . . There wouldn't be much traffic then. Inside there would be trees and tombstones near that road where he could hide. If he just told her to come through that gate and walk straight ahead until she met him that would give him the advantage. He could pick his spot, jump out, and grab her. If she screamed, there was nobody but him to hear her. He didn't like using a place without checking it out first, but he didn't have much choice. He hurried to a gas station to use the outside pay phone.

Sharon was sitting on the couch with her legs tucked under her when the phone rang. She stared at it, didn't take it from the charger until the third ring. The cop sitting across from her put on her headset.

"Hi, baby."

"DeVonte." Her stomach began churning.

"You sound out of breath."

"No. No. I was just sitting here." She covered her mouth, belched, tasted bile.

"Are you okay, baby? You're not sick, are you?"

"No. Nothing. I'm fine."

"I'm glad to hear it. I've got something for you to do. Listen well. You're going to meet me near Evanston, at Calvary Cemetery."

As Sharon listened, she watched the officer taking notes. The FBI would be listening, too. They were going to try to catch him, but he had gotten away before and this time he had Iris and Lynn Ella. As soon as he knew the police were on to him, they were dead. Marti hadn't seen the expression on his face when he tried to kill her. He was excited, happy, and angry all at once. None of them knew who they were dealing with, but she did.

"DeVonte," she said, interrupting him. "You . . ."

The cop was standing in front of her before she could tell him her car wasn't working and that he would have to come here.

"You're talking faster than I can write," she said instead. "Slow down."

The officer began writing again, but did not leave her side.

Marti was typing in the day's reports when Vik took a call and said, "Pick up on this." As she listened to DeVonte's instructions to Sharon, the scope of what they would have to do to catch him became apparent.

"I thought he would come to her," Marti admitted when they hung up.

"Me too."

"It's eight twenty already," she said. "He wants Sharon to meet him at eleven. That gives us about two hours to plan this operation and have everyone in place. We'll have to notify Evanston and Chicago. The cemetery borders both cities."

She made the call and explained the situation. Evanston said they were having a busy night, but could provide six uniforms and two detectives. Marti requested that they wear civilian clothes and guard the perimeter in case DeVonte got away. She wanted officers from her own department with her inside the cemetery.

"How big is the cemetery?" Vik asked.

"About ninety acres."

He whistled. "Why didn't we think of this?"

"I should have considered the possibility when I told them to tow the car," Marti agreed. "I thought he'd just take the train or steal another car." She closed her eyes for a moment, visualizing the main entrance of the cemetery on Chicago Avenue. Three arches, a large one flanked by two that were smaller, all with gates. The rear gate faced Sheridan Road and the lake. There was a post on each side of a wide concrete path with a gate that closed in the middle.

We'll have to climb a spiked, wrought-iron fence, but it's not high," she said. "There is one central path, from front to back, it's . . ."—she ticked off the Evanston streets—"six blocks. He didn't give her any markers or a meeting place, just told her to enter from Sheridan Road, stay on that path, and keep walking."

"Which means we'd need . . . what? Fifty cops along the route, maybe a hundred? And what's to keep him from spotting us?"

"I don't think logistics are that bad. The Chicago side of the boundary is Area Three." She thought for a moment. "It's got to be District Twenty-four." She called them.

"Well?" Vik said when she hung up.

"They can have four black and whites in the area as backup. And they will have ten guys undercover watching to see if anyone goes in."

"Great. So basically we're on our own. We call the lieutenant now, right?"

Marti decided to talk with the desk sergeant first.

"Nicholson left about twenty minutes ago," he said. "Deputy Chief Dirkowitz is still here. While you're talking to him—hint—I can see who's off duty and willing to come in."

Marti followed the sergeant's suggestion.

Dirkowitz agreed to her outline. "Sounds like a plan to me. Go for it."

"Is that an official heads up?"

"Sure is."

When the sergeant called back he said, "Geez, you guys are popular. We've got two dozen volunteers. Want me to keep calling?"

"No," Marti decided. "We've got Chicago in on this and Evanston. I don't want things to get too confusing. Why don't I meet with our guys in the parking lot in twenty minutes and we can head out. No departmental cars. This guy will recognize them. And nothing flashy."

She turned to Vik. "Okay, let's come up with a plan. We're talking about staking out a path four city blocks long. There are lots of hiding places. Mausoleums, statues, those tall pointy things, fancy headstones . . . there will be twenty-eight of us inside, including the decoy."

"Me," Lupe said.

"You're four inches taller than Sharon."

"How well lit is this place?"

"Streetlights around the perimeter. No lights inside."

"Give me fifteen minutes to go home and change clothes."

"You've got it." Marti turned to Vik. "Now all we need is a plan. Let's keep it simple. We'll all be in communication with each other. Hopefully one of the undercover cops will spot him going in. If not . . . South Boulevard borders the cemetery to the north. We'll have to drive those five blocks from the lake and decide how much distance we'll have between lookouts. They'll each have to find a good place to hide that's not too far from the path."

"And if DeVonte calls back and changes the plan?"

"We'll improvise."

Iris could tell that something was wrong with DeVonte. She didn't know what and she had no plans to ask. He was in the bed, wide awake, watching the clock, waiting. He seemed angry. She knew he was going to get the money tonight. Maybe it was just nerves.

She went in to check on Lynn Ella. The child had picked up on DeVonte's mood. She was sitting as far back in the closet as she could, hugging a pillow. Iris sat on the floor and leaned against the open door.

"You're scared, aren't you? There's no need to be worried about anything. You don't have to be worried or scared ever again. You're with me now. I won't let anybody hurt you again, not ever. I won't let anything bad happen to you either, no matter what. You hear me, girl?"

There was no answer.

"That's okay. You don't have to say anything. I'm just going to stay right here. Nobody will do anything to you unless they get past me, and they won't." She got the blanket and pillow off the bed and settled down on the floor in front of the closet.

"You're safe now, Lynn Ella," she said. "You're with your real mother now. I won't leave you again." Even as she said it, she wondered how she would keep that promise. She knew she had to.

Sharon sat on the couch with her feet tucked under her. She had a book, and turned the pages, but she wasn't reading. The cop sat across from her. How did they do it, sit hour after hour and just watch someone? Doing something like that would make her crazy. As she turned the page, she wondered what was happening now. It was almost ten o'clock. In another hour DeVonte might be in jail, or even dead. He had Iris and Iris's little girl. He would bring them with him to the cemetery. He would use them for hostages to try to save himself and kill them if that didn't work. And if he got away again, he would keep killing until someone did stop him.

She was the one he wanted now, the one who got away. And maybe he wanted Marti, too, since Marti had figured out what he was doing back then, killing women on the boat ride between Fort Lauderdale and Grand Bahama Island. But Marti would have Vik and a lot of cops to protect her. Iris and Lynn Ella would have no one, not unless she could get to him, let him take her hostage instead. Dying didn't seem like such a bad thing anymore. It wasn't like she had much to live for. Lisa hated her. Lisa was with Marti and there was no way she was ever going to come back. As for her, she would be running scared and hiding for the rest of her life if DeVonte managed to evade the trap Marti set for him.

"Coffee?" she asked.

"Sure."

"Are you going to be here all night?"

"No. Someone will relieve me at eleven."

Eleven o'clock. She was supposed to meet him then. It was ten minutes to ten now.

Sharon put on her slippers and went into the kitchen. She filled the kettle, turned on the gas burner, grabbed a dish towel, and wiped off the counter. Then she put the dish towel near the flame. Turning, she got cups out of the cabinet. She kept her back to the stove and blocked the cop's view of it at the same time. She filled the sugar bowl and was reaching for the tea bags when the cop yelled, "Fire!"

The woman came charging into the kitchen, pushed Sharon out of the way and yelled, "Call nine-one-one!"

"There's a fire extinguisher by the refrigerator!" Sharon yelled as she grabbed her jacket and her purse and ran out the front door.

Marti checked her watch, ten forty-five. She was standing about forty feet from the road behind a statue of Christ with his arms outstretched. There were several tombstones almost as large closer to the road, as well as a mausoleum and a Celtic cross at least eight feet high. The officer watching Sharon had called in with a report that she had set the kitchen on fire and ran out of the apartment. Her car was gone. Two Evanston patrol units were watching for her.

Between the Evanston and Chicago departments, the streets surrounding the cemetery were covered. Nobody could predict what would happen in here, but the plan was to take DeVonte, dead or alive. She hoped Sharon didn't get in the way. She didn't want a hostage situation. A standoff could take hours of negotiations and the outcome was never predictable.

Darkness seemed to envelop her. The moon was obscured by cloud cover. The streetlights didn't penetrate this far. The noise surprised her. She had always thought of a cemetery as a silent place, especially at night. Instead, she could hear occasional, muted traffic sounds, owls hooting and the sudden flapping of their wings as they spotted their prey. A cold wind made whistling noises and bare tree branches creaked and crackled. There were small animals here, too, who had not gone to sleep for the winter. She had even seen a deer picking its way among the winter-brown grass. Her radio was silent, but she didn't know if that was good or bad. It was almost eleven o'clock. Lupe would be climbing over the fence. DeVonte must be here waiting, but the undercover cops hadn't spotted him coming in.

DeVonte stood in a doorway on South Boulevard. He waited until a cop car went by, then crossed the street to the cemetery. He could have just vaulted the fence if his ribs weren't broken. Even with the tape, it hurt as he grabbed the metal bar near the top, and clambered over. He jumped to the ground, and hid behind the nearest tree, gasping for breath, feeling a sharp pain each time he inhaled. Codeine soon, he thought. As soon as he got back to his apartment.

He remembered the last time he had been in a graveyard. His mother's funeral. The sun had been bright that day. The mourners few. The neighbors who did come were more curious than sad. The minister seemed in a hurry. This place was much bigger than the burial grounds at home. And different in the dark.

When the pain subsided, he looked around. The smallest tombstones were waist high, the largest, taller than he was. Some were crowded together. Angels, Madonnas, even Jesus seemed to rise from the graves. He knew they were just statues, but in the darkness they seemed more like ghosts. He headed south, toward the center of the cemetery where he thought the path was. As he walked across the graves, he tried not to think of the people who were buried there, the coffins disintegrating, bones mouldering, flesh decomposing.

An owl hooted. He jumped. He should not have come here. This was a place of death, a place with spirits who had not found rest, souls still in search of peace. Or, like his mother, seeking vengeance. An angel, head bowed with folded wings, loomed ahead; beyond that, he could see the road. He remained among the headstones, and headed east, toward the lake. It was time. Sharon should be coming to meet him.

Iris looked in on Lynn Ella. The child was curled up under the blanket with her head on the pillow, asleep. She tiptoed from the room, taking her coat as she went past the bed. DeVonte had a ten-minute head start, but he had told her where he was going. She wanted to know who he was meeting. She wanted to find out what this debt was that Johnny owed, and why he owed it, and then find out whatever else this person could tell her about him. DeVonte only told her what he wanted her to know, and that could be nothing but lies.

She spotted the undercover cop as soon as she reached Juneway Terrace. She stepped into a doorway and watched for a minute. He was checking out the cemetery, not watching what was happening on the street. The cops were on to whatever De-Vonte was up to.

She headed west, turned north on Chicago Avenue, and walked until she found a place where the branches of trees, taller than Christmas trees, hung over the fence. Nobody would notice her here. As she scaled the fence, she wondered how difficult it had been for DeVonte. She didn't think he would let anything stop him.

It felt like something was banging in her chest when Lynn Ella ran down the stairs and went outside. She could hear a noise inside of her like someone knocking on a door. She didn't want this daddy or this mama to leave her. But they were both gone. She had to find them and go with them. They wouldn't come back. She followed this mama, stopped walking when she did, saw her almost go one way, then go another. When she got to the corner this mama was way ahead of her and going across the street to a park.

There were people on the street who were like the people who came to the last mama's house. People she didn't like. They talked funny and walked funny and fell down. Sometimes they got into fights on the bed. Mostly, they smelled. Lynn Ella went to the alley behind the houses the people were standing in front of. She picked up a stick to chase the rats with, but none of them left the bags of garbage to bother her. At the end of the alley, she peeked out, looked both ways, and saw the park this mama had gone to.

It was scary crossing the street because the bad people could see her. She didn't look at them, and she walked—but she wanted to run. This park had a fence around it. She walked until she came to a gate. There was a space where the gate was by something made of stone. She squeezed in.

This park was like magic. Beautiful stone people with wings like birds looked down at her but didn't move. A mama deer and a daddy deer were under a tree with their babies. She played a game with the stones, walking in front of one and behind another until she saw someone still far away but coming toward her. Then she hid behind one of the stones so no one could see her.

Sharon parked several blocks from the cemetery and walked along the lake. She hadn't had time to put on her shoes and still wore her slippers. Maybe, if a cop did drive by, he wouldn't notice and stop to ask questions. Her coat was long and flapped about her legs as she walked. When she reached the cemetery, she didn't want to go across the street, didn't want to go inside. She wished she had just stayed home. Then she thought of DeVonte. The others didn't know him the way she did. They didn't know how seductive, how persuasive he could be, how frightening.

She thought of Iris, of Lynn Ella, how terrified they would be while he was killing them. And he would. If he hadn't already. If they were still alive, she had to do something. This was her fault, all of it. Mr. Wonderful. She had brought him into their lives. She couldn't face being responsible for their deaths, but maybe she already was. Somehow, this had to end here, tonight, now. The killing had to stop. She had to make sure that happened.

She waited until a car drove past, then crossed the street and stood before the locked gate. Just inside she saw a tall cross, beyond that, white headstones, then darkness. She took off her coat, tossed it on the fence, and tried to figure out how to climb over. There were some bushes and a tree near what could be a chapel just inside the fence. She found a low branch that would support her weight, cat walked until she crossed over the top of the fence, then jumped down. She retrieved her coat, slung her purse strap over her shoulder, looked as far down the road as she could see, and began walking.

Lupe looked from one side of the path to the other and walked hesitantly, as if she was afraid. "DeVonte?" she whispered a few times. She would have spoken louder but then he might know she wasn't Sharon. She was wearing jeans, a jacket, and thick socks because her shoes had steel plates in the toes. A scarf partially covered her face. Both hands were in her pockets. One held the grip of her gun, the other a can of mace.

As she approached a statue of Jesus with a child on His lap and a child at His side, a man stepped into the path.

"DeVonte," she said, speaking into the wire.

He walked toward her until he was about twenty feet away. "You're not Sharon."

The shock in his voice surprised her. She pulled out her service revolver.

"I'm a police officer and you're under arrest."

He looked stunned. As he raised his hands, she thought, This is too easy.

"Daddy!" a child screamed. "Daddy!"

DeVonte looked to his left.

Lupe didn't take her eyes off him.

"Come, child," he said. "Come to Daddy."

"Don't do this," Lupe warned him.

"No!" someone shouted behind her. She didn't turn around.

"DeVonte! No! I'm here. They tricked me. The bank. They put a hold on the check and they called the cops. I swear to God."

Sharon, Lupe thought, just what she needed.

DeVonte was still looking to his left.

Lupe risked a glance in that direction. A little girl was standing where the grass met the path.

Then another woman was behind DeVonte, running toward them.

"Stop!" Lupe shouted. "Stay back!"

"Police!" voices called from behind her. They switched on their flashlights.

Then Sharon ran past her to DeVonte. "I'm here," Sharon said. "You don't need them, you've got me. I won't leave you."

The other woman kept running toward them. "Lynn Ella," she called, "Lynn Ella, come to Mama."

Lupe glanced to her left just as the little girl took a step toward DeVonte.

"Come," he said. "Come to Daddy."

The girl took another step toward him. Lupe didn't dare try to warn her away. It might cause her to do just the opposite.

"Lynn Ella," the woman cried out. "No! Come to Mama."

The child looked at her mama, hesitated, looked at DeVonte again, then ran to her mama.

Lupe kept her weapon trained on DeVonte as other officers began to surround them.

DeVonte looked down at Sharon, then turned to see Iris holding on to Lynn Ella. Bitches, all of them. None of them worth shit. But he couldn't stop looking at the child. She had wanted a daddy. He wanted her. And now she had turned away from him, too.

He looked at the woman holding the gun. There were nine cops now.

"Where is she?" he asked.

"Who?"

"MacAlister. I want to see her."

"No, DeVonte, no," Sharon pleaded. "You've got me."

"I want the cop," he said.

A tall male cop holding a gun took a step toward him. "Sorry," he said. "No can do."

Sharon sagged against DeVonte. "Jessenovik. Thank God."

"I won't let go of her until you give me MacAlister."

"Don't do this," Sharon begged.

"No," the tall male cop said again.

"No way," a voice said behind him.

DeVonte looked at the cops. They all had guns in their hands. He was surrounded. They wouldn't give up one of their own, not even to save Sharon's sorry ass. He looked at the statue of Jesus with the children. What a lie. Children were born alone, abused alone, died alone. There was no God. Then he looked at the cop standing in front of him. She wasn't even as tall as he was. And she was a woman. She wouldn't care if she had to shoot through Sharon to get him. The only way to deal with a woman like her was to kill her.

"Give it up," she said. "It's over. Give it up."

"No," he said. "Never." He couldn't spend the rest of his life locked in a closet looking through the bars. He couldn't let them watch while he was put down like a dog. He couldn't give any woman that satisfaction. Turning, he looked at Lynn Ella. She sold him out, just like the others. Woman, none of them was worth shit.

He looked at the guns pointed at him. The cop was gripping hers with both hands and was ready to pull the trigger. He shoved Sharon toward her, and pulled out the fake gun.

An ambulance took DeVonte to St. Francis Hospital. He was dead on arrival. Sharon sat in the waiting room, sobbing. At least there was one person to mourn him, Marti thought. She didn't make any attempt to comfort her. Iris asked to go to a friend's house, Lottie Hodge. The Chicago police insisted on taking her and Lynn Ella to area headquarters. Marti put in a call to Denise Stevens who agreed to drive down immediately. She watched as Lupe gave Holmberg her weapon, and Vik did the same. Then he walked over to Marti. They hugged. "I fired first, then Lupe," he told her. "It was my turn. You took out the last one."

23

As Vik drove down yet another rolling hill, a sign came into view: BEAVER RIDGE POPULATION 1,429. To his right he could see the bluffs along the Chicago River, to his left, a herd of sheep. He braked at a four-way stop. Two giggling young girls on horseback ambled across the road. The street narrowed as he entered the town. He felt like he was stepping back half a century in time. The gas station on the corner made him think of the *Andy Griffith Show*. Two pumps, a rusting chest painted red with a Coke logo, and two chairs on a wooden platform that served as a porch.

As he drove along, it didn't get any better. Main Street was a ragtag collection of storefronts. Even the post office was in a run-down one-story wood frame that also housed a notary, an attorney, and the justice of the peace. The house was so small that it occurred to him that they might all be the same person. He glanced at Mildred. She seemed okay despite the hundred-mile drive that had taken two hours.

He didn't see any street numbers. "Watch for a dog pound or a vet or something," he suggested. All this for a scraggly-looking German shepherd, whose picture Krista had helped her find on the Internet—a dog Mildred wanted immediately. "And let me know if you think you see a place where we can get something to eat without getting ptomaine poisoning." He didn't see anything that looked like an animal shelter.

After a block there was another rolling hill with small houses and smoke coming from the chimneys. The front yards were tidy, but in the back, old cars sat on blocks and tire swings hung from tree branches. Firewood was stacked against sagging garages. Vik turned, headed back. He spotted a restaurant, "Gert's Place."

"That's it!" she said.

"What? The restaurant. I see it."

"No, the place where the dog is. See the sign. It's that little building between the restaurant and the hardware store."

The sign was cardboard with STRAYS. DOGS AND CATS hand lettered with a blue marker.

"Maybe we should . . . ," he began

"Go inside," Mildred insisted.

He parked.

Vik was not pleased when they went inside. This was a real bare-bones operation, he decided. Beige walls, cracked brown tile with beige streaks, a gunmetal-gray desk with a black dial phone and one four-drawer army-green file cabinet. Then he took another look around. The walls were made festive with posters of dogs and cats, rabbits and squirrels. There was even a raccoon and a skunk, both of which Vik considered nuisances. He looked at Mildred. He could tell she was hovering somewhere between hope and anxiety.

An older woman wearing bib overalls and a plaid flannel shirt came through a rear door. A fat orange tabby followed her and jumped up on the desk.

"You've come about the German shepherd on our Web site," she said. "The sheriff found her wandering in the woods a couple of days ago. The vet spayed her right away. He said she's had at least one litter. We're not sure exactly how old she is. We think maybe a year and half to two. I'll be right back with her."

There were two chairs and a bay window. Mildred chose the bay window and sat. Vik remained standing. This did not sound good. He wanted a companion dog for Mildred, possibly one that could be trained to do something useful if she needed help. He was sure this wasn't the dog, but didn't know how he would convince Mildred.

The woman returned with the skinniest German shepherd Vik had ever seen. Her ribs were showing. The dog seemed confused as she looked around. She went over to the orange tabby. The cat looked at her and yawned. Then the dog looked at Mildred, took a few steps toward her, hesitated as if she was nervous, and then went over to her. The dog smelled. Vik moved away. No way was he going to make a hundred-mile, two-hour trip back home with this skinny, sickly, stinky animal in the back of Krista's S.U.V.

Mildred didn't seem to notice the odor. She offered the dog one of the treats Krista had put in a baggy. The dog sniffed it, but didn't eat it.

"Such a pretty girl," Mildred said, and began petting her. As soon as the dog leaned against Mildred's leg and closed her eyes, Vik knew that leaving without her was a lost cause. He could see that Mildred, who could hardly take care of herself anymore, couldn't wait to begin mothering this dog.

The woman in the bib overalls walked to Mildred and watched for a moment as Mildred petted the dog. "Got to take her in back and change her collar," she said. "It'll have a tag with our phone number on it. Let the phone ring five, six times if you call, in case I'm in back. Come on, girl."

The dog didn't want to go.

"It's okay," Mildred said. "Here, Maxie, I'll come with you."

Maxie. The deed was done. Mildred had named her.

The woman went to the desk, picked up a clipboard with several forms, and handed it to him. "I'll need you to fill out these."

The top sheet read "Adoption Application." Vik read through the questions, which included marital status, age, who would be responsible for the pet, where it would sleep, other pets in the household, number of adults and children in the household, type of residence, how many hours during the day the pet would be alone, how the pet would be reprimanded. Reprimanded? This dog was going to be a companion dog. He didn't think they needed reprimands. Maybe if he said please.

There were four pages of questions. He bet this was more than they asked when children were being adopted. The only thing lacking was a home visit. He turned to page four. Someone near Lincoln Prairie involved with dog rescues would follow up with a home visit. All this for Maxie, scrawny, sickly, and stinky Maxie. No, all this for Mildred, his heart.

He walked over to the doorway and looked into the room where the animals were kept. Each pen, or crate, had a brightly colored blanket and several toys. There was a hand-lettered sign for each dog and cat, as well as one pigeon, four rabbits, and, sure enough, a raccoon. The sign over the empty cage with the open door read: HI. I'M GENTLE AND AFFECTIONATE. I LOVE TO HAVE MY EARS RUBBED. I GET ALONG REAL GOOD WITH THE OTHER DOGS.

He looked at the dog. He knew as soon as he saw her on the Internet that she was going to come home with them. Maybe with a little fattening up and a bath, maybe. Not that it mattered. Mildred was already smitten.

It was after five in the evening when Marti and Vik met with Frank Winans at the Barrister Pub. Marti thought Winans chose some place informal to break the news that they were not being considered for the task force. Lieutenant Nicholson would not have given them a favorable recommendation. She was furious because they went to Dirkowitz for authorization to carry out the cemetery operation. Her anger was compounded when the *News-Times* not only printed the details about the serial killings, but praised Marti and Vik for their actions while calling into question her inaction. To make matters worse, a picture of Nicholson with former alderman Wittenberg appeared in the newspaper two days before his peers censured him. The EPA was also questioning Wittenberg regarding numerous violations.

After the waitress brought drinks, Winans said, "Judge Daniels flew in from Detroit. I asked him to sit in because there isn't anything he hasn't done in law enforcement in the past forty years. He started out as a beat cop, got a law degree, worked as a defense attorney and a prosecutor, and has spent the last seventeen years on the bench." He tasted his martini. "Not bad. What I want to do with this task force is have a prototype, something that we are confident will work, instead of going in and winging it and then somewhere down the line saying this is what did work, this is what didn't."

The waitress returned with their food. Marti and Winans had the shepherd's pie, Vik had his usual, bangers and mash.

"So I'm here to ask if you two will head up homicide."

Vik stopped and stared, a forkful of mashed potatoes halfway to his mouth.

"Us?" Marti said. "I didn't think we told you what you wanted to hear."

Winans laughed. "You didn't tell us what we expected to hear. You told us about something that is called thinking outside the box. We agree that is a critical criterion. That and risk taking, working independently, taking charge, handling adversity. And, after I talked with your boss . . ."

"Lieutenant Nicholson?" Marti and Vik almost spoke in unison.

"And Lieutenant Dirkowitz. But, you're right, Lieutenant Nicholson did have the most impact."

Marti looked at Vik. Neither asked why.

"You know," Winans went on, "the way this is set up, you two will continue to work for her; but, when you're working a case on the task force, you'll be in charge. She won't be your boss then. In fact, you'll be able to tell her what you want her to do. With Dirkowitz, that wouldn't be an issue. With Nicholson, it could be."

"And you think we can handle this?" Marti asked.

"Oh, I could tell that when I talked to her, and also with the way you wrapped up the case you were working on. I've got all the reports, yours, Chicago's, and Evanston's. Outstanding job. You two can handle this just fine. Nicholson might not be able to, but that'll be her problem."

*   *   *

"We got it!" Marti said as they walked back to their car.

"I thought for sure we blew it at that second meeting," Vik said.

"And Nicholson must have bad-mouthed us."

Marti was grinning as she unlocked the car door. She looked at Vik. This was the first time she had seen him smile in two weeks.

24

Marti listened to Momma humming and watched Ben setting up folding tables in the dining room. Theo and Mike were bringing in the chairs. When that was done, Momma pointed to the sideboard. "Lisa and Joanna, you get out the linen. When the tablecloths are on, show Lynn Ella where the napkins go."

As Marti watched, Ben coaxed Lynn Ella into the room. She was still a little wary of most of the women in the house, but she had taken to Ben right away. They had custody of her now. Sharon was homeschooling her and they were taking her to a counselor. Iris was living in a halfway house, but she'd be here in time for dinner. Iris's eleven-year-old daughter didn't want to have anything to do with any of them. Marti hoped that in time that would change.

"Theo, Mike, get out the silverware," Momma said. "I've got to get back in the kitchen."

Marti followed her, careful to stay out of the way. The turkey was ready and Cowboy was giving Slim a demonstration on how to carve a steamboat roast of beef. All of the traditional food would be part of the buffet—macaroni and cheese, candied sweet potatoes, collard greens—but Cowboy had prepared poached salmon, oyster dressing, brown rice pilaf, and a squash-and-pumpkin soup. Joanna had contributed three salads. Mildred, Helen, and Krista prepared the desserts.

Pleased that she wasn't needed, Marti went downstairs. Bigfoot, Geronimo, and Maxie were all in the den. She had not expected the three dogs to get along, but they did. Vik had hurried out of the office the day after they brought Maxie home and rushed her to the vet. She had a serious infection and was still on antibiotics. Marti had been astonished when Vik stayed home the next day to help take care of her.

Bigfoot and Geronimo seemed to sense that Maxie was still sick. Bigfoot was sprawled in front of the chair Maxie had climbed up on, and Geronimo was on one side chewing on a large bone. Even Goblin, their cat, had come in. Marti checked the three water bowls and food dishes and went back upstairs.

She stood just outside the living room and watched as Lisa and Joanna served mulled cider and wine. Lisa was living with them, too. Even today she was avoiding her mother. Sharon had been quiet ever since the night DeVonte died. She was living in the apartment over the garage for now. Marti didn't see much of her, but Momma did. And so did Lynn Ella.

Fred had been hesitant about coming, and reluctant to join the others in the living room, but Vik's son and Krista's husband got him talking about the places he had been—about thirty-eight states and all of the national parks, as it turned out, and he seemed to feel comfortable now. Fred would be staying on for a while. Cowboy had put him to work as custodian of his rental properties. They were going to veteran's stress-disorder meetings together. Best of all, Fred and Geronimo were together again. Cowboy was talking about going to Beaver Ridge to find a dog. Instead of trying to talk him out of it, Vik had given him directions.

Ben came up behind her. Marti leaned into him and he put his arms around her waist. Feeling him so close, and watching those she loved, she gave thanks. For this day and these people, for friendship and love, and even trials and pain and misfortune. "The fabric of life," Momma called it.